DRAWN UP
FROM
DEEP PLACES

GEMMA FILES

TREPIDATIO
PUBLISHING

Trepidatio books may be ordered through booksellers or by contacting:

Trepidatio

www.trepidatio.com

or

JournalStone

www.journalstone.com

The views expressed in this work are solely those of the authors and do not necessarily reflect the views of the publisher, and the publisher hereby disclaims any responsibility for them.

ISBN: 978-1-947654-23-5 (sc)
ISBN: 978-1-947654-24-2 (ebook)

Trepidatio rev. date: October 12, 2018

Library of Congress Control Number: 2018950329

Printed in the United States of America

Cover Design: Fredrick Richard / 99designs
Interior Layout: Jess Landry

Edited by Sean Leonard
Proofread by Scarlett R. Algee

DRAWN UP
FROM
DEEP PLACES

VILLA LOCUSTA

"When any Roman town was founded, it seems to have been standard practice to dig a trench, called the *mundus*, and throw offerings into it in order to invite the gods to watch over the place and its inhabitants. The trench was then covered with a stone. This *mundus* apparently evolved into some sort of subterranean chamber dedicated in particular to underworld spirits. Three times a year (in August, October and November) the stone covering was raised so that, it is claimed, the spirits of the dead had access to the world of the living, or as Cumont and Frazier put it, the 'door of hell was opened.'"
—R.C. Finucane, *Appearances of the Dead: A Cultural History of Ghosts*

Herculanaeum, August 24, A.D. 79—the ninth day before the Calends of September

When Marcilla wakes, at last, it's with Gnaius Vespis shaking her, hard enough to bruise. "Barbarian," he says. "Time to go, little wild girl; good enough time as any, anyhow. Now or never, like."

She turns over, groaning, to scrub thick sleep from her eyes.

Outside, there's still the same steady patter of tiny black stones falling down through the clouds around Vesuvius' crest, like some angry god's spittle. Last she remembers, Dromio and the few remaining house-boys were going up top to scrape Villa Locusta's roof clean, so it wouldn't collapse under this strange deluge's mounting weight; the yard itself was already carpeted thick and ankle-deep with them, grating beneath her sandals as Marcilla ran to the bath-house with her skirt looped up over her head, trying vainly to shield herself against harm from above. And now she reaches up to feel her scalp, only to find it still sticky in places from where the harder stones made her head bleed—while Gnaius watches, fair champing at the bit with impatience, like the half-mad war-stallion he still is.

"Is Chryse fit to travel, then?" Marcilla asks, voice hoarse with dust and heat.

"I'll *carry* her, she's not. Come on, barbarian—herself's still down below, praying more ruin on us all. We've one chance only, this, and don't think I'll stay much longer to convince you."

Again, the off-hand insult; great fool never *has* managed to learn even this meaningless name her captors forced on her, years before, in Rome's own main slave-market. Yet Marcilla can't fault him for it, somehow. He means well enough, in his clumsy way... like when he finally figured out how he'd got Chryse with a child neither of them could afford to keep, yet chose to stay by her nevertheless, instead of running off with the rest of Locusta's household.

She yawns, jaw cracking; levers herself upright in the too-bright darkness, groping under her pallet for a rough bundle of clothes, bread, a broken bronze knife hoarded from the kitchen while the head cook wasn't paying attention. Thinking at the same time, though never (of course) saying right out loud:

I had a son once too, Gnaius, ever hear tell of that? Oh, yes. 'Til a man like you stamped on his sweet little skull while it was still soft, because he'd've been too much trouble to keep alive all the way back to Rome, not to mention too unsalable at the other end. Not a sufficiently justifiable...investment.

Because that's what happens to babies bred from slaves, whether their fathers be cashed-out Legionnaires turned bodyguards, or brave young Icenii warriors so eager to die for their cause they don't even stop to think over what might happen to their wives—or children—afterward. When they fight the Empire's victorious hordes first-hand, and *lose*.

And why does Gnaius even want her along on this (no doubt) doomed venture? In case Chryse comes to time before they're well away, out in the woods or fields, with no surgeon handy? If they're caught, they'll all be killed, that's a foregone conclusion: Gnaius for stealing the Lady Locusta's property, Marcilla and Chryse for "stealing" themselves, as an example to the others. Which is fairly funny, come to think, considering just how few of those others seem to've hung around since the cloud first went up, and are thus likely to benefit from such a paradoxical lesson…

But at least it'll finally be out of her own hands, then. A sure and certain end, no matter how long they make it last before the climax; beyond her control, like so much else. And then the long sleep, forever—through Elysium's dark gate and back to her own country, one way or another.

Where I come from, things were different, Marcilla tries devoutly to make herself believe, as ever. Though really, it's been so long since she was last there that she finds it hard to recall exactly how, or even why.

Herculanaeum is no Rome, for all its pretensions. Yet Rome lies heavy on her still, like her first rapist did (and him not even Roman, or at least not so directly). It crushes out her every breath. She barely has enough strength to force herself through each day without turning the stolen kitchen knife on her own throat, her belly, the soft, scarred interior of her thigh, where a vein far too large and full of blood to staunch waits to be tapped, its very pulse like a rebuke. Hammering, with each fresh beat: *Why are you alive yet, traitor, and so many others not—so many more deserving, braver, better? How do you dare live on at all?*

But it takes so much effort to fight back, and so little not to; this is the one, the only real truth of her current condition. That simple. That dreadful.

So: "Let's bloody go, then," is all Marcilla says, finally. To which Gnaius looses a great gust of held breath, and grins his usual broke-toothed grin: *Good barbarian! That's the spirit, wild girl!*

"Praise be to all gods, you've seen sense. Thought I was going to have to throw you both over my shoulders and march away whistling, like Hercules Jupiter-get himself with his Amazon bitches."

"Wouldn't've got too far at that rate, would you? Not with your bad leg."

He claps her on the shoulders, fake-hearty. "Oh, never you mind *that*, little Pict. I'm surprising in a tight squeeze, me, often as not—just ask Chryse."

"Pass, thanks."

And out they set, together.

When Marcilla first came to the Lady Locusta's service, a year or so ago, this *domus* was already more than halfway as it is now: Sombre, denuded, empty as city streets on Lemuria feast-day, when ghosts are said to possess the upper- as well as the under-earth. Its halls filled with sadly pastoral murals, its rooms with dust and abandoned toys—and Dromio was quick enough to tell her the why of it, for all she hadn't actually bothered to ask; she'd learned long before that curiosity is seldom a well-rewarded quality in slaves.

"It was her son, see. The young master. Struck down by a cart on the fifth *cardo*, just north of the Suburban Thermae." He paused here, for effect. "And him only eight name-days old."

Longer than my boy lived, and far happier, I've no doubt, Marcilla thought. But: "Sad," she said, aloud. As she knew they expected.

"She wouldn't even let his pyre be laid," the head cook put in, here. "Just ordered him taken down to the *mundus*, and never brought him back up yet."

Gnaius, from the corner, oiling his leather armor: "Well, might be he lives still, down there. Crippled, like. That might happen."

Dromio shook his head. "I saw him brought home, held him up while she washed his face. He…could not have survived."

The cook again, portentously: "They'll come to stop her, you'll see—his father's kin won't have it. Such blasphemy can't go unpunished forever."

And yet…it did. Still does.

Didn't take long for the plain truth to out in day-to-day conversation either, no matter how many happy euphemisms Dromio might've originally tried to cloak it in. Widowed and childless as she is, plagued with debts on every hand, the Lady Locusta keeps her otherwise patrician head above water through a multitude of strange ventures, most having to do with the black arts: Necromancy, love potions, poisoning for hire, drawing horoscopes and casting the future, in defiance of all local temple strictures. For how can her servants think any different, really, seeing she's down in her family's private *mundus* at all hours, calling on infernal powers to work her clients' will?

Many times in the night's small hours, when no one else lies sleepless, Marcilla has pressed her ear to that cold stone lid. Beneath, her mistress's usually-soft voice rises and falls in horrid ecstasy, worshipping at the ancestor-shrine those long-dead first Locustii crafted from a fissure sprung agape in the too-active Vesuvian earth—a steaming gash kept open ever since specifically so those of her *gens* can use it to practice their personal brand of witchcraft. Marcilla has listened, heart in throat, while the lady scratches curses on sheets of soft lead and throws them into the smoking crack itself, surrounded by the tombs of her mothers and fathers, whose inhabitants presumably lie ready either to carry the message further below, or simply do the job themselves.

Locusta, usually so polite and kind, if a trifle absent—each word or move deliberate, never a hair left out of place. Her downcast eyes the same dull blue washed with faintest rose as a river's current made sluggish by sheer proximity, by merest implication, when it flows downstream from some ford choked by fresh corpses.

Since then, Marcilla is careful to keep her own eyes down whenever the lady of the house walks by, avoiding that empty gaze if she possibly can. But she can never quite make herself forget the last and latest thing her eavesdropping told her, that secret she will never tell Gnaius, Chryse or any of the others, not even if they think to ask: that she has heard another voice answer Locusta back, here and there, amongst the wailing. A lisping boy's voice, small and cold and still, which answers only when asked directly—

Are they here yet? The others?
Yes.
Will it be soon?
Yes.
What must I do?
Only wait. Pray. And...

(be ready)

That awful voice, and then Locusta's again, stone-muffled in deep darkness. Declaiming string after string of strange titles, pseudonyms Marcilla neither knows, nor wants to: *You of the whispers. You, Empty One. You who sew things, each to each. You who wear us as robes. You, Render from Above. You who seed without regard. You, who harvest everything. Seasonless ones, timeless ones, faceless ones, nameless ones...*

Let it all come down, now. Let it come to an end, and quickly. Quickly!

Let this world be remade at last, or destroyed utterly.

She keeps herself to herself, Marcilla, at the best of times— but these are not those, and haven't been for quite some while. It began back when the month first turned, with a series of small signs: Springs and wells turned salt, dried up, a constant stench of sulphur on the summer air; little tremors shook the rim of the Bay, hills and gorges alike convulsed by Triton Earth-shaker's wrath, splitting open here and there like a dying man's lips under the strain.

After which came the rumours, flocking in on every hand like psychopomp birds, equally impossible to discount as to prove— black wonders and obscene miracles enacted across the whole of Herculanaeum, without apparent cause or cure. Fresh plagues breeding necklaces of buboes that burst open, mouth-like, to whisper poison in their sufferers' ears. Fearsome dust devils blowing back and forth through the empty streets, scooping stragglers up into that misery-colored sky and dropping them again days later, half-eaten. Cicadas singing dirges in the trees before dawn, their voices almost understandable. A luminous vapour leaking in over the water each sunset, dissipating wherever it reaches the shore...

Or that day two weeks past, when Dromio sent Chryse to market for the last time, only to see her come home late beyond hope of excuse, empty-handed, fix-eyed and panting. Claiming: "Market was gone."

"What are you talking about, you stupid slut?"

"I couldn't find the old road, I swear it on Juno's breasts, though I looked everywhere—just some other, wide and well-laid, like it'd been there for years. But...I didn't take it."

"Why not?"

"...It looked...wrong."

So that night they made do with food from the storehouse, and Chryse was beaten—not over-hard, for her child's sake, though Marcilla saw Gnaius bite his lip at every stroke. Just like she heard Dromio and the head cook whispering about it, afterward: Dromio reckoning the Villa's accounts on his wax tablet, cook shelling peas, neither looking at the other directly. Firelight painted both their faces as red-tinged tragedy masks, impossible to read aside from whatever their voices let slip.

"End of the world, that's what they're saying over at Piso's Retreat. What d'you think, Dromio?"

"I think the world's always ending, or so someone always claims. That Jewish preacher in Rome, twenty years ago—Petros, his name was—said the exact same, and all he got for it was crucified. Head-downwards, by his own request."

"Suppose you're right."

"Yes, well—Jews always prophesy calamity, and lo and behold, calamity usually comes. It makes the cheat all the better: Any omen might mean any one of ten thousand disasters, and your god decides which it was." A pause. "But all the same, this man was no ranting lunatic took with heatstroke visions; seemed sane as you or I, or saner. Didn't speak of the world's end as tragedy, only salvation—the return of his savior, that false Jew-king Pilate did for."

"Must not've done his duty too well, he had to return for a second go at it."

"You know he didn't. The legions smashed the Jews' high temple for good and all, nine years gone."

"So things never improved, one way or the other?"

"Not for them."

To which the cook shrugged, tipping the last of her husks together into her drawn-up apron. And said, rising—

"Doesn't sound like much of a god to *me*, then...hardly one worth dying for, anyhow."

Thus confirming something Marcilla's always suspected about her captors, especially given their habit of routinely deifying dead emperors, whether or not said rulers were mainly loved or feared during their lifetimes: that when all is said and done, *lares* and *penates* aside, the only thing Romans really worship is themselves. Which certainly makes some sense, considering the way they tend to treat everyone else they come across.

Since then, there've been no more market expeditions—Locusta's servants stay inside, bide their time, arrange their days to coincide with her own strange schedule: eat, sleep, pray. Watch the world darken, not least with the slow appearance of men they don't know at the very edges of her fields, eddying here and there like phantoms. They don't come much closer, don't seem to see the Villa somehow, not even when they stare at it directly: a testament to Locusta's power, perhaps, or to the power she serves. But they don't go *away*, either.

And then, yesterday—finally—the worst thing yet. A cloud arching up over Vesuvius like some funeral pine, spreading its branches to blot out the sun...

Whatever the Lady Locusta's drawn down upon this city, and no matter her reasoning for doing so, Marcilla knows she's already lingered far too long in its path to get away clean. But she's not ready to watch Gnaius Vespis and his Chryse die as well, not just yet; not when they want so badly, the both of them, to live—with each other. *For* each other.

And then there's the child, who has no say in any of this at all. Surely someone should think to speak for it, while—

(if)

—there's still time.

They find Chryse upstairs, at last—still asleep, hands pressed tight to her distended belly, and no amount of Gnaius' whispering or caresses seems to wake her. Finally, he gives in and does his fabled demigod act after all—hoists her up high and drapes her across himself like a senator's toga, limping more than ever under the strain, so they can creep back down and out through the peristyle *interiora*, Locusta's hidden garden, through which they might yet hope to reach the *posticum*, the bath-house, the road and trees beyond.

By the water clock in the atrium, night has already eked past into morning and beyond, not that anyone left awake would be able to tell the difference. The cloud around Vesuvius' summit has blocked out the sky, turning it a lowering, vivid grey so dark it seems almost purple. Sometimes the clouds part far enough to admit a brownish-yellow shaft or two of the sort of light which comes during an eclipse, even as juddering sheets of lightning continually spit and tangle above the torrent of ash and pumice, in flashes so bright they seem to cut Heaven wide open.

The rest of Villa Locusta is darker and even more silent than before, eating their footsteps like a sacred grove. Marcilla runs her hand along the wall as they go, tracing the painted river; on better days, this ribbon of bright, meandering blue "flows" so clear you might almost think you see fish flicker beneath its surface, poised to jump. Now it's opaque, shadowed by dense and over-hanging green foliage, behind which—if you pause incautiously long enough to study it too closely—a series of almost-familiar faces sometimes seem to peer out at you, baring their tiny phan-tom teeth.

As they clear the peristyle's entrance, Chryse stirs, gives a rat-tling sigh. Asks, in a thin little voice: "...Gnaius?"

"That's me, lovely—Marcilla, too. We're here to get you free of all this, the both of us, tonight."

Her drooping head turns, eyes still shut, white lids blind in the cloud's erratic light. "'Cilla...it's dark yet? Must be morning, by now..."

"Long past, Chryse; go back to sleep now, will you? Baby must need it, I'm sure."

But Chryse's pleasant face sours at that, her brows wrinkling; she tries once more to wrench her lashes up past half-mast, only to flop a fresh tangle of sweat-slicked hair back over them instead. And:

"...'S not..." she says, at last. "...I mean, I think, 's *not*..."

...What? Gnaius' baby? Hers? Or, perhaps, not even—

(*a* baby?)

Then, to Gnaius: "I had that...dream...again..."

She doesn't need to explain which one, of course: The dream of the Empty Eye, the Open Gash, a hole opened up to the world's heart and deeper, with a blazing light at its bottom. The dream that stops people sleeping.

"We've all of us had that dream, Chryse," Marcilla says, shortly.

Gnaius, obscurely insulted: "*I* haven't."

But Marcilla just elbows him in the ribs, not stopping. "Go faster, fool," she orders. "And *quieter*."

That he understands, at least; you can always get Gnaius to do what you want, Marcilla's observed, so long as you make yourself sound like his drill sergeant. Gnaius hoists Chryse higher and moves, fast and quiet both. Soon enough, they leave the skewed light and thick air of the peristyle for a brief jaunt through the oddly honest gloom of the bathhouse, *calidarium*, *tepidarium* and *frigidarium* alike all empty but for dust. And then the courtyard, as empty as the peristyle but wider, its cobbles sifted over with ash and slippery with fallen sky-rock. Marcilla lets something that might be hope stir to tentative life as she spots the doors, standing open to reveal the road beyond—

—which is, of course, *exactly* when Dromio moves out into that same doorway, Gnaius' spare *gladius* gleaming in his hand.

A moment's shocked silence, indignantly broken by Gnaius: "That's *mine!*"

Dromio tilts the blade to catch the horrid, bloated light. A half-dug shallow trench by his feet reveals what he and the others have been doing all this time, and while there may be no Legion's SPQR brand on his shoulder, the lethal competence of his stance is unmistakable. "No, Gnaius Vespis," the slavemaster corrects him. "This is the Villa's—like her, or her. Or you, come to that."

"Step within my reach, old man, and make that claim again."

Marcilla takes a step back, automatically, at the snarl in Gnaius' voice; Chryse barely looks up, hugging Gnaius closer, which undercuts the challenge's immediacy somewhat. But Dromio merely shakes his head, as though he'd expected as much.

"Where was it you three thought to go, exactly?" he asks, almost sadly. "There's nothing past here but Gods-wrath and Chryse's wrong-looking road, children; believe me, I've already checked."

"We'll take our chances."

Another head-shake, sadder still. "Can't let you, I'm afraid. You must know as much."

Gnaius gives a strange sort of full-body shrug, a great cat poising to spring, and shifts Chryse so his arm's around her waist, freeing his sword-hand. "Come on, then," he says, and raises the blade so its shadow crosses Dromio's from above, the way Vesuvius' does them all.

But: "Enough," a third voice puts in from where the garden wall runs to darkness, kitty-corner to the bathhouse door. And the Lady Locusta herself issues forth, unhurriedly—earrings chiming cool on this dust-laced wind, long train of her summer-weight dress trailing forgotten over the ashy grass, the turned-up earth. To her right, Marcilla sees a shallow, new-dug trench running from where the *mundus*-lid stands slightly open, for once; a shovel stained with new dirt leans against one edge, no doubt abandoned by Dromio, who must have been the last to use it.

"More runaways, Mistress," Dromio informs her, unnecessarily. "Gnaius and his whore, the Pictish girl…"

"So I see."

"Cowards, all of 'em, to leave you like this. Should cut these ones down here and now, for the insult to your family name alone—"

"Don't be ridiculous, Dromio." Locusta is close enough to lay her hand on his blade now, urging it gently downwards. "I hope you trust me capable of disciplining my own slaves, should I feel they merit it…but unnatural times call for unnatural measures, so you need not bloody your blade tonight. Gnaius, Chryse and Marcilla are all entirely free to go; you too, if you wish it." Then adds, turning to Marcilla: "Though if you, in particular, were to stay and help me one last time, I would be very grateful."

They make a pretty group for just a moment, posed together against the looming sky: Dromio gaping, Gnaius uncertain how to react, Chryse barely able to stand. While Marcilla, similarly caught by surprise, finds herself abruptly looking straight into the lady's particolored eyes, unable to fall back on her normal policy of self-protective dumb insolence. Thinking: *She has charmed me, surely. I must fight it, her, must break free, before…*

But she finds she does not know *before* what, no matter how she strives to grasp the concept. Is unable even to form the question, let alone answer it.

"*Will* you help me, Marcilla?" Locusta asks once more, softer still, and sweeter. "It is such a small thing I ask for, you see—but I cannot do it by myself."

Marcilla shivers, for all that the cloud-bound garden grows increasingly, oppressively hot. Thinking, yet again: *But why not? And more importantly…why me?* In, as you say—

(*particular*)

19

Though there is this, it suddenly occurs to her—Locusta was a mother too, once. Locusta has shared her grief, that indigestible stone which sits always in the pit of Marcilla's stomach, changing everything she tastes to dirt. That strange power of hers again, perhaps...the power to make even her slaves feel sorry enough for her to jeopardize their own safety and freedom to help her. Or, yet more simply—

Where would I have gone, after all, anyhow? Marcilla catches herself wondering. This—

(she)

—is all I have left.

"Tell me what you need, Domina," Marcilla answers, finally. And is mildly surprised to see Locusta's weird gaze sadden slightly, as she does. *Had you hoped for more of a fight, my lady? Should've asked Gnaius instead, if that was what you wanted.*

But Locusta says nothing to confirm this nor disprove it. Only inquires, as Marcilla could never have expected her to—

"Does this world please you, Marcilla? Do you love it?"

What?

And here it is, in one cold flash: Every bad thing that's ever happened to her sent flooding back at once like a sharp stick thrust between her legs, into the very softest part of her, the secretest wound. Thrust in deep, beyond its hilt, and twisted.

Marcilla swallows, hard. "No, Domina," she husks. "I beg your pardon; no."

"No, no, never apologize—you are right not to. This world is a cruel place; it always has been, from the very beginning." Here Locusta pauses, allowing a tone that Marcilla has never heard before to enter her otherwise murmur-calm voice—not upset, not urgent, so much as *definite*. "But it will all change, Marcilla, I promise you. It *will* change."

Can this be sympathy? It smells a bit like it, or like Marcilla remembers it smelling; perhaps she is simply fooling herself, one more time in a long string of times. Yet it feels good nonetheless, Locusta's stainless fingers resting against her cheek, cupping her jaw. This unlooked-for feeling of...support.

"You are kind, Domina," she hears herself say, voice cracking. "You do not have to be. I thank you for it."

But: "Oh no, Marcilla. Thank *you*."

And then—a movement, so fast Marcilla can barely register it before she hears Dromio gasp and Gnaius curse: a slim flash of polished bronze against her neck (Knife? Hair pin?), followed by searing pain. Marcilla falls forward, hands at her throat, powerless to stem the flood. She sees her own blood gush into the trench, drunk by the thirsty mud, and it hurts so badly, so badly...

...Until suddenly, with a snap, she's outside herself, separated and apart. Locusta with her red hands, Dromio vomiting to one side, Gnaius hugging Chryse's face to his chest—she still *knows* them, yes, but none of it means anything more or less to her than anything else: the cloud above, the wind in the trees, those same black-clad men slipping in across the fields again, making their way towards the apparently now-visible Villa. Or that endless road which, Marcilla realizes, spirals out around peristyle, bathhouse and *mundus* alike—smooth like blown glass, black like night-water, overhung at intervals with poplar-high iron trees whose single, double or triple clusters of fruit give off an eerily unblinking glow: scarlet, green, yellow, white.

And beyond that, even more marvels: great buildings looming wherever Marcilla looks, mountain-high, ten thousand phantom temples to ten thousand unknown gods. And light at almost every window, spilling forth in unbroken waves, pure and dreadful, implacable as the impending moment of death.

With only slightly more interest than she would have shown in anything else, Marcilla watches a coil of something ooze its way from the displaced *mundus*-cover to her discarded flesh, before thrusting itself—wormlike, with a subtle clockwise screwing motion—inside. Watches as the corpse straightens stiffly, humping up from the ground like a worm, its throat still gaping open. Sees it crouch again to lap its own blood from the shallow groove in front of it, smearing its—

(*her*)

—lips with dust and gore.

The black-clad men are very close now, moving crab-like, shadows on top of shadows. With such a far more significant show to witness at close range, however, Marcilla cannot count herself too surprised if no one inside Locusta's garden notices their approach.

Locusta, voice even higher, that note of certainty more pronounced: "Speak, I constrain you. Is it now? Has it come? Is this it?"

The body looks up, wipes its mouth with the clumsy back of one hand, only making things worse. And from Marcilla's flapping second mouth, a cold, pale voice drops words like lumps of rotting flesh:

"Too...late."

Locusta's hand goes to her mouth. Her eyes shine, wide and wet. "You lie."

"No. Too...late." It straightens again, seeming somehow taller—looming over her, almost, while its own shadow spills out around both their feet in a lapping flood.

"Who tells you so? My master—"

"Ah, but there are others of his kind too, are there not? Seven, to be exact."

So tall and growing still, its face shimmering with darkness, eaten away from within; Locusta gives a stark cry at the sight, falls to her knees, buries her face heedlessly in her polluted palms and smears them back and forth, back and forth. Lets her well-coiffed hair rush down to straggle in the blood-mud, without regard for the result.

With bleak glee: "Did you really think none of us would also come when you called, little lady?"

For: *Ah yes*, Marcilla thinks. Those *others*.

You who sew things, each to each. You who wear us as robes...seasonless, timeless, faceless, nameless...

Perhaps the world does end tonight, after all—in one way, or another.

And: "Bugger all this," Gnaius says, hoisting Chryse once more, so he can run faster. But before he's so much as taken a single step, the black watchers are already on him. They bring him down, and her, as Dromio just stands there, frozen. While the ghost-clad thing that was Marcilla simply laughs and grows on, unstoppable, and Locusta sobs over the wreckage of her grandest plans.

Time to go, Marcilla reckons. Yet finds herself hovering on, still somehow obscurely sorry for her former mistress, almost wanting to touch her, to offer comfort.

Beside the lady, a new spectre rises—smaller, wavering, yet just as uncomfortable. The half-crushed figure of Locusta's son has exited the *mundus* unnoticed, on unsteady tiptoes. His grave little face is a bloodless parody of hers, aside from the eyes: like purple butterflies set sidelong, opening and closing their spotted wings as lashes, pupils golden in the gathering storm.

"I failed you, master," Locusta weeps, burying her face against his tiny feet. "It goes on and on, the same as ever. I failed."

"You could not help it," he says, and touches her ruined hair, gently.

The Marcilla-thing shakes itself, impatiently. It sends its shadow out further yet, summoning its acolytes from their work; to a one, they leave Marcilla's former friends where they've fallen and gather close, surrounding Locusta and her lich-baby alike. Their teeth gleam, reflecting lightning.

But you and she are done, nevertheless, it says, no longer bothering to speak at all. *The door is closing. This stops here.*

"Oh, yes," the little boy agrees. "It does."

And his gentle touch on Locusta's shaking shoulder wakes a last thunderclap that rips the night asunder, as a wall of boiling mud vomited up from Gaea's guts rushes down out of the dark. Walls shatter, stones fly; slate tiles burst in the heat; bodies curl fetally and parboil into shells, black mirror of the wombs in which they once dreamed. The lid slams down over the *mundus*-pit, its foulness and its secrets locked away once and for all as molten earth drowns and buries it.

The pyroclastic flow rips through Hercules' city, scouring all in its path away forever.

After, Marcilla feels herself peel away up into the exploding sky. Sees Locusta engulfed below her, along with what's left of Dromio, Gnaius, poor Chryse and her child, if child there even was.

She briefly finds time to hope, absently, that someone—her real son, perhaps?—will care enough to show Locusta which way to go, so she doesn't wander eternally. Her intentions were better than might be expected, especially from a Roman.

First the flow, the flaming gases, followed then by mud, by rock, by time. The city will be seeded over and forgotten, found again by chance, unearthed once more, visited, studied. The Villa Locusta will become only one of many necropoli, each equally important. Each equally misunderstood.

She knows this, somehow, just as she somehow knows her own

sad tale to have been only one of many near-apocalyptic stories—all of them different, all of them the exact same. Except, on occasion, for some minor difference in the way they reach their appointed end.

Herself, however, Marcilla is free, of all of it. Of everything: pain, past, world, time, name. Too free even to appreciate her own freedom.

Simple and plain, free and clear; here, then not. And then, at long last, very gratefully indeed—

—gone.

TRAP-WEED

For their land-longing shall be sea-longing and their sea-longing shall be land-longing, forever.
—An old legend of the Orkneys, concerning those seals who shed their skins to become women and men

Any selkie can be Great, if he fights for it when challenged. We are by no means a democracy.

But for myself, I did not care to, and was driven forth, into deeper waters. So I swam until my fat and fur could no longer warm me, 'til the chill had almost breached my heart. I swam 'til my lungs gave out, then sank, deep into darkness.

When I woke, I found myself aboard-ship, peltless and doubly nude. A lean man stood looking down on me, his elegant face all angles, while others watched from behind, above...so many, for this creaking wooden shell to carry oceanbound in safety. I had never seen such a number before, all in one place.

(For we stay as far from human men as possible on Sule Skerry, if we can, unless our instincts drive us otherwise. We know their works.)

I was gasping, painful all over, in strange places—burnt and scraped, as though I'd been dragged over rocks. Indeed, my arm had a chunk torn from it, neat and triangular—nipped straight out at the point where it blended into shoulder, that same place I saw most mariners adorn with tattoo-work. I gaped at this a while, then tried to touch, and flinched from the sting of my own fingers' salt.

"I wouldn't do that," the man advised, without sympathy. "Call it the price of your salvation—a lesson either to keep to shallower waters or learn to hold your breath longer, when you choose not to."

Though it had been some time since I tried for human speech, I found it returned quick enough. "Where...am I, sir?"

And this he smiled at, grimly enough—no surprise there. Since in their hearts, most men like the pap they call courtesy, that sorry salve to their impossible pride.

"This scow of a brig's mine, by right of seizure," he replied, sweeping a contemptuous little bow. "*Bitch of Hell*, some call her, or *Salina Resurrecta*, since she's cobbled from shipwrecks. While I myself am Jerusalem Parry, captain: a pirate, as you suspect. You were *drowning*, meantime—a sorry sight, in one sea-bred. Yet Mister Dolomance here brang you up, before mortality could quite take hold entirely...and while I misdoubt he did you as little hurt in the performance of it as he might have, we must always recall how those he comes from are not known for their restraint, in general."

"Mister Dolomance?"

"Aye, that's he, hid over yonder, where he likes it best—you'd be dead if he hadn't found you, or if he was still able to do as he wished, instead of how I tell him to. For which you should, in either case, be suitably grateful." Fixing me with cold, pale eyes, then, like two silver pennies salt-blanched to the color of water-cured bone turned coral: "And what are we to call you?"

You could not say it if you tried, I thought. But since I seemed compelled to answer, I rummaged for the last human name I'd heard—the one that boy I'd pulled from his boat's kin had called after him, its syllables dissolving down through water into meaningless sound by the time they reached the cave where my sisters kept him tethered, forcing him to sire a fresh crop of younglings. What they did with him after I never witnessed, for I was already at the sparring by then, about to choose discretion over valor, exile over family. Indeed, it only now occurred to me, I might not see

26

them again, in his company or otherwise.

In that moment I knew myself alone, entirely, lost amongst those who normally hate and prey on us—who either club us dead to steal our skins in error, thinking us only animals, or make away with them when we're foolish enough to leave them unguarded and detain us for *their* pleasure, breeding children who will never feel at home on either sea or shore. And so, seeing no other way out, for the time being—

"You may call me Ciaran, sir," I said, at last.

To my left, I heard the thing Captain Parry called Mister Dolomance give out with a disgusted little noise from his hidey-hole—half snort, half spit—and turned, abruptly far more angry than bereft, to confront whatever creature had dragged me up onto this rotting, lurching mass of timber held together mostly by barnacles and forward motion, at the still-sore price of its snatched mouthful of flesh.

I found him squatting on the weather deck in a strange nest made from two massy coils of rope with a tarpaulin slung over top, keeping himself moist by angling into the splash from a nearby cannon-port's mouth. Standing, he would be half as tall as Captain Parry but a good two hands broader, squat yet sleek. With doll-eyes and an almost lipless mouth hiding a serrated bear-trap bite, he sported what some sailors called "a drowned man's pallor," close-wrapped to save himself from burning in direct sunlight. It was that sea-bed dweller's skin of his, I later found out, which had left me so raw, drawing blood from frictive angles on the very briefest of contacts.

I know you now, I thought, meeting that lidless black gaze, if only for a moment; he well might mock, since his own kind were known to scorn names entirely. So the fact that he answered at all to that mockingly polite and inexact one the captain'd applied to him showed just how puissant this man's magic must be, when reflected in "Mister Dolomance's" grudging obeyance, his infinitely resentful loyalty. Or, for that matter, the mere fact of Parry being yet alive, having not only bent this tadpole version of a Great White shark to his will, but forced it to assume a (mostly) human form, while doing so.

I have no doubt but that Mister Dolomance perceived both my terror and my pity, though his waverless glare rejected them both.

27

And so we stood a while, locked in mutual regard: one cold-blooded, the other warm, doomed to meet for the first time in assumed shapes, confined to this creaking hulk. Me with my man-shape like a secret weakness revealed, as though I'd been forcibly shook inside-out; him with his man-shape imposed from the outside-in, never more than cruel illusion. For beneath it, he remained all rough muscle and horrid teeth, a terrible hunger, not even held together with bones.

Though we suffered the same privations, we could never be allies. I was prey to him, as much as any other thing without Captain Parry's power to protect it.

"Well, then, gentlemen," my captor told me, meanwhile, and Mister Dolomance as well—I could tell from the begrudging liquid grumble Mister Dolomance gave Parry back, by way of a reply. "Shall we retire to my cabin, and speak a bit further?"

And since there seemed no option but to go, I bowed my clumsy, fresh-made man-head, and went.

"I will trouble you for my skin, sir, if I may," I ventured, when the door was safely closed behind us.

By the look of his possessions and on closer examination, I gathered that Parry had once been of some quality, as humans reckon such things—regally slim, his fine hands sword-callused and ink-stained, not roughened with rope. If he went un-wigged, that seemed to be by choice; the hair thus revealed was still mostly brown, though shot through with hints of grey. There were also more books in his quarters than I had seen in my whole life, though, grantedly, the sea does not treat such objects well.

But the captain only shook his head. "No, I'll take care of that awhile yet, as I hold most of my crew's effects in trust for them. For we are none of us here entirely by choice, you see—not even me."

"Surely, though, it can matter little to you if I remain. I am no great hunter, like your...Mister Dolomance, there; my place is near the shore, not the open sea. And while some of my people have magic, of a sort, I am not one of them."

Parry sniffed again, prim as any cat. "I have all the magic I need already at my disposal, 'Ciaran,' and little liking for competition.

You would provide me a very different service; less a tool to my hand than an object-lesson for others."

"But what use can I possibly be of to you, bound *or* free, when you have one of the ocean's greatest nightmares sworn to your service already?"

"You undervalue your own impressiveness. My men fear me, and rightly, because I have a way with supernatural creatures, so adding a selkie to that roster cannot do me ill, even if it does me little comparative good."

Having no arguments left, I resorted to simply pointing out: "I...am no sailor, sir." To which Captain Parry gave merely a chilly smile, as though to say that was both of no matter, and hardly a skill requiring great genius to master.

"Oh, you'll soon learn," was all he replied, and waved me away.

Thus I found myself press-ganged, after a fashion; I betook myself to the quartermaster and begged my share of the ship's labour, setting myself to it with energy, if not much effect. Yet the crew, on the whole, were kind—perhaps because they were sorry for me, a thing so far out of its place, if not its element.

And always I could just glimpse Mister Dolomance stalking attendance, following at the captain's heels even while his gaze roamed after me. The farther we went from land, the happier he seemed, his sharp grin less a threat than a promise. While I wished myself increasingly back with my kin, fighting for supremacy I neither craved nor thought myself fit to hold, on that bloody rock; anywhere with land and sea alike, in close enough proximity to swim between.

As my despair mounted, I prayed outright to the eel-tailed Maid of the Sea (whose teeth are fishbones and whelk-shells, whose wet breath smells only of salt, and cold, and death), though She was far more likely to answer Mister Dolomance than the likes of me. But then again, my elders had taught me his kind do not trust in invocations to free them from mishap, if their own strength proves unequal to the task. For they are a harsh people, the sleepless ever-moving ones, even to themselves—unwilling to incur debts they do not wish to pay, even to the goddess who watches over all such wrack as we, the fertile ocean's muck and cast-offs. Its children, lost at sea, or out of it.

As time wore on, meanwhile, the quartermaster grew friendly

with me, giving me leave to eat raw fish from the common net, and stroking my hair as I did. "Do not be sad," he would say, "the captain will tire of ye soon enough, like any other toy he plucks from the deep. 'Sides which, were you bound for anywhere in particular? No? Then it'll serve you just as well to stay a while wi' us; just drift along, as if current-borne. See where *that* takes you."

"Do I have a choice?" I asked him, sullen, picking bones from my flat, blunt man-teeth. Only to have him laugh aloud at my bitterness, matching it with his own.

"Do any of us?" he asked me, in return.

The answer, of course, being no. We all existed entirely subject to the captain's whim, just as he himself was inwardly consumed by a seemingly-constant quest for novelty, sharp-panged as any mere bodily famishment. Those silver-penny eyes of his always scanning away at the horizon, seemingly incognizant of Mister Dolomance crouched like some lump of pure hatred made flesh at his side—though not so much *ignorant* of his closest companion's feelings, I eventually came to see, as simply content to ignore them.

Rumours followed Parry, as with any other fatal man, so I listened to them whenever they were offered, eager for any possibility of escape. "Captain's cursed, is what I 'eard," the second gunner said at mess, as the rum-cup was passed 'round one way, the water-cup the other. "'Twas laid on 'im 'ow 'e can't set foot on land..."

The first gunner, impatient: "No, fool, for I've seen him *do* so, to his cost—it's that he can't *stay* on land, or he starts to bleed."

"Aye," the quartermaster broke in here, nodding sagely. "I was there as well, that same occasion, and saw what come out—enough t'fill a slaughterhouse trough, and him so pale t'start with! Which is why he stays afloat, these days, and sends Mister Dolomance out scoutin' for prizes instead, settin' him t'bite through anchor-ropes or gnaw holes in some other ship's side. For it's wrecks the captain wants, as we all know, and there's no earthly reason why he should be content t'wait for 'em to happen natural...not when he has so many other ways to make it so."

But to what purpose? I almost asked, before thinking better of it. Answering myself, as I did, with the sudden realization: *To cobble*

*this ship of his ever-bigger with them, of course. To grow his king-
dom—or increase his prison's capacity, at the very least.*

Salina Resurrecta, Bitch of Hell; Parry's Doom they called it as
well, whenever they thought him too deep-engaged in his arcane
business to notice. A blot of a thing, literally engorged with flotsam from every prize it took and scuttled, hull gaping open maw-
like at Captain Parry's gesture to suck in whatever items he—or
it?—most took a fancy to. Thus it increased in size, steadily, over
the months I spent as just one more item of that literally damnable vessel's cargo—sprouted fresh decks and hulling, masts and
port-holes rabbit-breeding 'til the whole ship sat taller against
the waves with a veritable totem-pole of figureheads to guide it,
a corpse-fed trail of destruction left behind in its ever-widening
wake.

I remember the captain standing high in the foredeck, shaking
that hex-bag he used to raise fog and draw storms out into the
wind, full to its brim with less-than-sacred objects. These I saw
variously, at differing times, when he would reach in and with-
draw them for specific tasks: a wealth of red-gold hair, braided and
knotted nine times nine (this aided in illusions); some dead babe's
finger, pickled in gin (he used it as a pointer, to navigate). An
eyeball carved from ivory, set with the skull and crossed bones in
fine black jet, was all that was left of the *Bitch*'s legendary former
Captain Rusk, fashioned to replace one lost in battle and plucked
from his barnacle-torn corpse after Parry had him keel-hauled,
scraping him dead on his own ship's bottom-side—a trophy for
luck, perhaps, though Parry sometimes raised it to his ear and gave
that cat's-wince smile of his, as if it whispered advice to him.

But then there was an idol of dark wood, too, so gnarled one
could barely ascertain its shape and studded all over with rusted
nails, staining its weathered skin like blood—who had Parry stolen *that* from, and why? Bone fragments, sea-glass, scrimshaw,
plus what I took to be a serrated tooth from Mister Dolomance's
smile, knocked violently free at its root. And deep down, far beyond my reach, though I caught the occasional teasing glimpse of
it, now and then...

...my skin, contradictory heart of all I was, reduced to one more
fetish, one more weapon in Parry's arsenal. One more tool to bend
my and the shark's great Mother to his all-too-human will.

"*Who* was it cursed him, though?" I demanded, eventually, scrabbing for some sort of detail to use against Parry, some way out of this closing trap. To which the quartermaster replied, musingly—

"Now, that I can't say, young Ciaran. Only that it happened quick enough, without warning, some time after he first took the *Bitch* in mutiny, I think, and laid our old captain down. So perhaps it was Solomon Rusk's work, not that I ever saw him do for any who rose against him with weapons other than sword and fist, previous. Still, keel-haulin' is an ill death, a singularly painful end... and it does give you time t'think on things, I can only s'pose, when you're down there under-hull..."

"How foolish he'd been to bring Parry on, in the first place," I suggested.

A nod. "Maybe so. Rusk took him off a Navy prize, y'see—found him down in the brig like cargo, iron-collared, and knew him a magician bound for the next port of call, to face the king's justice: be burned alive or hanged in chains, depending on the Admiralty's fancy. Those other blue-coats who swore the ship's Articles t'keep their lives were mightily afeared of him already, sayin' how he was accused of all manner of wizardous ill-doings—necromancy and doll-makin' and catchin' gales in a sieve, the way most sailors think only women do. But Captain Rusk, he wouldn't be warned away, not once his temper was up, or his interest piqued. He'd have a man-witch at his beck and call, or know the reason why."

"Most magicians die in the uncollaring, don't they?"

"Aye, for them rigs don't have locks, just seams—the witchfinders put 'em on hot and force 'em sealed, so's they'll waste all their effort on one last spell to keep from dyin'; Captain Parry keeps his cravat high for a reason, t'hide the scars all 'round his neck. But Rusk broke it open, with his hands; he was a strong man, and always knew the trick of twistin' where a thing was weakest."

"I 'eard this tale, too," the second gunner chimed in. "'Jerusha, I'll call ye,' he said, 'seein' you owe me all.' And Parry just snapped at 'im, like they was two gents in a drawing-room: 'Sir! I have not given you permission to use me thus, familiarly!'"

"No, and he never did, did he? Though Solomon Rusk, bold bastard that he was, wasn't a one t'ever pay such niceties much mind..."

So Parry had begun in servitude himself, of the same sort he practiced on Mister Dolomance and me—a slave turned slave-master who, just like the shark-were, had no sympathy for his own past weakness, let alone the weaknesses of others. *I fought free*, he might say, if questioned; *do the same, if you can...and if not, stop your whining.*

(Yet for such a creature to base his power in the sea, where nothing is permanent, ever...not the shape of land, the ebb and flow of tide, or even any clear distinction between what makes one more itself than the other...)

I think you court destruction, sir, I thought, allowing myself the very faintest beginnings of hope. And would almost have risked a smile to myself, had I not been so afraid he might be watching.

On those few brief occasions when we put ashore to trade, re-stocking with food and weaponry, the captain always hung back, with only Mister Dolomance (who had an instinctual distrust of anything under his feet which did not move according to the ocean's in- and out-breath) for company in his watery exile. And though other times women might come aboard, for the crew's recreation, the captain never indulged himself, though he might have had his pick—being not only undeniably handsomer than any other man on his ship, but having far better manners.

Instead, the two of them would retire early, and I would peep in through the window's crack to discover them bent together over parchment, Mister Dolomance squeak-gurgling away in Parry's ear while his master scratched away furiously with pencil and charcoal, checking and re-checking measurements with various instrumenta-tion. And slowly, I came to figure they must be making a map to-gether, hopelessly impenetrable to any land-dweller's eyes: a grand survey of the ocean's most uncharted areas, from the *bottom up*.

"He seeks for a place more land than sea, yet neither," was the quartermaster's theory. "Only there might this bane of his be lifted, and he find peace, if that's indeed what he's after."

"Do you doubt it?"

"With the captain? Where he's concerned I doubt all things, 'til I'm told otherwise. 'Tis the best policy I've found, thus far."

I glanced away, just in time to catch my fellow captive—listening too, as always—shoot me what passed for a smirk on that mask-like parody of a human face of his, as if to say: *What fools!*

Indeed, it did often seem to me the crew barely knew whereof they spoke, notwithstanding the fact they'd spent far more time under Parry's rule than I had. And one way or another, for all my researches, exactly nothing they—or I—had discovered about him could in any way free me from my situation. I remained trapped, his possession, his slave; yet still worse, for I was not even of any great interest to him, of any particular *use.*

It galled me to realize this, almost as much as it galled me to realize I cared, either way. But perhaps Captain Parry was not altogether human either—partly dragon, maybe, for his twinned love of gold and fire, his magic, his damnable arrogance; partly wolf, for his love of blood.

Or he was just a man like any other, plundering this great sea-womb and stealing its children, using power he had no right to to bend our Mother herself to his selfish desires. Would that make things better, or worse?

I could not fight him, either way—not I, who had declined to fight even my own kind, against whom I might have stood some chance of success. So I must find some other, more subtle, way... think myself out of this trap, like the man he'd condemned me to pretend to be, instead of the seal I so heartily wished I still was.

So I thought, and thought again, and thought yet further. Until, at last—I found a way.

One night, while Mister Dolomance swam his own discomforts away in the sea below's black bosom, I threw a rope over the ship's side and shimmied far enough down to face my fears—plunged my face into the water and took a deep, drowning breath, opening my mouth wide enough to let words leak out, trusting the water to carry them to Mister Dolomance's ear-holes, translated thus into speech we might both understand.

We must work together, I told him, *to gain our freedoms.*

A gulp, and the reply came back, harsh even through silky fathoms: *Clumsy sea-cow in man-skin, born neither of one sort nor the other, you fat-greased, fleshy thing! What could you offer that I had any need of, save for enough of your meat to fill my craw, and your too-hot blood to wash it down with?*

I had expected nothing less, nothing more. Yet I spoke on, anyhow, and he...

...hard words aside, I could tell, even then: Mister Dolomance *listened*.

There was a long silence, after. So long I feared he might be swimming closer, too intent on an easy kill to truly mull my plan over.

But: *I accept*, he said, at last. Just that.

Good, I replied. And shimmied back up, before the crew might find me gone.

We did not consult long, Mister Dolomance and I, in forming our plans; I knew from the start just how ill-suited by nature he was to be anything like the planning sort. Yet it is always in their desires that men make themselves most vulnerable, and though Mister Dolomance had surely never looked to, we both understood he had already gained far more insight into our captor's yearnings than I ever would.

So—having extracted such intelligences about the hungers which drove Captain Parry as my co-conspirator was capable of giving—it fell to me, instead, to find a way to turn their direction to our mutual benefit.

It was not so much that the captain trusted Mister Dolomance (for in truth, he trusted no one, thinking no one equal enough to him to merit such a gift). Yet, as had already become rapidly clear, he placed a quite foolish amount of trust in his dominance over this awful creature, whose taming-by-force formed much of his own reputation.

"I think you are not entirely honest with me, sir," I heard him say, one evening, over those charts of theirs. "Yet so long as you do what I require, I find I care little what details you may think to withhold."

A mistake, on his part. And to not consider me, at all, in his equations...this was a mistake too, though he did not know it.

Not yet.

The *Bitch* made on, leading ever-westerly, with Mister Dolomance's grumbles our pilot's only guide for navigation. Islands grew scarce, and stores likewise; the crew grew unhappy, yet loath to express it. While Captain Parry kept his face carefully schooled, with only the dullish glint in those sea-burnt eyes to indicate a growing undercurrent of excitement—until the night when I saw him stride into the mess unexpectedly and swig lit rum from the communal store along with the rest, all of them too disconcerted by far to refuse him a part in their drunkenness.

Later, his back set against the foredeck's supplemental mast while the crew reveled down below, I watched him stare out over the topmost figurehead's shoulders at the dark billows Mister Dolomance hid in, and mutter to himself: "Hell gape to take you, Solomon Rusk, if it didn't that day, the way it should have—you had no stink of the true practitioner about you, trained or un-, that I could discern. How was I to know it hid in your blood, any more than you did, waiting for that very last breath to bring your death's vow of ruin on me to fruition?"

Here he actually paused a half-moment; I swear I saw him listen, as to an invisible companion. Then grimace at nothing and reply, pale face suddenly touched with heat—

"'Nice as a divine'...yes, you *would* say that. But here is truth: You took liberties with me, though I warned you not to, and this is the result. Do not think to deny it! I swore you ship-loyalty, nothing more, but you were not the sort to stint yourself and you have reaped bitter fruit from that decision since, dead man. So you may complain all you wish when drink opens my ears, but I have suffered long enough for your sins, as well as my own. I will have my place, got for me with the sea's help, and you—you will have nothing. Now stop your mouth, before I prison your ghost in a bottle and sink you further still; from this instant forward you may watch but not touch, not ever again, and choke on the sight."

All at once, the humid breeze seemed to turn sharp-cold, blowing in one bitter gust from where the captain sat to where I squatted, listening; I shivered to feel it pass by, as if touched by some strange hand. Behind us, meanwhile, the quartermaster took up with a chantey tune, fellow after fellow soon joining in as a bawling round. Quickly, I recognized in it a song usually attributed to Captain Kidd, here modified to fit a different, entirely predictable personage:

...Oh, 'Salem Parry is my name, as I sail, as I sail,
The root of my infame, as I sail, as I sail,
My faults I will display,

Committed day by day—
Damnation be my lot, as I sail...

For every legend, good or bad, warrants a song made from his exploits. But sailors are fatalists all, drowned men kept upright sheerly by luck's vagaries—and thus unlikely to stay long impressed by anything, or anyone, who claims to be able to cheat destiny forever.

...So we'll be taken at last, and then die, and then die,
Though we have reigned awhile, we will die—
Though we have reigned awhile,
While fortune seemed to smile,
We must have our due deserts, and still die...

If Parry found the implication insulting, however, he gave no sign of it; his fine-cut face stayed closed and stony, indifferent as always. And his thoughts, now he was done discoursing with Captain Rusk's ghost, remained his own.

The next day, we finally reached that place Mister Dolomance had described to me—a great knot of weed flowering up from the ocean's bottom, roots sunk two hundred feet or more, down to the darkness where blue-clear water becomes mulch-black sand. For even at its very deepest places, the sea too gives way to land, eventually.

(And might this have been the worst part of old Captain Rusk's curse, made all the more potent by his extremity—for if there were truly no place without land, how could the ocean ever be anything but a stop-gap, a salve between bleedings against pain that never fully died? Which, in turn, perhaps explained so much about Parry's manner, his stiff coldness, his constant distraction; things become clearest in hindsight, always, after the fact. *Long* after, most often.

(But since I am now coming near my own story's end, as you can no doubt tell, I judge I too may well be falling into a distraction. So I will take care to try and tell the rest of it through without embellishment, from here on.)

We nosed in slowly, seeking not to entangle ourselves, 'til the weed-forest's thickness made it impossible and we dropped anchor as best we might, hooking it in the crook where three branches grew together at the holdfast like ivy. Parry and a small party took to the boats, following Mister Dolomance, who merely gave that creaky laugh of his when Parry vented his doubts as to where, exactly, he might be leading them. For once, I felt I could tell exactly what he was saying:

If you believe me capable of deception, wizard, even when still so ensorcelled I keep this shape you've laid on me, then it is yourself you make look bad, not I.

At this, Captain Parry merely sniffed yet once more, forbearing response—haughty as the Devil himself, if with far less reason—and waved the oarsmen to their task, bidding them into the weeds' heart 'til all of them were eventually lost from sight. The remaining crew stayed on deck, watching after with weapons ready, lest their master send up some sort of signal for aid. But since I knew exactly what they would find if they only went far enough, I slipped down below and performed a few small tasks, while no one else was looking.

One boat came back, the quartermaster at its helm. "Captain wants ye, Ciaran-boy, and quick-smart," he called up to me. "To 'bear witness to his triumph,' or some-such nonsense."

"Coming," I said, and was over the side a second after, not waiting on a ladder or rope; I hit the water with a splash and let the man haul me bodily aboard, all uncaring of how wet I got these ill-fitting clothes I soon expected to no longer have to wear.

The captain's boat had moored, again by tethering itself to whatever was handy, right by a weed-clump so thoroughly knotted it had grown a sort of skin, fleshy-rough as any mushroom. A veritable floating island, such as crews tell tales of from one end of the sea to the other, never for a moment thinking to set foot upon its like in real life. And it was here that Jerusalem Parry already stood, boot-heels sunk just a bare quarter-inch into the spongey mass below; stood and swayed slightly, braced against pain, 'til he was sure no blood would come. Whereupon his bitter mouth finally stretched wide and he threw back his head to laugh, delighted as any child with the way his magic had brought him at last to that place he'd so long sought for.

"See?" he called to me, triumphant. "I stand victorious. Though Rusk stole the land from me, yet have I conquered; the sea itself delivers whatever I demand, no matter how impossible!"

"Mister Dolomance and myself, rather, to whom *you* now owe a debt of thanks."

Parry raised a brow. "Mister Dolomance has proved a treasured investment, undoubtedly," he admitted with surprising grace, "so much so I may even free him for it, one day. But you've given me little enough during your stay with my crew, aside from sullen looks and poor labour. Or am I mistaken?"

He thought to toy with me in his customary style, all aristocrat's drawl and fine vocabulary—as he'd done with Rusk, perhaps, who'd seemingly found it more attractive than I. But because I knew something the captain did not, for once, I met his insults with a similar grin.

"As it ensues, yes," I replied. "For instead of giving, I have in fact *taken* something, without your notice."

"Explain yourself, sir."

I shrugged. "Wait and see."

Out where weed gave way again to ocean, the *Bitch* floated low, lapped at by some gentle tidal gyre; we caught yet more music off its thronged deck, playing counterpoint to light laughter, scuffle and jesting. But all this changed a moment later, when—with a flash and muffled roar, like some cracked cannon's back-fire—its magazine, which I'd carefully set fire to before disembarking, went off, blowing her hull so far open her guts were laid bare. The mainmast went one way, the mizzenmast another, tearing wood like splintery paper; screams rose, as did smoke, and flames.

Had he been still on board, Captain Parry's magic might have turned the trick, but from here, there was no help for it; those careful bonds suturing wreck to wreck dissolved, leaving the ship itself to slide apart in chunks and sink, taking the bulk of his crew down as well.

Parry's smile became a snarl, his eyes two werewolf moons. "You flotsam scum," he called me, words ground out between his teeth like bones. "God curse the day I ever let you on my vessel."

"Yes, and that was entirely at your pleasure, was it not? Well, I wish you full joy of that call, just as you once wished Rusk's ghost joy of his, when you thought no one was listening...and joy of this new home of yours, likewise, for however long your stay on it may last."

Caught gloating as only fools do, I was so puffed with my own cleverness that I barely registered Parry's hand slipping inside his coat, though I knew what it was he kept there. But when he withdrew the hex-bag, brandishing it like a pistol, I at least knew to shy away; the boat rocked sharply, salt spray slopping in over the side, prompting the quartermaster—shook from his shocked silence, and grabbing for his oars—to swear in three separate languages.

Still: "Not so much as I wish *this* joy on *you*," Parry told me, coldly. And up-ended the whole mess into the waves between us—bottle-finger, eyeball, hair-rope, fetish, tooth and all else, useless to him in his current cheated state, except as one last weapon. Since, at the very end, yet another thing more came slipping out to feed the churn...my skin.

My skin.

I must confess I almost went in after it, just on the off-chance, before I recalled what lurked in wait below. But then I caught sight of Mister Dolomance, still crouched in his captor's shadow, tearing away at his own parody-of-human disguise in a paroxysm of painful delight: mouth already ripped to either earhole with new teeth sprouting up along the bottom jaw in a bloody spray, muzzle punching out triangular, while his eyes—already far too widely spaced for comfort—migrated to either side of his head, losing their minimal ability to blink entirely. Shoulders hunched and splitting down mid-line, too, as his fin's long-buried crest at last came arching up between...

All your bad works brought to ruin in the same instant, I thought, staring Captain Parry down, straight in his silver-penny glare. *All you've sowed bloomed up full, sir, and ripe for reaping; well, I do hope you relish the taste of it, you sad fellow sport of unnaturalness. What little you can swallow, that is, before the end.*

Beneath the captain's boots, the weed-island rocked and buckled, forcing him down on one knee. I watched it crack, pull apart at its weakest points, and remembered how Mister Dolomance had described the forest that supported it, where his kin (who do not of a custom flock, or even pair, at least for longer than it takes one to get a kit on another) glided so close they risked touching in order to graze the schools that fed on those mile-high weed-fronds. It was always twilight there, a purple half-night forever blood-tinged, the water itself heavy with rotting meat; a bed of infinite appetite upon which every prospective victim knew they would, at least, die full-stomached.

This was what Jerusalem Parry found himself momentarily balanced above—a chasm of open mouths, all waiting to take a bite, before what was left of him drifted to the ocean's mucky floor. Yet even as he summoned his last few shreds of power to stave that judgment off, if only for a breath, he opened himself to the surprise attack he should have *most* feared, all along: Mister Dolomance, leaping high in mid-spasm to bite deep into the captain's unprotected nape, severing spine and the spell which kept him man-shaped alike. The shared arc of that jump threw them both sidelong, dragging Parry off-balance even as Mister Dolomance's legs shrank vestigial, once more fusing to form a tail; the weight of it put them down together with a great slap, waves gouting high, and slammed shut a blue-water door upon them both.

It was done, then—our revenge, complete—and Mister Dolomance surely got the lion's share of spoils, though I was the one self-condemned to live out a false man-life 'til laid in some landbound grave. And since cowardice, at least, could never be counted amongst his sins, I somehow knew the captain would go down fighting, to the very last...that image bringing me a variety of pleasure, at least, even as grief for my own losses cored my buried seal's heart.

The quartermaster pulled to with a will, meanwhile, and I took up oars as well, helping him put enough distance between us and the *Bitch*'s overthrow to make sure we were well out of range before the true frenzy began. After which we drifted, delirious with heat and fever, with hunger our only company; it occurred to me more than once, during this phase, that if I had managed to regain my true shape then the man I shared this boat with would have slit my throat long since, and be already picking his teeth with my bones. But thankfully, another ship picked us up before he could fully recall what lurked inside me, instead of thinking of me only as a boy—a tender thing, more his kin than not, to be protected rather than eaten.

"Ye're one of us now, son," was the last thing he spoke to me, which I know he meant kindly. Yet I just shook my head, waiting until he slept to steal what few coins he still possessed to pay my passage and roll him out through the sluices with a splash so quiet

I reckon it was barely heard, either above-decks or under.

It was an impulse and no doubt an unworthy one, for I did feel bad after, if only a little while. But the feeling did not last long, confirming what I hoped was still true, even in my current skinless state: that we were *not* alike, he and I, no more than I and Mister Dolomance. That we never could be.

By ship after ship and voyage after voyage, sometimes spaced years apart, I made my long way back to the Skerry where I took up residence on the shore, gazing each day from cliffside across to the home I would never regain. I built myself a boat, and fished from it; I made myself a life, and lived it. At a midsummer dance, I told a girl my name was Ciaran, and married her. Our son became Young Ciaran, in his turn.

And then, one day, I pulled up my net to find a skin—*my* skin—inside it.

Now it is late, and the fire is almost out. In the other room, Young Ciaran and his mother lie sleeping; my tale is told, in almost every particular. So I sit here and stroke the long-lost pelt spread out upon my knees, so soft, so durable...barely a mark on it, though my own hide has grown rough from ill-use, and not even a tear to show where the scar I once took from Mister Dolomance's teeth should be. Indeed, it reminds me of nothing so much as its polar opposite, my former co-conspirator's skin, which—like Captain Parry himself, as one man learned, to ill-profit—could hardly stand to be touched at all, at least from some angles, without danger of wounding. Never without cost, of one sort or another.

Tonight, I think, *I will go swimming.* And I smile, even knowing what probably awaits me, out there in the dark stretch of water between beach and Sule—something cold-blooded, grown huge as a bull in its far-roaming freedom, with little about it to indicate it was ever forced to walk upright, bowing and scraping at the whim of a man whose magic kept it prisoned in a shape it never would have chosen otherwise. For unlike my own kind, Mister Dolomance was only made to be what he is, not what he could be; his sort have no use for contradiction, let alone for metaphor.

Yet we are both equally treacherous, he and I—just as our Mother the sea is, in Her changeable yet unchanging heart. We cannot be overborne even by the subtlest magics, as Jerusalem Parry learned too late; we cannot be trusted, ever, even by those who love us. And as the sea is my home, so I will be proud to die there, if I must...more proud than I ever would have been to die on land, had I been forced to, as for so many years I was certain I would be.

Perhaps, though...perhaps I *will* fight, this time, the way I declined to, so long ago. Why not? What more do I have to lose?

Little enough, in the end.

The tide turns. The fire becomes ash. I rise. And here—in silence—is where I take my leave of all you who listen, closing the circle with these words: Just as any man may seize power if he consents to pay for it, by whatever method, any selkie *may* be Great, eventually...

...if he cares to.

SOWN FROM SALT

They made a desert there, and called it peace.
—Tacitus

Reese woke after dawn, dew-stiff, with difficulty; so much blood had dried all over his face, while he slept, that his eyelashes were now almost too sticky to peel open. The hard Arizona sun pressed down on him. Aside from the song of flies, no other living creature seemed anywhere near.

Though there did not seem to be too much to bother rousing himself for, he sat up moments later nonetheless, and nearly threw up. A terribly familiar pain monopolized the centre of his chest, folding him up around itself like a half-screwed winch. Had he not known better, he might have thought the bullet in him still, lodged deep—a truly unlovely thing, harbinger of delirium and death. Yet neither of those was to be his portion anymore, as he was well aware.

There was a dead body lying almost next to him, one of several such—leftovers from the latest trip to yet another town, fresh and not-so alike, scattered where they fell after judgment—but he ignored it; dead bodies were everywhere. This world was a butcher shop at the best of times. He'd've been far more surprised not to find one, there or elsewhere, on top of the earth or under it.

Eventually, he made his feet and stood there swaying, squinting upwards. He felt for his watch, popped it open, checked the time and reckoned which direction might be north accordingly: left a bit, where that dry ravine-mouth hid the horizon, aided by scrubby bushes. Some hours' hard walking to anything resembling civilization, probably, which alone argued for getting going. Yet he stood there a moment more, unsteady, wishing with all his considerable might that he could simply lie back down and sleep, this time without fear of waking.

His mouth already too dry for spit, he drew a cambric handkerchief from one pocket and used it, fastidiously, to scrub his sticky lashes clean. His eyes burned.

Grimly, he staggered forward.

Never fully alone, even in this emptiest of places; as the sun moved overhead, shimmering mirages lit the corners of his eyes. Reese seemed to hear distant laughter, footsteps behind and whinnying horses ahead, even brief snatches of song—a plaintive hill-holler tune from old Missouri, Mother of Outlaws, sung in the most easily recognizable of light baritones:

I wish I wish...my baby was born...and sittin' on...his daddy's knee...and me, poor gal, was dead and gone...and the green grass growin' over me...

...at which point he fell, taking almost a whole half-hour to rise again. Lay curled 'round his pain once more, cracked lips fresh-split, and sang the chorus back in a bare whisper all the while, not even one-quarter so effortlessly pretty:

"...but that's not now, nor never will be...'til the sweet apple grows...on the sour apple tree..."

He had a man kept in his mind to go with that voice, same as always: last thing he'd seen before that dark crack between then and now first gaped wide, not to mention the only thing he'd remembered consistently, since. Those mocking eyes finding his, full-on, right before obscene pain broke his world apart in a spurt of gun-smoke. They had looked at each other, and then he had been looking at the ground, and then he had been looking at nothing. And then—

—and then, after…much later…he had woken up once more, dew-stiff and cold on the hard desert ground, his heart apparently having been replaced by an open wound. With someone else's blood dried to a sticky mask all over his stupidly dumbfounded face.

He rose back up, walked on, 'til the sun met the horizon. 'Til everything went gold, then red, then black.

The next town he crossed over into—sometime after sunset, under a mean sprinkling of stars—was so small he somehow knew (as he always did, these days) it only had one whore left working, and her kept so indifferently busy, she often had to take in piecework to make ends meet. They'd had setbacks, obviously, almost since foundation; a virtual parade of ill-luck with no apparent cause (or cure), forever conspiring to rob the place of reason for being. Hope of mining had first inspired settlers to congregate there, 'til the claims dried up. They'd then switched to raising livestock—sheep, pigs, cattle, horses—'til various sicknesses forced those not bankrupted outright to cultivate a host of crops, all of which similarly came to nothing. Now there was intermittent talk of the Railroad, which might (or might not) be drifting towards their territory.

Jesus, too, had persisted strongly throughout all of the above— camp-meetings, revivals, the occasional church of some Revelation or other always raising itself up and flourishing briefly before falling away again to ruin—though that in itself had never, as yet, proved much of a draw for attracting new citizenry.

He passed the gutted shell of one such project on the town's west-most outskirt. Someone had propped a sign against its door-lintel, done unpunctuated, in shaky red letters of varying size: *MaNy cry in Truble & Are not hEard But to there SalvatioN.*

"Saint Augustine," he said, out loud, recognizing the words as ones his former "friend" had once quoted him, in time of particular moral quandary—for the man in question did love to read, and loved even better to let others know just how well-read he was.

That struggle with his own impulses—let alone their shared actions—had been a passing one, he now recalled; easily overturned by sentiment, if not by argument. As ever.

Because: *We've all done things we regret, I expect*, his "friend" had allowed, though both of 'em knew full well the other probably didn't think he had. To which he'd paused and considered, trying his level best to summon even one instance in which he'd genuinely questioned himself. Replying, finally—

I do wish I hadn't stayed my hand, at Lincoln.

His "friend" smiled at that, narrowly: *Didn't much, from what I hear.*

Not too much, no. But whenever I did, I wish I hadn't.

And did he feel differently, now? Could he even tell *how* he felt, if—indeed—he felt anything, at all?

But here were the lights of what passed for a main street, at last: open doorways, noise and music, faces peering out to greet him as he limped towards them in his dusty motley, his sticky crimson finery. He aimed to at least reach that storefront which claimed a doctor resided within before he pitched over, face-forward, to wait for them to decide what best to do with him…and this he was indeed able to achieve, before darkness reclaimed him. The never-quite-broken-off song rising undimmed in his ears, like blood, like tide:

I wish I wish…my love had died…
And set his spirit roaming free…
So we might meet where ravens fly
And never longer parted be…

(But that's not now, nor never will be)

"Mister. Mister, do you know where you are?"

A gruffer voice, from some further distance off:

"'Course he don't, Doc—don't even know his own name, I bet. How long you think he's been walkin'?"

The doc sighed. "Couldn't rightly say, not without I question him directly. Help me shift him up on that table, will you?"

This last was followed by a vertiginous rush and roll of movement, balanced ineptly with a hand or two on every slack limb before he came crashing down again, his skull connecting table-top-wards with a sick little crack. And: "Not so hard!" the doc cried, fussily. "You'll tear his scalp open, start him back to bleedin'—"

Then came the gruff voice once more, chiming back in—someone in authority; Sheriff? Mayor? Or both? Saying:

"You sure that's all *his* blood, Doc? 'Cause he don't look too 'sanguinated to me, from where *I* sit."

He didn't have to open his eyes to "see" the doc's mouth crimp at that, unbelieving. "Well, I suppose I don't quite take your meaning, Mister Marten. For pity's sake, whose else would it be likely to *be?*"

"That's the question, all right," Marten murmured.

When he did open his eyes, some hours later, they came apart smoothly; someone had finally run a hot cloth over his face, paying special attention to all those varying nooks and crannies where the blood had collected most deeply.

He got up, still moving slowly—didn't seem to move any other way, these days. He remembered how his pulse had once run so hot, his every movement a fever, resting heartbeat faster than a grouse across level ground. In the pier glass above the wash basin, he saw his own pale visage blink back at him: bushwhacker hair to below his shoulders, meticulously groomed in anticipation of whenever the South might rise again, plus a narrow blond beard and luxuriant moustachios, a pistoleer musketeer; sand-light eyes under similarly bleached lashes, almost yellow from some angles.

And: *Why, Sergeant,* he thought, *I never looked to see you here, down amongst the dead men and the drifting trash. Not without your dear companion to spur you along in any necessary endeavors, at any rate.*

Oh, but it was bitter, too, no matter how he might try to smile at it; the pain inside him felt abruptly greater than before, not that it ever grew small. So hollow with grief and hate and longing that it fair came off of him in waves, the way heat boils up from the veiny crust of some fallow field at noon. In that one dreadful moment he at last knew himself little more than a husk set endlessly roaming this world, always in search of one who fled from him (as youth flees from youth, or shadow flees from light), and might well have wept at such terrible understanding, had the desert not long since rendered him incapable.

But now there was a knocking at the door, impatient for entry;

he stood there stock-still, unable to hide his true nature anymore. Spotting his guns slung over a chair by the bed-stead even as they kicked through, and knowing himself far too slow to reach them before they broke through their initial shock at seeing him laid thus bare, jumping forward all at once to take him down in a single sprawling pile.

Face-on, Sheriff Marten proved as bluff and craggy a Union bastard as any Reese'd ever plugged through the brain-pan, or anywhere else. Marten held up a broadsheet from which the same face he'd seen mirrored upstairs stared, wall-eyed; next to it his "friend" quirked just the slightest of smiles, as though thinking it a fine irony that they meet again this way.

"Your name Sartain Reese, same's it says here?" Marten asked.

"Sartain Stannard Reese, yes."

"Folks call you 'One-Shot'?"

"They do."

Marten's deputy, a clean-browed young man whose eyes were masked by little round-lensed spectacles, put in, at that: "You really at Lincoln, Reese?"

"When I was fifteen, yes."

"And I guess you was at Bewelcome, too," Marten said. "With Bart Haugh."

"...Yes."

"Uh huh. So where's that sumbitch now?"

Reese glanced down, head hung low, ridiculous hair falling between them like a shield; replied, carefully—fighting hard to keep any further tremor from his already-shaky voice, which thankfully might be put down to him having been punched in both throat and belly during their earlier tussle—

"Don't rightly know. We had a fallin' out."

"What happened?"

At this Reese looked up again, grinning against the pain, and tapped his chest one time above the breast-bone, neat and clean and hard, like knocking on a coffin's lid. Saying:

"Well, as to that...he shot me, Sheriff, just about here. You see it, where I'm pointin'? Right through my Goddamned heart."

Marten stared him straight in the eye, unimpressed by what he maybe took for mere rhetoric. "So how're you alive then, Mister Reese?"

Reese nodded, slightly. "How am I?" he repeated, without much emphasis. Having already asked himself that same question on many an occasion by now, and never yet received any satisfactory answer.

They beat on him some more for a while, after, before slinging him into a cell to wait on some judge they'd have to order from two towns over. The deputy (Jenkins, his name proved to be) sat there checking Reese's guns in front of him, stroking their chased silver hilts admiringly and sighting down their long barrels at nothing in particular, before locking them safely away with the rest of the sheriff's armaments.

"Wouldn't do that, I was you," Reese told him, carefully maneuvering one of his looser teeth around in its socket with his tongue-tip.

Jenkins frowned. "Why not?"

"'Cause unless you're planning on selling 'em, you probably don't want what comes along with 'em. They was at Lincoln too, after all."

Jenkins gave him a long, cool look. "I heard some things, about you and Haugh."

"Did you, now." A pause. "Well, since I think I know what, I don't suppose it'll do either of us much good to discuss it any further. Still—would you say I merited hangin' less or more, I wonder, you happened to find out they was true?"

"There's some would say more," Jenkins allowed, flushing slightly. "But I ain't with 'em on that one, necessarily."

"Kind of you. I *do* merit it, though, sure enough—for Bewelcome, and elsewhere. Make no mistake about that."

That shut Jenkins up, at least for a little bit; must've been something he saw reflected in Reese's eyes, under the lantern's uncertain light. They maintained silence together, oddly companionable, until he finally had to ask—

"Whose blood was that you had on you, Reese?"

"Oh, somebody from round here's, I expect. Didn't you recognize it?" A pause. "Listen, Jenkins—you and yours seem good people, on the whole, from what I've seen. But there's always a reason I run across places, and you have been unlucky, so might be that's 'cause there's other people here, ones that's just like me."

Jenkins, paling: "I'd know, if there was."

Reese really did have to laugh then, torn mouth bleeding just a bit as he did, streaking his smile like rouge. "Would you? How, exactly, saving the Word of God? Men lie, Jenkins, even when they *don't* have something to hide—so how much more you think they're prepared to do to cover true sin up, 'specially if they don't want to have to keep on runnin' from its consequences?"

Which brought silence again, for a spell. Reese drank it in, leaned his head back against the cell wall, and waited.

As it soon turned out, the rest of the townsfolk didn't plan on putting anything off for simple lack of a judge. Instead, they came for Reese at midnight, with guns and torches; shouted Marten and Jenkins down, then hustled him back down Cow-track Avenue and hanged him from a tree outside that same burnt church he'd passed on his way into town. They also proved inexpert enough at this particular form of semi-judicial murder that his neck failed to break on the drop, which meant he dangled there a while—tongue out and blackening, face a-swell, some awful noise issuing forth from his throat like a half-swallowed rattlesnake—before Jenkins finally lunged forward and hauled at both his legs together 'til the crack of bone rang out at last.

This last mercy loosed a flood of piss that ran down Reese's fine trousers to foul them from the crotch down, soiling dirt and deputy alike; as he thrashed, strangling, his gay shirt flew open in front, revealing to all and sundry the black miracle of his wound...that awful fleshly Advent calendar with only one day left celebrated, laid open like a little bone window so everyone in town could see the cold pink meat framed underneath its ragged hole, unbroken yet unbeating.

He heard more than one woman or close-hugged child shriek out in terror at the sight, while many more than one man blasphemed in gutter-language he recognized from Lincoln, Dodge City, Bewelcome itself. But then the penultimate buzz was in his ears, drowning out even that damn betraying song, at long long last:

The owl the owl...is a lonesome bird...

It chills my heart with dread and terror...
That's someone's blood there on its wing,
That's someone's blood there on its feather...

Then Reese was not,
  nor never would be,
    strung to rot like fruit
      from a gallows-tree.

But it wasn't the end, of course; never was. Not since he'd woken that first morning with blood in his eyes, his mouth, his hair—with an open wound where his shot-through heart should be, and Bart Haugh's faithless name still curdled on his lips.

By dawn on the third day he was deep in unhallowed ground, sand and stones piled haphazardly atop to ward off coyotes. But the morning opened dark above his grave, only to grow steadily darker, a storm lowering constantly overhead yet never breaking fully into much-needed rainfall, while ball- and sheet-lightning chased each other up and down the sullen, swollen sky.

And just after sunset, once more, was when Reese came limping into town again, up the main street to Marten's office, covered in the same dirt and piss they'd buried him wearing. His tongue black-tinged yet in a still-torn mouth, when he opened it to wish Sheriff Marten and Deputy Jenkins alike a raspy—

"Good even, gentlemen."

Marten gaped. "Sweet King Christ Jesus, 'One-Shot' Reese."

"That'd be a 'no' to the first, 'yes' to the second," Reese replied, with all the bleak coolness of his condition. Adding, to Jenkins: "Now, I'd much appreciate havin' my guns back, deputy, if you don't mind; they were a gift, you see. And the plain truth is, I'm sentimental about such things."

Jenkins nodded a tad at this, as though he quite took Reese's point—but Marten drew his own sidearm instead, aiming it straight at Reese's midsection. Blustering: "*You* can just go right on back to Hell and *stay* there, this time, you damned murderin' secesh—"

Reese shook his head, dusty gold hair flapping a bit with the gathering wind. "I believe there's some following behind me may want a few words with you, Sheriff, on that very same subject."

He said it gently, though—perhaps too much so. For under cover of that howl-din which suddenly rose up all around them, a great chorus of disembodied plaint knit to a hundred skittering shadows, Reese's warning seemed almost entirely lost on Marten, whose eyes grew wide and crazed. Even as Jenkins turned to inquire if he was all right, the sheriff found himself abruptly surrounded by nothing and borne away in some phantom twister of screams, kicking and yelling, bound for whatever black country Reese had already left behind.

Now it was Jenkins' turn to freeze, face slack and wondering. For all over the rest of town, similar harsh magic was being worked: a new-made widow far too infatuate with her state over here, a rival whose dispute had been settled through apparent chance over there; one veteran who boasted, another who did not; those with unsupported claims to their pasts, as well as those who never spoke of what had brought them there at all. Interestingly, almost none of Reese's own lynch-gang were to be counted amongst the judged—save for one or two Jenkins knew had once delivered other, similarly rough, instances of frontier "justice."

Reese—who had seen this same drama played out many times previously, in many different places—ignored it all, strolling past Jenkins into the sheriff's vacant office, where he broke the weapons cabinet's lock with Marten's empty desk chair. As he walked back out, adjusting his holsters down low on his hips, he found Jenkins there to meet him…and paused, courteously, barely flinching, to let the deputy bury a few slugs in his gut; the very least he could offer, as recompense for the night's awfulness. Nothing poured from the wounds except for a few slack streams of sand and reddish dust, admixed.

Reese peered at Jenkins, frozen once more, some vague semblance of sympathy in his yellow eyes. "Feel better?" he asked.

Jenkins swallowed. "Why him? Why not me?"

"Well, he had blood on him too, I expect; you don't. Not yet, anyhow." Turning away: "Better look to keep it that way in future, don't you think?"

He left Jenkins standing there—probably the town's best

choice for new sheriff, now—and made off, without much haste, down that muddy cart route which might never quite pass for a true main thoroughfare, while dark tides of vengeance eddied back and forth all about him, leaving few but him (their harbinger, their slave) untouched. Musing as he did on how Bart Haugh, always over-proud of his Eastern university learning, had once read from *Bullfinch's Mythology* the tale of King Cadmus, who killed the dragon guarding the river outside Thebes-to-be, knocked out all its teeth and sowed 'em in the nearby fields...like seed, like salt. Then stood there astounded when men came up instead of crops, all over armor, and did what men in armor do best...

Amusing once, now the story was only bitter true: He knew himself a walking dragon's tooth, sent to lie in other folks' earth a while, and see what might rise up along with him, afterwards. And yet, even supposing some variety of judgment (divine, or otherwise) drove what he did, he could never count what he brought along with him as vengeance, not even for whatever the people there might wreak on him beforehand; as he'd told Jenkins, *that* was only what he deserved. If he were to be hanged in every town from here to Missouri, it still might not be enough to wash him clean of everything he'd done.

On reaching the western-most border of town, Reese paused again, craning his neck to the sky. And cried out, to no one in particular—

"There. Am I done yet? Can I *stop*?"

Silence, only; the lightning's flash, clouds a-boil like lava. Reese felt it twist in him, knife-like, 'til he could not restrain his next demand, torn cold and bloody from the dry hole where his perforated heart should keep time still, unbreached. Screaming up at those hidden, condemning stars, 'til his throat fair cracked:

"Look, just—where in the Hell *is* he, Goddamnit? So I know which way to go, at least! You want me to keep on working Your will much longer, You surely need to tell me, *right damn now*—"

But: Nothing replied, as he'd come to expect, save for the thunder, which cracked the vault above him open, wide, to loose the promised torrent. A scarlet, sticky rain, warm and salty, which fell only on him, soaking him from tip to toe with the leavings of his own sin. Covering him completely, erasing all he was, or might have been.

An answer, of sorts—long-expected, bitter in his torn mouth, on his blackened tongue. So Sartain Stannard Reese bowed his proud bushwhacker head to the wind of comeuppance, prepared to walk until he fell. Knowing that by the time the sun rose he would wake yet again, dew-stiff and cold, crusted all over with blood not his own. That he would seek his "friend"-turned-enemy Bart Haugh eternally and never find him, for vengeance...once that most satisfactory of all commodities...was no longer his to administer.

Not now. Nor never.

He set his raw feet to the desert's hard road, therefore, that same song dinning ceaseless in his ears. And let darkness take him, praying that this time—this time, of innumerable other occasions—

—it would not be so unkind as to even play at letting him go, once more.

TWO
CAPTAINS

"One captain to a ship, always, or that ship flounders." It was good advice...most especially so, in hindsight.

"Found somethin' for ye below-decks, Cap'n," the bo'sun told him, with a wink. And thus, with little warning, Solomon Rusk's last great set of troubles began.

"Something" soon proved a man in rags, enchained, with a possessed saint's face and a cough that racked him stem to stern, shaking him like a high wind. He attempted to rise as Rusk pushed the door to, barely making his feet before falling back again, panting slightly. This creature's feverish eyes were the same shade as silver pennies bleached almost to pale green by tarnish; they so well caught the light that Rusk all but thought he might be able to see himself mirrored in them, if he only moved closer—and *wanted* to, the sudden impulse deep-set, like a bone in the throat.

"You put me at a...disadvantage, sir," the man managed, after two attempts at speech, both equally exhausting.

To which Rusk replied: "You'd seem to've done that yourself, already, given where I find ye." Continuing, as the man arched a fine-cut brow: "We've searched this whole brig and found nothing t' warrant our investment, save for rats, rot—and one prisoner. Might such an estimation be correct?"

"Having not seen the rest of this ship since they...brought me aboard, I...couldn't possibly say."

"Well. And what am I t'do with *you*, then, exactly?"

The man snorted, setting himself off once more. Then snapped back, nonetheless, far too haughtily for any ordinary prisoner: "As you please, I'm sure! *I* obviously can't prevent it."

A bit too sharp to count as showing proper respect, though since Rusk could only assume the poor bastard was in pain, he forgave it. Yet here the captain felt his own eyebrows hike, fast as sparks striking from cold flint, and peered closer, suddenly aware how that shadow the man was trying to hide beneath his close-held blanket was, in fact, the rim of a collar—cold iron over puffed scar, with portions of it adhering yet to the sadly tormented skin below.

A wizard, Rusk thought. They'd meant him for Admiralty justice, obviously—been taking him on to the next lawful port, where he'd be burnt or hanged, or both.

The man did not seem to notice; he was deep-engaged in trying not to cough again, pale face flush-blotched with sudden, indignant scarlet. But looked up again nonetheless, when Rusk told him—"You interest me, 'sir.'"

"I...do not mean to," the man replied, regaining some sense of caution.

"No, y'wouldn't, and yet—maybe I've not wasted my men's time entirely, in playing out this lark. For any prize comes wi' a man-witch already netted in its hold is one well worth the taking."

Quick-touched by Rusk's implication, the man perhaps wished to say more—opened his prim mouth to, at least, baring teeth like a cat, a harbinger of equal-sharp words to come. But even as passion undid his better judgment, sheer sickness overtook the rest; those pale eyes rolled up and he fell forwards, into Rusk's arms.

Frail, and slim, and steely. The man smelled ill after his captivity, but Rusk wondered what lay under that. His cabin had a tub, liberated from some Moghul vessel and sold in the marketplace on Veritay Island, back near where his kin had slave-holdings; to fill it with hot water would take more effort than simply sluicing the man with a bucket of brine, but it wasn't as though Rusk had so much to do that he could entirely discard the notion of entertainment.

So: "Bo'sun," he called back, through the open door. "Them as takes the Articles may come along; kill the rest, then scuttle her. And make ready t' cast off sharpish, in good time, that the *Bitch* not grow restless."

"Yes, Cap'n."

With that, Rusk hoisted his newest personal possession high, and left—a bad choice, as it turned out, but he wasn't to know. Not that such foreknowledge ever stopped him, anyhow.

For we must do as our natures dictate, seeing we cannot do otherwise, he would think, much later. And conjure up the bitter memory of a smile on lost lips, so ghostly now—so rendered down by time, along with various other complaints—that he found he only barely remembered just what such an expression should feel like.

Rusk had seen sorcerers aplenty in his time—they were in no short supply out here, on the very rim of all civilized things, where prejudices of both King and Church held so little popular account: not so much feared as coveted, though treated with the same caution one would accord any other exotic beast. Yet never before had he encountered one collared, which proclaimed that the main error of this man currently still insensibly a-toss in his bed had resided in trying to hide what he was in plain sight, by joining one of the primary institutions which hunted his kind out most effectively.

"Jerusalem Parry, that's 'is name," one of the new recruits offered, when quizzed on particulars. "Ensign, 'e was, mobbed in at Portsmouth. Comes from some bloody smuggler's hole in Cornwall, set up smack in the middle of a marsh; well-learnt, too, in all manner of books and languages. 'E'd've made a parson, if the local squire 'adn't ruled his mother be 'ung for...you know."

"Whoredom? Theft?"

A circumspect look, like the recruit expected to find Parry standing in the shadows, listening. "No, though there might've been some of that, too; the...same as 'im, they do say."

Rusk understood the man's implication well enough, though

from what-all he'd seen, blood seldom told quite as indubitably as most fools seemed to think, in *that* way. Christ knew, there'd been a scandal of the same sort 'round old Judas Rusk, his clan's progenitor, born fatherless in the Witch-House at Eye, in old Scotland, with his dam already Fire-bound. There were tales on how, in every generation since, some Rusk woman (or, far less frequently, man) would be able to raise storms or read minds, blast with a word and tame with a touch, dream the future—and he himself had seen it happen so, though never on the white-skinned side of things. Yet if such tricks truly lingered in his own veins, Rusk couldn't claim a shred of proof for it; his primary skills lay in sailcraft and slaughter, qualities which had gained him his ship *Bitch of Hell*, amongst other things... young Master Parry, most lately, very much included.

The man in question stayed insensible 'til a week on, however, when he puked blood, and the chirurgeon gave him up. "Iron-poisoned and sick with it, unto the very death: he'll not survive without help of a sort plain human men can't give. This wizard of yours is doomed, Captain."

Moments after, the drunken sawbones dispatched back to his own place, Rusk stood staring down at this fever-thrashing by-blow of uncanniness he'd thought to make a pet of, cursing himself a fool. Thinking: *Were this a woman, you'd've had her already five times over, consequences be damned; hell, put to port, nursed her healthy, and forced the bitch's hand in marriage if you wanted, or not...*

(The very idea of which, snake-striking him from the side—some neat spinster, hands folded prim over skirts, staring up at him under her lashes with Parry's same moon-eyes and finding him wanting, contempt immediate as lust—was enough to stick him in some vital point, and *twist*.)

All right, then.

Rusk put both hands on either side of Parry's throat, feeling for the collar's seam with his palms spanning jaw to collarbones, one rough thumb grazing the clavicle. Parry strained that odd gaze of his open, squinted to focus, demanding: "What is't you...do here, sir? What...are y'about?"

"Your freedom, man-witch. Now shut that pretty mouth, and let me t'my work."

"I will thank you not to...use such terms with me—"

"Yes, yes. Shush, or I'll clout ye back asleep."

'Round and 'round, over and under, the metal warming beneath his touch. 'Til at last, he felt some sort of spark prick all ten fingers at once, and knew where best to pull—the collar shivered itself apart, Parry gasping as strangulation's threat went unfulfilled, and came away in sections, taking an uppermost rind of scar along with it. Thus revealed, the resultant inter-braiding of wounds was red, white and a sort of angry bluish-pink combined, a souvenir Parry might well never find himself rid of, no matter how long his recuperation; he put up his own hand as he fell back, reflexive, and spasmed at the feel, face disgust-contorted—the insult of owning such a Cain-mark far more immediate than any pain, at least for him.

Rusk shrugged, cracking his knuckles. "There—now cure your-self or die, for not one of us here can do it for ye."

"I..." Parry turned his head for what must have been the first time in weeks, that handsome skull of his flopping 'til his sweat-wet hair smeared the sheet, then found himself too weak to lift it back; the words came haltingly, at cost. "I am not...trained, in such matters. Never knew, for sure...not 'til the finders called me out, and then..." He spat at the collar's two broken halves, carelessly dropped beside him. "*Then*, may all such bastards rot in Hell, I...spent every native jot of power I proved to have in keeping myself alive, while they put *that* on me—"

Rusk shook his head, unsympathetic. "Can't help ye there, what with you bein' the cunning one. So ye'll try and succeed, or try and fail; there'll be no man aboard my ship don't earn his keep, either way."

"God damn you, I don't know *how*!"

"An' you never will, ye don't damn well shift off your narrow arse and *try*, ye bloody lazy bugger! So *do*. See what happens."

Parry cursed, volubly, inventively, the words triply profane be-tween those lips; Rusk leant forward and watched, fascinated, as he strained to summon magic from his pores, sweating it out like blood while continuing to damn Rusk at every turn. It crept along every limb, polishing his sickness away, burnishing him 'til he gleamed like metal heated too high to touch. His verminous prison-clothes crisped off and went floating away in a burnt husk that sprayed ash everywhere, peeling him dimly naked under a smeared coat of grey. Then cooled again to safe degrees, skin firming and paling slowly 'til he lay there once more in need of a bath, but otherwise immaculate—breath slowing, fever gone. When he opened those eyes again, the tarnish-green tinge was cured at last, leaving nothing behind but silver.

My mirror, Rusk thought.

And: "Done," Jerusalem Parry told him, only slightly hoarse, each drawling divine's vowel a bared blade. "Are you satisfied?"

"Not entirely," was Rusk's answer. And before Parry could think to stop him, he'd already mashed their lips together, knocking mouths so hard he could fair feel their teeth grate.

Parry sprang as far back as the bed would allow for, slapping Rusk 'cross the face with enough force it made the captain laugh out loud; Rusk'd wear the mark some days, and gladly. Spitting, as he did: "Sir! I have not given you permission to use me thus, familiarly!"

"No more y'have. Still, ye do owe me somewhat, my Jerusha— for that's how I'll call you, seein' ye owe me all for pullin' ye from a straight-made path t'wards stake or gallows, and teachin' you the use of your own skill, in the bargain."

Parry gave his own laugh here, less pleased than bitter. "So, are you God, now, pirate?"

"I like that notion."

"I'm sure. And me with no daughter to kill, on your altar."

"Aye, well—there's other payments might be negotiated, easily enough."

Parry shook his head, abruptly sullen. Said, all unaware of his own ridiculousness: "I swore your Articles, Captain; my oath and my loyalty are yours already, as a Navy man. What right have you to demand more?"

"Oh, none, probably. But them as stay dumb don't get their will, as you yourself may've had occasion t'note. And besides which..."

"Besides which?"

Rusk watched the man stare up at him, so innocent, in his odd way: this trick-box thing, crammed shut with impossible secrets, a puzzle ripe for forcible solution. It made him smile. Then lean in further—so close his breath might almost warm the man's tongue— and add, his grin grown all the larger:

"...whoever said I was *askin'*?"

Foolish as it might ring, given his looks, it soon ensued that Jerusalem Parry—so neat, finicky and otherwise over-learned—had been given pitiful little education, thus far, in fleshly matters; perhaps parsons kept their vows differently in Cornwall than they did in all the other places Rusk had made shore, in that they actually *kept* them. So Rusk delighted in taking his time with the man's first few lessons, not least because it so amused him to chart Parry's responses, those oh-so-winning little gasps and snarls, not to mention the blue- and green-flickering jolts of what he took to be power expelled along with 'em—magical might as purest product, undirected and aimless, unable to give itself substance as long as he carefully kept its master far too distracted to form spells, even in his own mind.

Licking down along the collar-scar, feeling the wizard's sex jump in his hand like a fish while he stirred him from inside out, puffed hard himself as any iron stew-ladle by the very feel of Parry's intactness giving way; Rusk pressed him back down even as Parry strained up, bruise-sudden, seeing him flush with an embarrassed admixture of pain and pleasure combined and thinking, happy: *If that's your poison, Master Parry, then I believe I can well-afford t'supply your needs...for I do like a bit of tussle myself, y'see, both in bed, and out of it.*

After, Parry huffed into the sheets' rucked nest, gave one long shudder, and made as if to laugh, before thinking better of it. "Do you treat all your guests thus?" he asked, at last.

"Only those as strike my fancy. Ye may call me shark, my Jerusha, with all manner of creatures my meat, once they've fallen into my grip."

"You mistake yourself, sir, as ever; there is no way in which I am yours."

"Certain parts of your corpus might argue the point, I think, if you're honest." Adding, as Parry hissed: "Yet let us not be cross wi' each other, Hell-priest—I've done you some small service as well, after all, have I not?"

"Aye, and gotten full measure for it."

"Oh, not quite yet—for there's more than one reason I brought you out of bondage, and we've yet t'negotiate those terms. Now tell me: Can you raise storms?"

Parry sighed, turning over, and studied the cabin's roof-beams awhile before answering. "Apparently yes," he replied, at last, "since that's what the finders charged me with, after those Navy sheep branded me a Jonah. It's instinct—easy enough, even without ritual."

"Hmm. And a ship—could you raise such as that?"

"One wrecked already, you mean? Perhaps, if you gave me her name, or something from a survivor—I haven't tried, certainly. But—" He pondered, seemingly glad to have something to consider besides the ways in which he'd just been so thoroughly outraged. "—it seems likely, with preparation enough."

"A man from the dead, then. Could ye raise *him*?"

"Not for long, for none can; never *permanently*, if that's your aim. Death is the great leveller, the one boundary all magicals fear to cross."

"Then I know aught you don't, for I've seen whole factories full of men brought back upright and set t'work, mouths sewn shut lest they taste salt, and wake."

"Yes, well: Those men aren't actually dead to begin with, in the main..."

Rusk gave a wolf's smile. "What a treasure y'are," he said, "well worth the finding, and cheap at twice the price."

Some more sport ensued, to which Parry—perhaps not seeing the point, given how intent Rusk was on ignoring his protests—raised little immediate objection. After, however, he demanded fresh raiment, then complained (once supplied with the only clothes available, scaled for Rusk's own long body) that they didn't fit.

But: "We're aboard-ship," Rusk pointed out, blithely, "and even I cannot conjure things entire from the air whilst in transit—not like some."

It was enough. The next time he saw him, Parry was making ginger little steps 'cross-deck, arrayed head-to-toe in the neat, well-tailored black he'd once aspired to wear for slightly less nefarious purposes. The breeze lifted his brown hair, untied and disordered; his eyes, narrowed against the horizon, cast back its light like a cat's. Rusk all but wanted to take him again there and then, right on the fo'c'sle, in full view of any who might aspire to liberate him from their current arrangement.

Yet when he hove in for only the briefest embrace, Parry showed himself unamused.

"No."

"Come, don't be foolish; you liked it well enough last night, same as I."

"Convinced yourself, have you? And still I say no, nevertheless: you've had all you will from me, in that respect—consider my price of passage paid. So I'll keep my own place from now on, if you'll be so good as to allow me the privilege."

"Ship-mates only, eh? And that'll last, ye reckon? Very well, then, Jerusha, don't take on so. I'll require no more...liberties, not without invitation."

"Which you will not gain, sir, know that now."

"Ah, brave words. For all things change at sea, Master Parry, as She herself be wont to; the sea is deep, after all, and little-known. You'll learn."

Bitch of Hell put in at Porte Macoute, to re-stock and recre-ate. Parry would have refused to go ashore entirely, but that Rusk promised to introduce him to a practicing sorceress of his ac-quaintance. This was his "cousin," Tante Ankolee, who'd helped her *maman* nurse Rusk up along with his elder siblings, before eventually buying her way free of the whole familial mess; she and Parry sat and talked, quietly, Parry minding his manners far more with her than he'd ever bothered to with Rusk, regardless of the bone through her blue-lined lower lip and the bells in her stiff-locked hair.

When they were done, she sent Parry off with a serving wench to pick and choose amongst her wide collection of fetish-objects for seeds to grow his own personal hex-bag from, then poured Rusk a shot of rum, lit it, and watched him sip it down, tent-ing her clawed fingers. "What-all you know of that man in there, Solomon Rusk, save for he make your trousers tight? That's some trouble you done brung on, little half-me-blood; may have saved him the rope, sure, but I bet he ain't thank you for it."

Rusk shrugged. "There you'd be wrong, big sis—for 'tis my experience thus far Jerusalem Parry always recalls his courtesies, whether he means 'em or no."

"Oh, eh? Well, he a pure devil in the makin', set t'grow up tree-high once he come into his full power, no mistake—but better yet, he hate you bad, now an' forever. You show him what him nah want t'know, an' he don't find you charmin' for it."

"Ah, he'll forgive me soon enough, once he finds there's no other way; poor creature was raised Christian, after all."

"You think?"

"'Tis a certainty."

"Nah, I don't believe 'tis. 'Cause that a man of *pride* you got yourself there, chuck—the sort holds grudges and plots on 'em too, remorseless, no matter what the way him feel in your bed make you want t'believe."

"Let him plot! 'Tis my ship we sail on, no way 'round that."

"And what you think he care?" She gave a snap, contemptuous. "*This* much, like any other cunning-folk. 'Sides which, 'twasn't always so. Was it?"

True enough. So instead of bothering trying to deny it, Rusk merely demanded—"Tell me how best t'protect myself, then, witch. Or leave me t'my fate."

"Chain him up an' sink him deep, that the best way. But you won't do that." Sighing, as he shook his head: "Well, then...give me that eye o'yours and I work me will on't, rub it wi' the blood we share on me mirror, an' see what rise up in the reflection. For we do be the same line, after all, wi' that one ancestress of yours puissant as any ten o'mine; should help, to a point."

Given how little its loss troubled him, these days, Rusk felt an almost foolish stab of surprise to hear her even mention the gewgaw's mere existence. But he popped it free nonetheless, and handed it over—ivory inlaid with jet, the skull and crossed bones winking back up at him from his own salt-rough palm. "I'll wait on the beach, shall I?"

"As ya please," Tante Ankolee replied, all blissful-unaware how she parroted the same man whose ill-wishes she sought to keep her roguish "little" half-brother safe from.

Rusk lay on the sand, stretched out and warming himself, 'til the sun dipped low enough to turn everything behind his lids deep red. At which point he heard crunching to his right hand and knew without even looking how Parry drew near, his booted steps sure and light as any other stalking thing.

"She has your looks, on close examination," Parry said, settling himself beside with arms wrapped 'round his knees, "for which, one can only assume, she is hardly to be blamed."

"A misfortune most Rusks share," the captain agreed, still not opening his eye. "Her dam and mine were bed-mates, of a sort, though seldom sharing the same one at the same time."

"Ah, so your father kept slaves; well, then. Perhaps that explains it."

"Explains what?"

"How you have no qualm treating others thus, free *or* slave. But then again—if that was truly what you wanted, in my case, you would have done better to leave the collar on."

At this, Rusk did rise up, casting both his remaining eye and the empty socket a Frenchman's sword had left behind down Parry's way. He saw the man's fine, lean face even more set than usual, his shoulders stiff, ever-so-slightly a-tremble in the dimming light, and felt something soften in himself, if only for a moment.

"Nay, Jerusha—much as I may covet t'see you on your knees, it's little use you'd be t'me that way. And while I run no charity, to work a ship, any ship—pirate, Navy, the most mundane-lawful tub ever sailed—is indenture, as all aboard her know, with me no exception, my captain's colours aside. For so long as she's mine to command I'm owned just as sure, by the *Bitch of Hell* herself."

For a moment, Parry had nothing to offer by way of reply—and indeed, that moment stretched on so long, Rusk almost thought he had made him understand.

But then:

"This is easily said," Parry told him, coldly, making his own feet and meeting Rusk's half-gaze straight-on. And turned a black-clad back on him, spine no longer anything but ramrod-straight.

That night, when Tante Ankolee gave him back his eye, Rusk felt it sting slightly as it went in: her "protection," no doubt, and just as well. For from what he could see, he would probably need it.

The bag Rusk's cousin had helped him start grew apace, along with Parry's powers, and he and the captain settled into an uncomfortable sort of working partnership, accordingly. Since the wizard was learning on his feet, however, this arrangement did not come without dangers: when they ran into doldrums, Parry raised a wind to nudge them free that quick-swelled into a full-blown storm and almost swamped them, whilst a glamour meant to slip them close enough to a prize to board her unawares lit them up with ghostly flame, which had the exact opposite effect, drawing cannonballs like hail.

Still, even Rusk had to own himself impressed when Parry split the ship they'd just been almost sunk by down its midsection like a hot knife with one wave and used the two halves to cobble a new hull from, shelling the *Bitch* in strange wood; the result dressed them permanently in false colours, making them seem no threat at all from a distance so they might make striking range at double-time, then run up the black flag.

At the revels, after, Parry sat alone and un-drinking, on the very edge of the crowd. When Rusk passed him the rum he refused it: no surprise, there. "I seldom imbibe," Parry told him, shortly.

"'Seldom' still leaves me aught t'work with, ye realize."

Caught unawares, Parry had already half-started to laugh before he could quite stop himself but choked it off a second on, quick enough to rasp in the throat. "To proclaim oneself abstemious entire aboard a Navy vessel would have been foolish in the extreme," he said, at last. "Assuming you care to know my logic on the matter."

"Ah, it always does me good t'hear ye use such large words in casual conversation, my Jerusha; broadens the mind, it does, and lifts me own vocabulary likewise." Thus rebuffed, Rusk drank the dram down himself, and sighed. "Still, I cannot but think from your manner that ye have not yet forgiven me my trespasses, as that Book you once studied says ye should. What say you?"

"That you may count yourself entirely correct, in such a conclusion."

"A pity. I'll leave you to your brooding, then, shall I?"

"Please."

Rusk sketched him a bow, received a haughty nod in return, and withdrew some few paces, taking up a watchful position. When the fires burnt low enough, his crew began to pair off—some with native girls, some with each other—and he returned, softly, to where Parry now dozed on one hand, his grim head nodding. Then waited 'til even a sharp clap next to one ear was no longer sufficient to rouse him and gathered him up, retiring to what he'd begun to think of as their cabin.

Morning found them both stripped down and well-ensnared,

with one of Parry's fearsome cheekbones dug deep above where Rusk's black heart beat strongest through the fur of his chest. As far as Rusk could tell, the delights of the night had been entirely mutual, in their moment—but by the time Parry's eyes opened fully he was angry again, small hairs all over his body fair lifting with painful little blue-green sparks yet generally schooled to a cold stillness almost more frightening to witness than any full loss of control, as though he knew himself far too badly-enraged to give way to his passions, lest they stream from him so strongly they ripped the very ship 'round he and Rusk to shreds.

"I see you have broke your word to me, sir," he managed, at last, teeth so hard-set Rusk could hear their grind in every syllable. Determined to stay unaffected, however, he merely yawned and stretched himself before inquiring, all lazy charm—

"What word would that be, exactly?"

"That you would trust I keep my oaths and let me do as I list, so long as I bend my skills to support your ventures. That you would not require—this of me, as a simple measure of respect."

"I required nothing; showed my gratitude, only, for yesterday's assistance. And from what-all I saw, 'twas entirely your own idea t'accept the proof of it so...embracingly."

Parry bared his teeth, silver-penny gaze now gone truly dangerous. "I'm sure! Yet enlighten me, nevertheless: What was it failed to convince you *I am no one to be thus trifled with*, Solomon Rusk? Surely even a barbarian idiot like you must grasp that small fact about me, if nothing else—"

"Aye, I grasp it, well enough!" Rusk snapped back, rolling them both in one quick twist, so he wound up once more most securely on top. Then added, right into Parry's face, as the man all but bit at him like a trapped weasel: "Yet I can't help but note, powerful as y'are, at no point in the preceding did I ever once see you try to stop me doin' as I wished, not s'long as it was makin' ye jump an' sing! So don't play the re-stitched virgin wi' me, 'sir'—'tis hardly my fault I choose not t'believe these lies ye tell yourself, 'specially when I have such *hard evidence* t'the contrary—"

—and here he reached down between them, taking hold of the "evidence" he referenced with force enough to make Parry start back, as if scalded. Which Rusk was later forced to admit might *not*, in fact, have been the best possible way to calm the man's ruffled dignity, rather than rouse his ire to its furthest possible pitch—

Still: "*You will let me* go!" Jerusalem Parry roared at him, springing only momentarily naked from the bed, before a single gesture restored at least the illusion of clothing. "You will leave me be from now on, you bloody-handed bastard, or I will stave this Bitch of yours in and go down along with her, gladly—this I so swear, by every star above and demon below! Do you *hear* me, *Captain?*"

His pale face bright-flushed as it'd been during his first fever, lips near shaking, clerk's hands clawed like some fee-cheated Tortuga whore's. And how Rusk found himself driven to outright laughter at the sight, guffaws ringing both long and loud, hilariously unimpressed—which again, in retrospect, might well have been a certain grade of error, on his part.

"As ye say," he replied, finally. "Or perhaps I'll just wait 'til you're next in need of a good, long swive and see what happens then, shall I? When ye shut your eyes and lay back, waitin' for me t'overbear ye—play devil t'your saint and give ye what ye really want, in a way that deeds me the lion's share of guilt whilst you stay safely clean, my sweet Jerusha, at any cost; all high and mighty, with your vicar's ways and your Hell-born powers. What a life it is ye've made for yourself, man...so sadly complicated, wi' mine th'exact opposite! Yet if that's what ye *require*, I s'pose, 'tis the very least I can do..."

Too much, too far; no time left for any sort of apology to mend the rift he'd just ripped wide with words between 'em, even had Rusk thought to make one. In the sudden silence, Parry simply widened those eyes at him and vanished, winked out, so fast Rusk thought it unlikely he'd meant to, beforehand.

Snorting at these dramatics, therefore, Rusk turned over into their shared warmth and drifted back asleep again, all blissfully unknowing of events to come, which he himself had already set in motion.

Things did not play themselves out immediately, in terms of Parry's retribution for what he considered Rusk's many insults—but then again, they almost never do. In Rusk's sleep, the *Bitch* whispered warnings to its master that he did not care to hear and thus did not remember upon waking; told him how he was trapped and where best to twist if he truly wished his freedom, only to find itself ignored. After which, having done all it could, it creaked a sad song to itself as it cut the water, knowing him fore-doomed.

Far behind, Tante Ankolee felt the Bitch's mournings nudge at the corner of her own dreams and stole a quick look through Rusk's witched eye, shaking her head at what she glimpsed there: Jerusalem Parry, back always kept carefully turned to the man who still thought them lovers, his neat mind deep-engaged in plotting out the arcane mechanics of his revenge.

Hearing Rusk's voice in her own mind, bluff and hearty, so completely self-deluded: *He'll forgive me soon enough, once he finds there's no other way. 'Tis a certainty.*

And thinking, sadly, in her turn: *But here's ya worst mistake, little half-me-blood, for that man wasn't never no true Christian, ta begin wi'. What he knows best he learnt nah from the books he study, Good or no, but at his own witch-dam's knee, her he saw swung in the wind for wantin' freedom 'bove all from the same fat squire got 'im on her, in the first place. Him in he fancy coat, who sign her death warrant whilst drunk then don't even stay ta see her neck snap.*

And would I help ya, I only could? For you yourself, brother mine—aye, mayhap. But then I think of my maman, an' yours. Of the man made us both, but let you run free soon's ya told him that was ya will, an' kept me chain at the neck to raise him other bastards, 'til at last I make enough ta pay him for me freedom...

Between Rusk's narrowed lids, Tante Ankolee caught sight of Parry looking back over his shoulder, studying the small reflection that moved there with care. Felt Rusk notice and smile, all teeth, as though he truly believed such attentions meant for him—and he did, of course. Of course. Since Solomon Rusk, like every other man of his line, had lived his life thus far in a world where all things bent to his desires, eventually.

Parry too, though—yes, even now, when he thought he'd been taught better. Which was, she supposed, just the sad damn pity of it.

Whites like hissin' roaches, spreadin' out all 'cross this world wi' no regard for any dream but they own, an' always thinkin' they know best. Yet there be surprises ahead for both ya stubborn fools, in this bed ya make together.

No help for it, on her end; those watery miles between would prevent any useful intervention even if she didn't have other business, which she very much did. So she sighed and withdrew, leaving them to it.

Some days on—a period which had seen Jerusalem Parry shun Rusk's company almost entirely, except where simple lack of space made that option an impossibility—Rusk noticed a new recruit, close-wrapped in layers of rags, whose looks disturbed him on some level far beyond mere instinct: squat but hunched, his eight grey-skinned fingers webbed and nailless, pallid skin visibly touched with chill. He did his work clumsily, forever turning a too-thick neck to train first one wide-spaced, lidless-seeming flat black eye on the task to hand, then the other; even what little of the currently sinking sun was left appeared to pain him, making him bare a double-jawful of serrated teeth in an aggressive sort of wince, as though he wanted to take a bite out of it and bring on a far more comfortable flood of dark.

"That man suits me ill," Rusk told the bo'sun. "Who is he?"

With a grimace of his own, equal-uncomfortable: "Mister... Dolomance, Master Parry says 'is name is, Cap'n."

"And is *Master Parry* engaging hands, now? We will have words, he and I, once he sees fit t're-evince himself. Where's this troll of his hail from, exactly?"

"Over the side, Cap'n."

Now it was Rusk's turn to frown. "Off another ship, ye mean? That last prize? What was the name—"

"*Jocasta's Sin*, and nay, sir. 'Twas up, he came, that one—from the water."

Spurred by angry surprise, Rusk turned back to the rough semblance of a man in question, barking: "Aye? And what gave ye the notion you were wanted, fish-belly, t'scale my ship's sides without due invitation?" No reply; the man barely seemed aware he was being spoke to, prompting Rusk to peer closer, checking whether his ears were over-muffled, slit—or even there, to begin with. "Are ye deaf?" he demanded, raising his voice, with no visible effect. "I am captain, here; answer, damn you!"

But: "He cannot," that same cold voice he'd so often hoped to hear told Rusk, from his elbow. "Nor would he if he could, seeing he works for *me*, not you—I, who made him thus."

Rusk looked down on Parry, eyebrows quirking. "Mute, you mean?"

A small, grim smile. "Not as such. But then, his sort has very little use for speech, in the normal way; not here above the water, any road."

The "recruit" made a creaky, squeaky noise deep in his throat, straightening to the extent his bent spine would let him—half a squeal, half a snarl, and nothing near to human. And suddenly, Rusk knew this thing's profile, its silhouette, glimpsed often enough before, under very different circumstances; bent ever-so-slightly out of skew through the ocean's lens, and deformed by threat and motion. How that groove between its shoulders marked where its fin should arch, whilst those awful teeth would fit key-into-lock neat with almost any shipwreck survivor's wound Rusk had ever seen treated, those men crazed from time adrift and torn everywhere that flesh had touched water, worn down to raw flesh and exposed bone by what less predatory sailors were wont to name the Wolves of the Sea.

Parry crossed his arms and nodded, a satisfied schoolmaster. "Ah, I see you finally take my meaning, sir. Indeed, to quote you yourself, on another occasion—you may call him *shark*, Captain. With all creatures being his meat, that take his fancy."

They stared at each other a long moment, during which Rusk could feel the bo'sun—along with every other man on deck, aside from Parry's creation—cast eyes his way as well, waiting to see what might come of this confrontation. And though the wizard knew enough to school his face, Rusk nevertheless took due note of how his fingers flexed all unconscious, blue and green St. Elmo's fire dancing between and similar-hued sparks set dancing 'cross their knuckles as a clear demonstration of just how much they longed to form fists.

"Oh, Jerusha," Rusk said, almost sadly, his own hand moving to caress his sword's hilt. "What is't you've done now, ye mad bitch?"

"Freed myself at last from you, I venture, albeit at Mister Dolomance here's expense. Yes, I teased him up, bent him to my will, re-made him, as you see...slaved myself one of the sea's fiercest monsters, and without even a collar. For the which he now hates me, true—but then, I require only his obedience, not his affections. He will do my bidding from now on, neat as any devil but without the contract, thus posing no threat to my immortal soul beyond the immediate; guard my body in all matters, most particularly from those who lie, and cheat, and do not keep their promises."

"By which you mean myself, I suppose."

"Do you? Well. If the shoe fits."

Such a wild tone, lurking at these last words' very back, knit from equal parts despair and triumph; the bo'sun took a half-step back at their sound alone, though Rusk made himself stand fast. Telling Parry, as he did—

"So you're angry wi' me yet, as I knew already. But this is my ship, whose Articles you swore to on your honour, as a Navy man. Does none of that mean naught t'you, anymore? What's your intent?"

"Can you not guess? Then I will be plain: Since you have had your way with me, sir—and on several different occasions, no less—now it is both turn-about and catch-who-can, as the old phrases go. And thus, while the play involved may not perhaps be entirely *fair*, by some standards, yet it is just enough, to my mind."

"Mutiny, then. Ye seek the captaincy, in my place."

"If the crew agree."

"And ye think they will, between us—pick you over me, ye bedwarmer, who never went over-side or fought hand-to-hand in your life? Ye sly jest of a jumped-up Cornish marsh-witch's get, wi' your fake vicar's airs and graces?"

"They've little enough choice, considering. As little choice, almost, as you gave me."

At this last blatant ingratitude, however, Rusk drew himself up full height, unsheathing, while Parry reached for his hex-bag just as fast, whipping it free, aiming it like a pistol. "And who was it popped your lock, Hell-priest," Rusk heard himself declaim, "when you would've died like a sick bloody dog, iron-yoked still, had I not? For which reason alone ye'll do well t'keep a civil tongue in your head, damn your eyes!"

"*I have been civil with you throughout*, the more fool me! Would to God I had been less so, seeing all the good it did!"

A man of pride, Tante Ankolee had called Parry, once—and wasn't it so, Rusk only realized now; wasn't it, though, by Hell and blast. Pride poison-rich as any stingray's sac, the sort that'd make a man always more willing to break than bend, no matter what might be gained from doing the latter. Which meant, well though he suddenly understood the full range of his own mistakes, that there'd been no way for him to've ever had his will with Jerusalem Parry and walked away after with both 'em content, let alone happy...

I did have ye, though, sure enough, Rusk thought, meeting Parry's silver eyes, almost sure the man could hear him. *Made ye like it too, in our congress's fullest bloom. And by the very way you behave, 'sir'—no matter all your most fervent protests t'the contrary—I'd say I have ye still.*

Once more, he watched Parry nod, slightly. Thinking, in return: *Perhaps. But where magic is concerned, things go both ways, or so that cousin of yours tutored me. So here is my curse, pirate, my gratitude made flesh for all you gave, and took...*

(What you put in me, I put in you; what we share I turn against us both, accounting my own pain of no moment, so long as you suffer. By the bond between us I bind you fast and draw you down. Draw out your life's root, and sever it.)

So, you admit it: Ye'd have nothing at all, not even t'curse me with, were it not for me.

Rusk felt the spell's price flare behind his eye, a split coal screwed deep in the empty socket, and knew exactly what it was costing Parry to work it, in that very moment—a sick joke, overall, spurring him to laugh yet one more time, full in the man's self-sorry face. Scoffing, as he did—

"An apology, then, for givin' ye what you weren't canny enough t'know ye wanted? Because I took *liberties*? Well, be that as it may: in this case, as in all others, I scorn t'defend my actions, except with steel!"

Here he lunged forward, sword's point aimed straight towards the pale shadow of Parry's neck-scar, where it peeked from his cravat's high twist. Only to meet something else halfway, come barreling into him sidelong like a leaping whale: "Dolomance," Parry's curst creation, its teeth suddenly all ablaze with sorcerous fire, snapping-to like a trap about his wrist and biting the bone of it through entirely, in one fell *chunk*.

The pain was so severe Rusk swooned, coming to again in his own vomit, his nauseate agony set to the cracking, snuffling sound of a shark-were at its repast. Spasming, he jack-knifed left and came nose-to-snout with the thing, its bloodstained mouth still unnaturally aflame, and managed, groaning: "Wh-what, wh—*why*—?"

Standing above, too damnable calm by far, Parry paused to order first one cuff, then the other. "The process," he said, at last, "is called cauterization."

Rusk spit bile. "Because ye...want me t'live crippled, is...that it?"

"Because I want you alive, yes, for now. 'Til I say otherwise."

"And just how long will *that* be, I wonder?"

"A fair question. How long can you hold your breath?"

"No ship can have two captains," the *Bitch*'s former master used to claim, before Rusk overtook him. "'Tis not natural, and the sea bears no unnaturalness." Which was good advice, certainly, or always had been, before...

That man never had the ill-luck to meet with such as Jerusalem Parry, though, let alone make the supreme error of lying down with him, in both the phrase's prime senses. And Rusk thought he might well've given thanks for avoiding that opportunity, had he only found himself still far enough above-waves to venture a verdict on the matter.

"Others might maroon you," Parry had told him as the crew's four strongest members bound Rusk's pain-stiff carcass, all apologetic, to the *Bitch of Hell*'s anchor-chain. "But I am not over-merciful by nature, as you have no doubt noted, and have no interest in giving second chances. This ship is mine, from now on; your death will christen it with blood, as is only loreful."

Oh, aye, Rusk thought, far too wearied by dolour to summon much of a struggle. Still, it would all be over soon enough, if not immediately...

(and there was that vaunted lack of mercy showing through, in the very proclaimed method of his demise—for keel-hauling was one of the illest deaths imaginable, a terror seldom more than threatened, combining as it did all the varied and central terrors of drowning, great bodily suffering and utter humiliation)

Soon enough, yes. Or so he had believed.

"I *should* thank you, I suppose," Parry said, while they hauled him up, "for this change my durance seems to've wrought in me, since truly—even at my lowest, in that gaol-ship's brig—I never looked to be so powerful as I am now. Then again, my mother's marsh was salten, so perhaps I was always destined to find my power's depth at sea."

Rusk touched a too-dry tongue to bleeding lips, and eked out: "Hmm, might...be. So...will ye?"

"Give thanks, to you?" Parry cast that cold metal stare his way, one last time, lips pursing in a way Rusk would once have found intolerable for very different reasons. Then, at last: "I think not."

But this, too, was very little surprise.

"Stay...ever as y'are, my Jerusha," Rusk croaked while the weeping sailors heaved to, swinging him over the side. "I'll...miss ye."

"I cannot say the same, sir," was Parry's reply.

Then Rusk closed his eye, and let the water take him. Only to learn that for some unlucky few—himself very much included, it turned out—death was not always as he'd been previously given to believe, prior to shedding his mortal coil.

Now that he was no longer encumbered by the flesh, Rusk could easily see everything he'd never been privy to: lines of power leaking from Parry to Mister Dolomance and back again, a double set of chains; from his own ruined wreck of a body to the *Bitch*'s hull, in the brief instant Parry stooped to pluck Rusk's still-witched eyeball out and slip it in his bag, like spoils of war, before directing "his" crew to shove their former captain's corpse off-deck through the scuppers same as so much other rubbish. Or the curse he'd never known he was capable of placing on sweet Master Jerusha bleeding out from that same bespelled item, tainting every other hex-ingredient and entering Parry's heart through the breast-pocket, where it soon commenced to circulate through his system like any other humour.

Seem you the same sort'a Rusk as me after all, no matter the size o'that piece 'tween ya legs, or what-all it pull ya fiercest towards, Tante Ankolee might have said, had he ever thought to ask her. *Born of bad angels on one side an' bad men on th'other, a ten-mile-long chain o' witches, pirates, and pirate-witches—an' just like that Master Parry o'yours know all too well, t'him an' your cost both, 'tis never no fit measure ta look only at what a man already done ta foresee what him yet may do, under th'exact right circumstance. Why is't ya think y'have such a hunger for him, anyhow, but that ya finally recognize y'own kind?*

(*Which maybe explains it th'other way, too,* Rusk's traitor thoughts would have chimed in, if so. *Why he felt the same pull as regards to me, and just as strong, though Christ knows he'd do anything not t'admit it.*)

Anything and everything, yes. As current circumstances only went to prove.

When the *Bitch* returned to Porte Macoute, Rusk's ghost stood watching from her deck when Parry tried to come ashore, only to start bleeding out at every pore the second his boot-soles touched land. Saw Mister Dolomance drag him into the surf and swim back at double-time, inhumanly swift, that same passage rubbing Parry raw 'cross the chest and inner arms against the shark-were's sandpaper skin, even with two separate layers of clothing between.

Later, with Parry cocooned in healing power just like that first night they'd shared together, Rusk stretched himself invisibly alongside and passed a gelid ghost-hand down his beloved murderer's side, touching each of the wizard's organs in turn and saving that one he liked best for last. Stroked him once more from the inside out in an entirely different way, sowing gooseflesh over his blood-smeared new-grown hide, and whispered, in Parry's fever-bright ear:

Shield yourself from me all ye please, in whichever ways ye choose, yet I am here always, nonetheless. The Bitch *is my command as much as yours, forever, Master Parry. A sad truth, and one which must drag it down eventually, bringing you along with it...*

How it comes I know not, but know this: I will be there that day, that hour, at the very striking of your doom; we will meet again beneath the water, where I will hold you tight, as your own flesh casts you free. I will never let you go.

And so it did come to pass, eventually, but not for years yet. The which is another tale completely, told by one who would never know—or care to know—what you now do: how two equal-obdurate men may always be the death of each other, fast or slow, especially when magic is involved.

Said Solomon Rusk to Jerusalem Parry, licking this last truth—with a wintry ghost-tongue—directly onto the drum: *Shouldn't've killed me on me own ship, my Jerusha, ye really wished t'be rid of me.*

And while Parry moaned and tossed in sorcerous sleep, all un-knowing of why he felt so cold, the *Bitch of Hell* sailed on, secure in its two captains' care.

JACK-KNIFE

TABLEAU ONE: CORRESPONDENCE GONE UNAN-
SWERED

A WOMAN'S SCREAM. It begins with a gasp and peaks until
ragged, breaking off at its height, then trails into an ugly, liquid
gurgle, and is gone.

THE MAN KNOWN AS JACK
(Very clear, polite)
From hell, Mister Lusk, I send you half the
kidne I took from one woman, prasarved it
for you, tother piece I fried and ate it;
was very nise. I may send you the bloody
knif that took it out if you only wate
while longer. Catch me when you can,
Mishter Lusk.

A LARGE SPLASH dies away slowly, the drops of water dispersing over the stones by a river's side.

FADE UP, very slowly, a HISSING, PULSING noise—like the sound of the sea but darker, more interior.

BRING UP a HEARTBEAT. The sound resolves itself into that of blood circulating inside someone's head.

> JACK
> (Slow, sleepy whisper)
> It's so. Cold.

HOLD the BLOOD SOUND a few more seconds. MODIFY it to become—

TABLEAU TWO: LESSON THE FIRST—UNMENTIONABLES

—the soft sound of a cloth squeezing water into a basin.

A CLICK, like a lid opening. Pure, slightly warped MUSIC begins in mid-phrase: A MUSIC-BOX tune ("Oh, Believe Me, If All Those Endearing Young Charms..."). A woman (JACK'S MOTHER) HUMS ALONG.

> MOTHER
> "...that I gaze on so fondly today
> Were to fleet in an hour and fade in my arms..."

> YOUNG JACK
> (Outside the door)
> Mother! Mother, I'm home!

> MOTHER
> In here, darling.

YOUNG JACK
(Bursts in, out of breath)
Mother, it was wonderful, we—
(Sees the basin)
What's that?

The lid shuts, with a SNAP; the music stops.

MOTHER
My washing. Tell me about your trip.

YOUNG JACK
(Distracted)
Yes, we—
(Peers closer)
—but it's all...red.

MOTHER
Dear, you're flushed. Really, you mustn't concern yourself...

YOUNG JACK
(Realizing)
Red—it's blood, isn't it? It's full of blood!

MOTHER
(Soothing)
There, there—
(He continues to gasp; she shakes him)
Stop that! Listen to me, will you? Will you listen?

YOUNG JACK
Of course, I...
(A beat)
Whose blood is it?

MOTHER
Mine.

YOUNG JACK
Oh no, oh God! I'll get Father—

MOTHER
(Sharp)
You will *not*.
(Soothing again)
No need to trouble him; it's nothing to be afraid of, you know.
Simply an indignity we ladies must suffer, now and then.

YOUNG JACK
(Fascinated, despite himself)
All ladies?

MOTHER
Every one of them. And I'll tell you a secret—as long as we do,
the babies come.

YOUNG JACK
(Pause; whispers)
But you'll *die*.

MOTHER
(A little sad)
We all will, my precious boy. Eventually.
And there's no cure for that.

She tips the basin out into a sink. The SOUND OF WATER
GURGLING away down the drain.

TABLEAU THREE: NOTOREITY, AND ITS CONSE-
QUENCES

FADE IN, OVER: NIGHT SOUNDS, London, 1888.

JACK is WASHING his hands at a public sink, breath fast and
rough. A HORSE NEIGHS and shies behind him.

MAN
(Yelling)
Here, over here! Christ, it's awful!

WOMAN
Get the Peelers!

VOICES
The Ripper! The Ripper! The Ripper!

POLICE WHISTLES, SHOUTS, RUNNING FEET.

FADE UP the GURGLE OF WATER down the drain,
DROWNING OUT the rest.

A new woman's voice surfaces, OVER:

MRS. BENTHAM
Was that true?

JACK
I can't remember.

MRS. BENTHAM
Whether it happened that way, exactly?
Or whether it happened at all?

JACK
...Either.

MRS. BENTHAM
(After a moment)
Then...I suppose you'd better tell me
what...*might* have happened...next.

FADE INTO the rush of a river in flood.

TABLEAU FOUR: TWO LADS AT PLAY

FADE IN the sound of two BOYS LAUGHING by the river's side. COUNTRY NOISES, BIRDS. They are dragging the river for things to sell.

FIRST BOY
I found a shoe!

SECOND BOY
(Appraising it)
Too big for me.

FIRST BOY
Nice leather, though—

SECOND BOY
(Dismissive)
Too big for you, too.
(Ducks)
'Ey, easy with that stick!

FIRST BOY
Coward.
(Sees something)
Here, what's this?

SECOND BOY
(Uninterested)
A deadfall full of weeds, molly-brain.

FIRST BOY
No, look closer—

He SPLASHES into the river.

SECOND BOY
(Alarmed)
Wait up! Wait—ah, to hell with it.

He joins FIRST BOY. They try to shift the deadfall.

FIRST BOY
(Grunting with effort)
It's under—here—

SECOND BOY
(Grumbling)
What is? Nothing, that's what. Split your bleeding gut over
noth...

He trails off, spotting JACK pinned underneath.

SECOND BOY
...ing. God almighty...

FIRST BOY
Nothing, eh?

SECOND BOY
Come on, give us a hand! Jesus, a drowned man. Don't just
stand there, get him up on the bank!

FIRST BOY
What for? Not like we can help.

SECOND BOY
It's not what we can *do*, fool, it's what he's got on him!

SPLASHING SOUNDS as he starts dragging JACK out.

FIRST BOY
All right, all right—I'm not stupid, y'know.

MORE SPLASHING as they get JACK onto the bank; TWIN
THUMPS as they collapse. SECOND BOY begins going
through his pockets.

SECOND BOY
Bloody hell, what's this? No rings, no cutter, no bloody nothing!

FIRST BOY
Looks a right toff, though. And that red hair.

SECOND BOY
Unlucky. Besides—

A WATER-CHOKED COUGH interrupts him. Dead silence.
Another, deeper cough.

FIRST BOY
(Dumbstruck)
He's alive!

SECOND BOY
I see that, booby! All right, all right. Run and get the doctor.

FIRST BOY
Up at the madhouse?

SECOND BOY
Is there another? Come on! I'll stay and watch him.

FIRST BOY runs off. JACK keeps coughing until his fit sub-
sides. Ragged, uneven breathing sets in.

SECOND BOY
(To himself)
Yeah, I'll just watch him.
(Rummaging in JACK's coat)
Hah! Knew he'd have something.
(Pulls out the WATCH)
Nice work. Bet it keeps good time. Only fair I have it, really,
seeing how I saved him and all—

He flips the lid open with a CLICK. The same tune JACK'S
MOTHER sang begins to play, WARPED AND DISTORTED
by its time under the water.

SECOND BOY
(Surprised)
I'n't that pretty.

Jarred by the sound, JACK stirs.

JACK
(Hoarse)
Am I...alive?

SECOND BOY
(Terrified)
Sure you are, mister. Lucky to be so, too. That river's a killer.

JACK
(To himself)
Alive.

He SCREAMS—a long, inarticulate howl of triumph, rage and despair. The watch's lid SNAPS shut; the MUSIC CUTS OFF.

FADE UP: THE RIVER, over JACK'S scream, until it drowns him out.

TABLEAU FIVE: GENTLE MEDICINES

FADE INTO the NOISE OF A GURNEY, being wheeled quickly through the ECHOING HALLS of DR. PURL'S ASYLUM.

BOWKER
(Breathless)
Got his head?

LEAN
(Equally blown)
Just. Christ, this fucker's strong!
(JACK BITES him)
Ow!

BOWKER
Watch the teeth.

LEAN
Thanks, ever so.

They BUMP THROUGH DOORS into PURL'S operating room. The gurney SQUEAKS into position beside PURL'S "MA-CHINE," an electric generator used for primitive shock therapy. We can hear it HUMMING FAINTLY.

BOWKER
(To JACK)
Here we are, darling, all safe and sound.
We'll just wait here a while for the
doctor to come fry your bloody loony brain.

JACK howls and thrashes.

LEAN
Stop baiting him, Bowker! He's going for
my hands again, and I only got the two!

BOWKER
Easy cure for that, mate—

DR. PURL and MRS. BENTHAM enter.

PURL
I hope you're not assaulting the patients again, Bowker.
That'd be two times this week alone; I might have to let you go.

BOWKER
Won't be necessary, Doctor. I was just—

PURL
I know full well what you were "just," Bowker, so do be quiet.
Mrs. Bentham, the headpiece, if you please.

MRS. BENTHAM
Doctor.

PURL
Where'd they find this man, Lean?

LEAN
Picked him out the river, sir. Been like this
ever since.

PURL
From London, then...probably a failed suicide.

JACK screams again.

LEAN
I'd top myself too, I had a headful of whatever he's got.

PURL
I don't doubt it. Well, we'll soon clear his cranium. Mrs. Ben-
tham!
(To BOWKER and LEAN)
Hold him straight.

SOUNDS OF STRUGGLE, as they do. MRS. BENTHAM fas-
tens the headpiece onto JACK with a SNAP; JACK'S cries become muffled.

PURL
(Through gritted teeth)
All right, that does it. Mrs. Bentham, the switch!

MRS. BENTHAM
Yes, Dr. Purl.

She pulls the switch. The faint HUMMING of the generator
RATCHETS UP; a SHARP, ELECTRIC CRACKLE erupts
over it. JACK'S cries become a SUSTAINED, MUFFLED YELL.

The CRACKLE stops, the HUMMING dropping back to its previous level. A THUMP as JACK collapses onto his gurney.

> BOWKER
> Here, he's bitten through his lip—

> PURL
> No matter.
> (To MRS. BENTHAM)
> Again!

The same crackle, LOUDER this time. JACK HOWLS THROUGH CLENCHED TEETH, in even more pain. The crackle stops. JACK THUMPS to the gurney, harder this time. He MOANS softly.

> LEAN
> Doctor, his eyes are gone all white!

> PURL
> (Excited, vicious)
> You really *must* show me your license to practice medicine sometime in future, Lean.
> (To MRS. BENTHAM)
> *Again*!

The LOUDEST CRACKLE YET.

TABLEAU SIX: AND I AWOKE AND FOUND ME HERE

FADE INTO the sound of a cloth being TORN, then DIPPED into yet another BASIN OF WATER.

BRING UP the SOUND OF BIRDS outside the windows of JACK'S room.

> JACK
> (Gradually stirring awake)
> Uhhh.

MRS. BENTHAM
Sssh. Don't try to move.

JACK
Who—

MRS. BENTHAM
I'm Mrs. Bentham. You're at Dr. Purl's, in the country,
and you're here to get well.

She squeezes the cloth out, and daubs his forehead with it.

JACK
(Barely awake)
I...the river...

MRS. BENTHAM
That's all over now. You were saved. With God's grace,
you'll soon be yourself once more.

JACK
You're kind.

MRS. BENTHAM
As my position requires. What's your name?

JACK
(Freezes)
I—I don't...

MRS. BENTHAM
...Wish it known? Understandable, given the circumstances—

JACK
No, what I mean is—I don't believe I know it myself.

MRS. BENTHAM
Not at all?

JACK
(Not really answering)
Mmm. And yet...my mind's so *clean*, suddenly. So clear.

MRS. BENTHAM
That would be a result of Dr. Purl's treatment. Well, it will all
come back, I promise you.

JACK
Must it? Perhaps I don't want it to.

MRS. BENTHAM
You will, soon enough. Go to sleep now.
(Puts the cloth back in the basin)
Stephen—that was my husband's name. I'll call you that for
now, shall I? How does it sound?

JACK
(Falling asleep)
Very...nice.

As MRS. BENTHAM squeezes out the cloth once more, water
in the bowl SLOSHES back and forth. OVER WHICH WE—

BRING UP the SOUND OF WAVES LAPPING GENTLY,
drowning out the BIRDS. HOLD for a moment.

OVER, as before:

JACK
I remember *that*.

MRS. BENTHAM
As do I.
(A pause)
But...what about this?

FADE INTO: the SOUND OF BLOOD in JACK'S head again,
propelled by a DARK HEARTBEAT.

TABLEAU SEVEN: IN MILLER'S COURT

FOOTSTEPS on courtyard stones; a woman DRUNKEN LAUGH. She fumbles with a key.

> MARY KELLY
> (With a faint Irish lilt to her speech)
> Here it is, your honor. Not much, but I call it home—
> when I've the rent.

They move inside. While staggering around, in a bad parody of genteel hospitality:

> MARY KELLY
> Fancy a drain of gin? Only got the chamber pot to offer it in.
> Still, we're all friends here, ain't we? What with me in nowt but
> my unmentionables, an' all...
> (She giggles again, as though embarassed by her own repulsive-
> ness)
> Or p'raps you're admiring my etchings. That's what I call 'em,
> There's been so many 'round to see 'em.
> (JACK doesn't laugh)
> Not much fun, are you?

> JACK
> No.

A CLICK as he opens his bag. His HEARTBEAT SPEEDS UP.

> MARY KELLY
> 'Ey, a bag. You a doctor? What d'you got in there, anyways?

> JACK
> A cure for anything.

There's a WHICKER of air as JACK whips his knife out and around, striking in the same motion. A SOUND OF IMPACT. MARY KELLY GASPS, then CHOKES LIQUIDLY, GURGLING.

This comes at almost the same time as a THUMP: her falling onto the bed. Cloth rips, chased by a WETTER, MEATIER sound, like a butcher at work. Liquid SQUIRTS and SPLASHES.

Finally, JACK'S HARSH BREATHING and RACING HEARTBEAT drown out the sounds of his work.

A LAST BREATH comes up, MODIFYING into the ELECTRIC CRACKLE of PURL'S MACHINE. It PEAKS. SILENCE.

OVER:

> JACK
> (At last)
> Oh yes, that happened too—
> (Quieter)
> —more than once.

TABLEAU EIGHT: WHEN THE GREEN FIELD COMES OFF LIKE A LID

BRING UP the SOUND OF BIRDS in PURL'S garden. JACK is planting rosebushes, humming slightly, atonally (the MUSIC BOX tune). FOOTSTEPS ON GRASS, as MRS. BENTHAM approaches.

> MRS. BENTHAM
> Good morning, Stephen. A lovely day, isn't it?

> JACK
> Very. Won't you sit down?

> MRS. BENTHAM
> Just for a moment. Did Dr. Purl tell you to plant those bushes?

> JACK
> Bowker said I might, if I kept out of his way.

MRS. BENTHAM
Such a heavenly smell. I'm told you do very good work here,
in the garden.

JACK
As my position requires.
(Off her reaction)
The truth is, I enjoy it. That makes me try harder.

MRS. BENTHAM
Fair enough.
(A beat)
Oh, I had meant to ask you: Did you tamper with Asa's
bandages last night, by any chance?

JACK
I rewrapped them, yes. They had been tied much too tightly;
it was cruel, not to mention unprofessional.

MRS. BENTHAM
You must trust the doctor with his own work, Stephen. He
knows best what needs to be done.

JACK
You think so? The man's knuckles were black with blood.
Any first-year charity ward intern might have done better.

MRS. BENTHAM
(Surprised)
Stephen, were you...are you a physician?

JACK
I...don't think so. My father...
(Pauses)
...no, forgive me. It's gone again.

MRS. BENTHAM
(Rises)
I must tell Dr. Purl.

JACK
Must you?

MRS. BENTHAM
Well, certainly—this might be a clue to your identity. Don't
you want to know who you truly are?

JACK
No.

MRS. BENTHAM
Whyever not?

JACK
Perhaps because...I may already have some idea.

MRS. BENTHAM
I don't take your meaning. Besides which, I must confess, *I*
would still like to know.

JACK
Are you so sure?
(Tired)
Go on, then. Please. Don't concern yourself about me.

MRS. BENTHAM
But I do, Stephen; knowing your true name won't stop me
from continuing to do so. Until supper.

JACK
Until then—goodbye.

She leaves. He starts humming again. It begins as a snatch of the
MUSIC BOX tune, but soon trails off into the barest beat of a
rhyme: A, B, A, B, A... JACK begins to sound it out aloud, hesi-
tantly.

JACK
I'm not...a butcher, not a Yid, nor...yet some foreign skipper...
But I'm your own dear loving friend, yours truly...

He stops, puzzled. Then repeats, over and over—

JACK
Yours truly. Truly yours. Yours truly, truly, *truly*...

SILENCE.

TABLEAU NINE: LESSON THE SECOND—NAKED, YET
IN RAGS

A CLICK: the watch's lid, opening. The MUSIC BOX theme
starts yet once more, warped at first, then gradually purifying. It
echoes slightly, as though being played in a large, bare room.

FOOTSTEPS hurry down the corridor, then enter; a door
SHUTS behind them, with a hollow sound. The watch SNAPS
SHUT as well, music cutting off in mid-note.

JACK'S FATHER
Late again, I see.

JACK
Yes. The traffic was—

FATHER
Don't give excuses; patients brook none. Bear in mind that
yours would be dead by now.

JACK
I will, sir. Are we—is it ready?

FATHER
Of course. Are *you*?

JACK
...Certainly.

His FATHER snorts and throws back a sheet, revealing the
corpse they are about to dissect.

FATHER
Let's begin, then.

JACK
(After a pause)
That's a woman.

FATHER
How astute.
(Impatient)
It *was* a woman, yes. Now it is merely a subject, the same as
any other you've dissected thus far.

JACK
Mother would have disagreed.

FATHER
Your mother is dead.

JACK
So I recall.
(Turns to go)
Goodbye, sir.

FATHER
Stop where you are.

JACK does. His FATHER CROSSES to him.

FATHER
I must admit I don't entirely understand such squeamishness;
how can one possibly expect to operate on a live patient, if one
is unable to face even a corpse? Yet I suppose I should have fore-
seen this inherent...infirmity of purpose, in you.
(A beat)
The fault lies in my own judgment; overestimating your
abilities, I *had* hoped to postpone any thoroughgoing discussion
of such tedious and disgusting matters until it might prove utterly unavoidable. Now I see that day has come.

JACK says nothing.

FATHER
There is science and there is superstition: these twin currents,
alone, direct the flood of history—hot blood through the world's
vessels, refreshing and animating what religion and suchlike
poppycock seek to let remain a dead and rotten corpse. All else is
mere sophistry.
(Indicates the body)
Regard this—object, with care. Each of us stink the same once
the worm's been at us, petticoats or no. My wife, your *mother*,
could tell you as much. Do you think *this* a mystery? Only cold
meat on a slab, with no more power than you give it. Don't be
blinded by desire, for that is skin-deep at best; you're fated to
go so much deeper. To finally see what lies beneath—not
just the clothes, but under the skin itself.
(He hands him a knife)
Make your first cut.
JACK
I can't.

FATHER
(Grabbing his arm)
You will.

99

JACK
(Tries to break away)
I won't!

FATHER
(Hisses)
You *will*. I've lost too much already to let you fail me now!

They GRUNT in STRUGGLE; then FATHER forces JACK'S hand down. They plunge the knife in together with a SICK LIT-TLE SOUND.

JACK
Let go, sir!

FATHER
(Gritted teeth)
No. You have to *see*. Look!
(While JACK still struggles)
LOOK!

A LONG, WET RIPPING SOUND as FATHER PULLS THE KNIFE DOWN, parting the woman's chest.

MODIFY to become the SOUND OF CLOTH RIPPING.

MODIFY to become a LOUD ELECTRIC CRACKLE.

OVER, as it FADES:

MRS. BENTHAM
And there we have it.

TABLEAU TEN: SLIGHT DIFFERENCES OF NOMEN-CLATURE

BRING UP the NOISE OF BIRDS outside PURL'S office win-dows.

PURL
Have what, exactly?
(Unimpressed)
So your "Stephen" has a bit of medical jargon under his belt.
He could be a sideshow quack for all we know.

MRS. BENTHAM
You don't find it in the least...intriguing?

PURL
Intriguing, yes. Hardly proof positive.

MRS. BENTHAM
I'm aware I can't match your expertise in these matters,
Doctor, but I feel—

PURL
You *feel* too much, Mrs. Bentham. That is your sex's curse,
and its charm.
(Dismissive)
At any rate, you've spent too much time with this man already.
He's taken to the treatments, does his work and stays quiet;
there are many more who don't. It is they who require
your attention.

MRS. BENTHAM
...Yes, Doctor.

She EXITS, her BOOTS TAPPING AWAY down the hall.

BOWKER
Sir—
(Hesitant)
—this "Stephen," he seems quiet enough, but...well,
You've been to London.

PURL
What has that to do with anything?

101

BOWKER
I'll come right out with it then—

PURL
I wish you would.

BOWKER
Lean and me, we think he's the Ripper.

PURL
Well, how stimulating: Two equally absurd theories in one day.

BOWKER
But it fits, don't you see? It's been all over the Peelers think
he's a doctor.

PURL
Or a butcher, or an abortionist, or a Jew, or a Freemason...

BOWKER
You can laugh all you want, sir. Still, what if—

PURL
I'd have quite an achievement on my hands then, wouldn't I?
The river brought us a howling mad harlot-killer, and we
clipped his wings—with science.

BOWKER
Did we, though? That's what I'm worried about.

PURL
(Bored)
Put your mind at rest, then; I'm sure you need it for other things.

He rises, moving to exit.

> BOWKER
> You'll tell Mrs. Bentham what I said, though, won't you?
> (PURL brushes past him, not bothering to answer)
> *Won't* you?
> (Nothing. Under his breath)
> Bastard.

BOWKER stalks away in the other direction. A door SLAMS shut.

BRING UP the NOISE OF THE RIVER. HOLD a moment.

OVER:

> JACK
> Did he need to?

> MRS. BENTHAM
> Warn me? I suppose. Yet I'm uncertain whether it would have helped. Like the doctor, with his theories—we tell ourselves tales, then bend the facts to fit them.

> JACK
> For men such as the doctor, their work comes to depend as much on faith as it does upon science.

> MRS. BENTHAM
> Yes. Well, then...
> (A beat)
> ...tell me.

TABLEAU ELEVEN: RIVER-SIDE

BRING UP the NOISE OF THE RIVER. HOLD a moment.

FADE DOWN the RIVER. FADE UP the BACKGROUND NOISE OF LONDON—muffled hooves, wheels on cobblestones, newsboys crying the latest headlines. Slowly, these become audible, though overlapping:

FIRST NEWSBOY
In the earliest hours of the morning, while all Whitechapel lay asleep...

SECOND NEWSBOY
...he drank the cup of his strange obsession to the dregs, perpetrating...

THIRD NEWSBOY
...most horrid and abominable slaughter, perhaps brought on by...

FIRST NEWSBOY
...a softening of the brain due to rampant venereal infection.

SECOND NEWSBOY
(Quieter, a commentary)
Sin is a contagion upon us. Inhuman minds breed inhuman deeds, as the Good Book holds.

THIRD NEWSBOY
(Almost sad)
Surely, these are Judgment times.

CHILDREN'S VOICES slide in OVERTOP the shouts, a ragged choir singing a sniggering tune—

CHILDREN
Jack the Ripper's dead!
And lying in his bed!
He cut his throat with shaving soap!
Jack the Ripper's dead!

This doggerel dissolves into cruel laughter, trailing quickly away. At the same time, we BRING UP JACK'S BOOTS coming down a deserted street.

JACK
(Shivering)
So cold...

From a nearby alley, a familiar voice.

MARY KELLY
Here, who's that? I'll soon get you warm, mister.

JACK
I beg your pardon?

MARY KELLY
Oh, you should.
(Moving closer)
Don't be sorry, though—just come this way. The sure cure for
cold's right up my alley.

JACK
This fog's so thick, I can barely see you.

MARY KELLY
Aw, but you don't need your eyes for the close work, do ya?
Just your hands, and...whatever else.
(A beat)
What's wrong with you, anyway?

JACK
I'm lost.

MARY KELLY
Step under the light.

JACK does. MARY KELLY RECOGNIZES him.

MARY KELLY
Oh ho, well. You *are* lost.

JACK
Do you know me?

MARY KELLY
Don't you know *me*?

JACK
I don't—think so.

MARY KELLY
Fair enough. Take my hand, mister; I'll show you where
you ought to be.

FOOTSTEPS, as they walk together. The RIVER'S noise becomes LOUDER.

JACK
God, I'm so tired.

MARY KELLY
Gets to you, does it? The walking?

JACK
The searching.

MARY KELLY
Mmmm. Well, we're all lookin' for something, ain't we?
(Their FOOTSTEPS STOP; they're at the RIVER'S edge)
Here you are, then: Try it over. Maybe you can rest, you do it
right this time. Or maybe you never will.

JACK
Who *are* you?

MARY KELLY
Oh, we've met before.
(The sound of a dress being PULLED OPEN)
Take a good look.

JACK
You've...no face.

MARY KELLY

No face, no belly—not much of nothing, now. Cleaned me
right out, you did.

JACK

I—I don't even know you.

MARY KELLY

Don't suppose you do; not by name, any roads. None of us.
Not Polly, nor Annie, nor Long Liz, Kate or me. But I've a name,
mister. It's Mary Kelly, Marie Jeanette to you. I never wanted
to die. Just needed money for a glass, and my rent, with winter
coming. And my baby. Remember this?
"What's in your bag, mister?"

JACK

A cure...

MARY KELLY

...For anything?
(Mocking)
Oh, and I'm cured now, all right. Ain't I? But you know, I think
you liked the doin' of it just a bit too much for comfort, my lad.
A sight too much to call it anything like mercy.

JACK

Get away from me!

MARY KELLY

Easier said than done; can you get away from *me*, that's the question. Are you still that slippery?

JACK

(Not listening)
Get *away*!

He STUMBLES, FALLS. A HUGE SPLASH. Bring up the
SOUND OF THE RIVER as he sinks deeper, MARY KEL-
LY'S voice FADING IN warped, through the water—

MARY KELLY
There you go, love. There you go...
(Colder)
But don't come up again, for you'll just end up here, eventually.
And I'll be waiting.

MODIFY to the PULSE OF BLOOD in JACK'S brain. BRING UP his HEARTBEAT until it's VERY LOUD. Then stop.

The RIVER'S NOISE, CLEAN again.

TABLEAU TWELVE: MORE GIFTS FROM THE WATER

FADE IN the sound of TWO PEOPLE—a local POACHER and his son, the SECOND BOY—WADING in the river.

POACHER
Best catching's a little more this way.

SECOND BOY
Hold on, I can't keep up—

POACHER
Not trying then, are you?

SECOND BOY
Aw, *Dad*...

POACHER
(Hisses)
Keep it down! You want the whole bloody village to know?

SECOND BOY
(Grinning)
Think they don't? Half of 'em were down here last week.

POACHER
You shut up, or I'll take my stick to y—*ow*!

He's STUMBLED OVER SOMETHING.

> SECOND BOY
> What's wrong?

> POACHER
> There's summat caught under the water.
> (Fumbles around)
> Wedged under a stone. Help me, will you?

> SECOND BOY
> Oh, Lord. Not again.

With a GRUNT OF TRIUMPH and a great SPLASH, the POACHER pulls something out.

> POACHER
> Look, it's a bag! Must belong to that Doctor Purl.

> SECOND BOY
> What'd it be doing here, then?

> POACHER
> Who cares? Might be a reward. Come on!

He SPLASHES towards the bank.

> SECOND BOY
> To the madhouse?

> POACHER
> There and back again, with coin to show for our troubles.
> Here, boy, catch.

A THUMP as the bag hits the SECOND BOY; he clutches it, reluctantly. Muttering:

> SECOND BOY
> And here we bloody go....

They SPLASH away. A rumble of THUNDER. It starts to RAIN HEAVILY.

FADE UP the rain, until it becomes louder than the river.

TABLEAU THIRTEEN: LESSON THE THIRD—RED ALL OVER

MODIFY to become the sound of RAIN on PURL'S OFFICE WINDOWS. There's a KNOCK at the door.

PURL
Come in.

MRS. BENTHAM and JACK enter.

MRS. BENTHAM
See who's come to see you, Doctor.

PURL
(Rises)
The famous Stephen. To what do I owe this visit?

JACK
Your roses bloomed. I've brought you some.

PURL
Well.
(Takes them; at a loss)
I suppose I'd better put these in water.

MRS. BENTHAM
I'll do that.

She FADES into the background, pouring WATER from a pitcher.

PURL
You're happy in the garden, then?

JACK
Very.

PURL
This recent weather must have spoiled your work somewhat.

JACK
It comes back, though. That's what I like best about flowers.

PURL
The triumph over Death.

JACK
Facilely enough, yes. It's what we all strive for, isn't it? Cut and
burn and inoculate as we may, eternity remains in all its vastness,
uncharted: decay, rot, nothing left over. The end of all flesh.

PURL
Ah, but then we can serve as fertilizer.

JACK
I've had worse ambitions.

PURL is slightly taken aback by this revelation. Luckily for him,
MRS. BENTHAM intrudes.

MRS. BENTHAM
(Placing the flowers on his desk)
Here we are. Very nice, aren't they?

PURL
Indeed. I hope—

The door BANGS open. BOWKER, LEAN, POACHER and
SECOND BOY enter.

PURL
Has knocking become a foreign concept, Bowker?

BOWKER
(Surly)
These men want a word, is all. They say they've found
something—

POACHER
(Offers the bag)
Here 'tis. We thought it was yours.

PURL
This? Whyever would you?

POACHER
Well, uh...'cause you're the doctor, an' all.

PURL
(With fine contempt)
Oh, of course.
(He examines it)
You got it from the river, I presume.

POACHER
(Suddenly wary)
...Yes.

PURL
Calm yourself, man; I'm not about to ask on which side. However—Mrs. Bentham, have I lost a bag recently?

MRS. BENTHAM
Not recently, no.

PURL
No. And on closer examination, I don't believe this *is* mine, either. At least...I can't be entirely sure, one way or the other.

LEAN
Why don't you open it up and see?

PURL
Why not, indeed.

As the clasps SNAP open, a BOLT OF LIGHTNING strikes nearby with a searing crackle. Everybody gasps.

SECOND BOY
Holy Christ.

MRS. BENTHAM
Oh, ah.
(Sick)
Is that...?

PURL
No.
(Shakes head, tries to close it again)
Oh, *no*.

BOWKER
(Grabbing it from him)
Let's us just all have a good look, shall we?

He spills the contents out across PURL'S desk: A RATTLE OF KNIVES, blunted by cloth, plus the sound of a GLASS JAR FULL OF LIQUID, sliding over wood.

POACHER
God, what a stink!

MRS. BENTHAM
So much—blood.

LEAN
What's that in the jar?

SECOND BOY
I think it's...a baby. Before it's been born, like.

BOWKER
That last one—she was expecting, or so they said.

LEAN
What d'you mean?

BOWKER
Obvious, isn't it? What kind of doctor hauls around a bloody
bunch of knives and a baby in a bloody jar?

PURL
Bowker, please don't do this.

BOWKER
Oh, it's not what *I've* done, doctor. *Sir.*

MRS. BENTHAM
Whatever you're suggesting, Bowker, it can't be true and you
know it.

BOWKER
Do I? Why'd he come down from London, anyways? Because
of his *treatments*, his *research*? Or was it because the heat got
a bit too high 'round Whitechapel way, eh?

POACHER
What're you saying?

LEAN
That he's the Ripper.
(To BOWKER)
Ain't you?

BOWKER
Take a good look.
(He raises the jar, lets it fall with a sick THUD)
Draw your own conclusions.

PURL
For God's sake, you can't believe him!

LEAN
Sure I can.

POACHER
So can I.

SECOND BOY
But, Dad—

POACHER
Shut up, you! There's his bag, that's good enough!

BOWKER
Right then—let's go.

MRS. BENTHAM
Have you all gone mad? Where to?

LEAN
To the river!

BOWKER
That's right—the river!

PURL
(As they drag him past)
Mrs. Bentham, for the love of God, the constables—

BOWKER, LEAN, POACHER
The river! The river! The river!

Chanting it, a ROLL OF THUNDER blends all their voices together in a SINGLE HOWL. They seize PURL and drag him
SCREAMING from the room. The door SLAMS.

MRS. BENTHAM
Doctor! *Doctor!*
(Dazed)
But they can't—my God, it's monstrous. It's not his bag, it
couldn't be.

JACK
No.

MRS. BENTHAM
It simply *couldn't* be, can't they see that? It's just not his!

JACK
No, you're quite correct: It isn't.

MRS. BENTHAM
(Turns, finally hearing him)
And how would *you* know, exactly?

JACK
Because it's mine.

MRS. BENTHAM is shocked into silence. We hear FOOT-
STEPS, as JACK approaches the desk. Something has changed
in his voice; "Stephen," whatever there was of him to begin with,
is gone. The KNIVES RATTLE as he runs a finger across them.

JACK
My father gave me these. Said my talent was for surgery. Anato-
my lessons—practice on the dead to make perfect on the living.
To cure death itself, as though that were even possible. His whole
life through, he never gave up trying. But...I did.
(Picks up the JAR)
My mother said this was the one thing no one could cure, and
she was right. Something inside, the wonderful secret. Blood.
Babies. It turned against her, and she died.

He dashes the jar on the floor, suddenly; it SHATTERS,
SPLASHING over MRS. BENTHAM'S boots. She draws back,
with a CRY OF HORROR.

JACK

That scares you? It's just meat. You were married; you should
know the depths of men's depravity. Or think of your doctor,
with his experiments—he knows we're all alike under the skin,
all the same color. My father taught me that. When we look
at each other, we see only the surface; we feel desire pulling us
together, to make life and death in a rush of blood. But the real
power lies inside, in mystery. Blood and flesh, miles of tubes and
organs which pulse and writhe down deep in the dark where
we can't reach them, without our knowledge or consent. Desire
comes upon us like a fever, feeds on us, changes us. This terrible
power. I saw it in myself, and it scared me senseless. All I ever
wanted was to see it in someone else, just once to catch a glimpse
of it. But there was never anything but meat, but blood. And this
rage would come over me, this awful fear that perhaps there is
no force behind it at all, nothing to direct or drive us. That it was
me, only me and always me, alone. Alone. *Alone.*
(Quieter)
Then it was enough to see red, everywhere. Red streets. Red
walls. Red hands. All mine. All mine.

MRS. BENTHAM
Stephen—

JACK

Do you think calling me that will make me him if you only keep
on doing it long enough? No more than me calling you by another name would make you *her*: Mother, perhaps. Or...Mary.

MRS. BENTHAM
Stephen, I—

JACK
What is your Christian name, Mrs. Bentham?
If I might make so free.

MRS. BENTHAM
...Clarissa.

JACK
Very pretty.
(A beat)
My name is Jack.

MRS. BENTHAM
Oh...God. Oh, my good God.

JACK
Is God good, do you suppose? He made the flowers, true enough.
But then—he also made *me*.

He chooses a knife and paces, shifting it from hand to hand with
a very light CHINK of polished steel that increases steadily with
the rate of his agitation, like a Satanic metronome. Is he even
talking to her anymore? Or just to himself? No matter. Throughout, MRS. BENTHAM—rooted to the spot by fascination, terror, or a combination of the two—fights to slow her own frantic
BREATHING, as though trying to will herself invisible.

JACK
(Faster and faster)
Steam under stopper, super-heated. My urge to peel away the
skin of the world undone by finding only red garbage underneath—the basest carnal urges, so low they contaminate whatever they touch. Rendering flesh just a shallow mask over life's
hideous facts: What *can* be fucked *must* be fucked, always and
forever, the result of that fucking being not life, but death. Death
in childbirth. Death in abortion. Death by syphilis. Death by
cancer. Death by murder. Death by death.
(He rounds on her)
But this talk of a "cure"—all poppycock, a stupid sham, a coward's way out and nothing more. D'you understand? I might have
done the first merely to see, yes...yet why go on, as though more
might be learned? Why all these others, worse and worse and
worse, 'til SHE—
(Stops short; then)
Because...it's what I want. *All* I want. Nothing more, or less.

He GROANS, horribly. MRS. BENTHAM gives a gasp, shies from him—he stops again, fixing her. Then gives a small, mirthless smile.

> JACK
>
> Oh, I *am* a sad object, without doubt. But you do well to fear me.
> (Brings the knife up again)
> Shall I show you why?

He EVISCERATES HIMSELF. Layers of sound tell the tale: FLESH PARTING, SPRAYS OF BLOOD, punctuated by corresponding GASPS, MOANS, and THUNDER. The RAIN drums on, as background. MRS. BENTHAM whimpers.

> JACK
>
> (Describing the cuts as he makes them)
> Glandula...thyreoeidea. Sternum. Plica...umbilicalis...medialis.
> Messenterium...dorsale...commune. Vesica...urinaris.

A SICK, CRACKING SOUND as JACK takes his own RIB-CAGE in both hands and PULLS IT APART.

MODIFY the RAIN to the sound of JACK'S PULSING BLOOD. BRING UP the BEATING of his EXPOSED, NAKED HEART.

> JACK
>
> (Screaming)
> Here I am; here I am; here I am! *Take a good look!*

He and MRS. BENTHAM SCREAM one more time, together. Their cries, the sound of RAIN and JACK'S HEARTBEAT all peak at the same time.

FADE TO SILENCE.

OVER:

MRS. BENTHAM
And so we say goodbye?

JACK
Yes...
(After a long moment)
...goodbye.

MRS. BENTHAM
Always the gentleman.
(Moves away, voice DIMMING)
No place now but the water, for both of us.
Don't you think, my gentle Jack?

But no answer follows, only a splash. Which makes a sort of marriage.

FADE UP INTO:

TABLEAU FOURTEEN: LETHE

The RIVER'S steady ebb and flow, giving way to the WHEELS of a traveling gurney. It STOPS, with a screech.

MEDICAL STUDENT
You'll swear to its freshness?

MORGUE ATTENDANT
Dead a day at most, sir—and there's nobody will miss its company, neither, not even were they to check the roster. Still, I wouldn't worry too hard over legality, I was you...your professors turn a blind eye already, don't they? Only stands to reason the law'll soon follow.
(He folds back the sheet)
So. How d'you find her?

MEDICAL STUDENT
Very beautiful indeed. A suicide?

MORGUE ATTENDANT
Picked from the river just this morning. Unlucky in love, as the old cant goes—but we can't know that, can we, sir? Be nobody left upright in London, if that was all it took.

MEDICAL STUDENT
I suppose not.
(A pause)
One always wants to say words over a body; death should mean more than just a chance for further study. And yet...any eulogy I might consider seems so trite next to the sight of her lying there like that, all alone. So—cold.

MORGUE ATTENDANT
It's a cold old world. Ain't it?

MEDICAL STUDENT
...I suppose.

He SIGHS, reaching for his scalpel.

A FEAST
FOR DUST

All that summer so far there had been no real hint of precipitation, just drought, flame, and the ash it left behind, cut with intermittent rumors of blood falling from the air.

As the place he'd started off from fell further behind, in every new township that Sheriff Jenkins added to his hastily drafted map of the surrounding territories, he found men and women who prayed for rain ever more desperately, berating first the Injuns who no longer occupied their lands, then whatever strangers were unlucky enough to wander by, then God and the Devil in turn, before finally turning—only at the last—on themselves.

Storm's coming, he'd tell them, once he'd done enough to grab their attention—then find himself constrained to add, after they inevitably greeted such a prediction with hopeful pleasure: *No, not that sort, sad to say; what it's bringin' is something you in no wise want, let alone him who brings it. Which is why you need to look to your sins and own your secret guilts right now, folks, this very instant, 'fore the curse of self-deception all but assures the bulk of you end up the way we did, back home...*

They cursed him for a false prophet, mostly, and tried to run him off. Sometimes it came to blows, or even bullets, while other times he got off with a few harsh words, weathering them stone-faced, same as the horse apples they chucked after him. In the end, it was enough to've made his speech, Jenkins reckoned; they were warned now, if nothing else, no matter what-all they might yet choose to do (or not do) with that same grim intelligence. And that least—the *very* least, sparse as it might be—was, frankly, the best he could probably aspire to do, given the circumstances.

Those were the good days. Bad days came when he made a sweep elsewhere, spanning as many compass directions as he might around his target's last legitimate stopping point, and found nothing but ruin: homesteads denuded, gore-soaked not from affray but from above, as though some wounded behemoth had floated overhead spraying grue every-which-way; graves exploded outwards and empty. All the now sadly predictable detritus, roster of attendant destruction tabled ever-upwards, with no apparent sort of end—easy, or otherwise—in sight.

For this was the trail of Sartain Stannard Reese that Jenkins followed, as he had since what was left of the man had passed through his own home, sowing similar awfulness in his wake. Sartain Reese, known as "One-Shot," with his bushwhacker locks and his odd-angled pale eyes; Reese, who had ridden with Bartram Haugh in Lincoln and elsewhere, leaving enough far more natural devastation behind them both to sow broadsheets emblazoned with their linked images from here back to Missouri. Reese, who Jenkins's predecessor, Sheriff Marten, had failed to prevent his citizenry-flock from hanging off their single still-viable tree, only to see him come striding back up Main Street a night and a day later, trousers stiff with dirt and piss, to demand the guns Haugh had once gifted him with as a seal on their marriage of sorts—Satan-approved and God-decried, just like in Sodom-town of old—before shooting Reese straight through the heart, treacherously self-loving as always, and leaving him in the desert to die.

That other sheriff was gone from this world for sure, now; Jenkins had seen full proof of it, more than enough, before prying the man's tin star free and taking on that charge. But as for Reese, driven hither and yon to do what Jenkins could only assume was God's judgment on every other blooded creature in his way, while truly seeking retribution on one faithless companion only...though he certainly bore his fair share of a corpse's qualities, Jenkins somewhat suspected that one could neither call Reese dead nor alive, at this very moment, and hope to be entirely correct in the verdict. He was a revenant, a harbinger, and where his steps took him blood followed, literally—down from the heavens first, then back up from the earth borne on a tide of hungry ghosts; a fatal crop seeded and brought to sudden bloom by Reese's own execution.

Whose blood was that you had on you, Reese? he remembered asking as they'd sat together in the jailhouse, recalling the sticky red coat Reese had worn on first entrance, before the doctor had cleaned him up enough for Marten to place his face. To which Reese replied, not even looking up, apparently too tired by far to bother being properly sociable: *Oh, somebody from round here's, I expect. Didn't you recognize it?*

Because, as Reese went on to point out—*You and yours seem good people, on the whole, from what I've seen. But there's always a reason I run across places, and you have been unlucky, so might be that's 'cause there's other people here, ones that's just like me.*

I'd know, if there was, Jenkins had maintained, steadfast-foolish, not knowing any better. And Reese had simply laughed, torn mouth bleeding enough to paint his lips, before asking: *Would you? How, exactly...*

(...excepting the Word of God?)

For himself, Jenkins had listened mightily hard for that Word these many weeks since, both daily and nightly, catching not the barest syllable of a reply. Indeed, he almost began to feel that all his former prayers had been in vain, seeing how the only true miracles he'd ever witnessed were of Reese's pitch-black variety.

Yet still he came on, ever farther from the vales he'd known, plagued by heat and thirst, sore in both heart and belly; he stopped only to rest, to pick stones from his horse's hooves and then walk a while, for what else was he to do? *Someone* had to warn them Reese was coming, giving them at least that slightest of chances in the face of impartial and awful justice, this sanguine Second Deluge. To protect the guilty from their guilt, the sinners from their sins, the weak from the consequence of their own weaknesses...

...thus doing, apparently, what the same absent Lord that Jenkins had been raised to praise no longer cared to.

The next "town" Jenkins reached, by nightfall, was so small it hadn't found itself a name yet: no farms as such, no real homesteads, just a combined whistle-stop and trading post which specialized in whatever the last transaction'd left behind. The fellow manning it was of origins so indeterminate that the definition of such almost seemed a puzzle set for unwary travelers by a vaguely amused and un-benign Nature. He was dressed in badly-cured hides which haloed him with stenchgood and currently deep engaged in cleaning one of a brace of lizards for immediate jerkyfication.

Jenkins introduced himself, while the counter-tender regarded him with disinterested distrust, slopping lizard guts up over his shirt-cuffs. He allowed as how he was hoping to meet up with a specific local someone, if possible, a concept the man either didn't appear to've ever heard of, or saw too little to approve in.

"Willicks, that was the name they gave me, back at Shortfall. Said he's your marshal, or close enough."

"Y'huh."

"But you wouldn't know him to look at, I'm takin' it. Or where-all he might best be found at."

"N'huh."

"'Cause I've been traveling a piece, sir, and when I told my story up Shortfall way, they said Fred Willicks was him I should make my case to, in *these* parts..."

"*Uh,*" the man behind the counter put in, with some force, like he maybe meant to follow it up with more—but didn't. Jenkins stood there a long moment, waiting for elaboration before sighing and touching his hat.

Then he turned, only to be confronted by another man entirely, abruptly conjured from nothing: cat-footed and far more elegant in his motions than his clothes' drab cut would suggest, a luxuriant beard blurring his face, one hand sure on his gun-butt and the other shading his eyes, themselves hazel with just a light touch of rain-grey.

"Poor Mahershalalhashbaz here's only got half a tongue to work with, sir, thanks to bad Injuns, and that cut sideways," the man—whose lapel bore, Jenkins now saw, a tin star as well—told him, gaze held steady. "Makes him tough to put questions to, let alone get any useful answers from. But you're in luck nonetheless, turns out: Fred Willicks is *my* name, as it happens. Which makes you?"

"Clarke Jenkins, Mister Willicks. I'm...well, I *was* from Esther, before. Not that there's much left there now."

"Which wouldn't make you much of a sheriff at all, then, given you lack a town to watch over."

Jenkins shrugged, hands held carefully wide and empty, letting his full body allow as how when considered that-a-way, Willicks might have himself a point.

"You want my star, I'll gladly hand it over," he said, "'long as you do me the honour of listening to what I've got to say."

Willicks contemplated this. "Hell," he said, at last, "it can wait 'til I've heard out the latter to decide on the former, surely; my wife does like to entertain, not that she gets much cause for it. I'll tell her to set one place more."

Jenkins felt himself start to relax, as Willicks said it—where he was from, men didn't invite one another to guest if they planned on doing 'em ill, after. But then again, One-Shot Reese had been a guest too, in a way, and the "good" people of Jenkins' home had swung him from a tree; bad manners at best, even if not quite worthy of what'd followed, at least under non-Divine law...

I do need food, though, he thought. *And rest.*

So: "Lead on," he told Willicks, allowing his lips to shape what was probably a singularly unconvincing smile, considering how long he'd fallen out of the habit. To which Willicks merely raised a brow, and did.

Where Willicks lived, it turned out, was up above the area's sole wilting tree-line, in a cabin that was ramshackle without but snug-made within. His missus was young, pink-pricked and crumpled like a late rose, with every part of her swelled up tight in anticipation of a second child; their first was a spry little boy of perhaps five years, changeable-eyed like Willicks yet cheerful-industrious as his dam, without even a hint of his father's hidden depths. The meal was salt pork, beans and a slab of flat-bread, which Jenkins—who hadn't eaten well in almost a week—set to with grateful pleasure.

After, with the boy dispatched to bed, Jenkins leaned close to Willicks by the fire and told his tale, in quiet measured tones.

Willicks listened without comment, up 'til almost the end.

"This 'companion' Reese spoke of," he began, then. "This man Haugh…"

"Bartram Haugh, yes, sir. Bewelcome's chief architect."

"They were in it together, shoulder to shoulder, is what I heard."

"Maybe so," Jenkins allowed. "I only have what Reese told me to go on, after all. And his testimony's—suspect, at best."

Willicks sat back, sighing. "Well, any rate. You've been tracking Reese a while now; what is it you think he's after, exactly?"

"You've already named him, Mister Willicks," Jenkins replied. "Was Haugh who set this off, far as I can figure—Reese bears the mark of proof right over his heart, or rather *through* it. He won't stop 'til he finds this false 'friend' of his, and visits the same judgment on Haugh for breaking their…pact as he has on every Haugh-less place he's sojourned in thus far."

"Then if you really want to stop him, Sheriff, it'd seem you're going in the wrong direction entirely. Following Reese won't help, or even hinder—it's Haugh you need."

Such a simple conclusion! The second Willicks let it drop, Jenkins saw his own errors at once laid bare, hideous in their utter inaccuracy. It was a slap to the face that set his ears ringing so, he barely heard what the man said next. "Sorry, again?"

"Do you know where this-all happened—the original shooting?"

"Not as such. But…" Rummaging in a waistcoat pocket, Jenkins withdrew the map he'd annotated, its modifications all shaky lead-pencil scribblings done mostly by firelight. "Here," he said, pointing; "this came before Esther, by near a month, or so them that was left told me—found it on my initial sweep, when I was still bothering to go backwards, having no clear impression which way Reese might've left town by after the storm. Granted, there's no assurance this was where he reached first, after whatever happened between 'em…happened, but—"

"—It's a good enough place to start." Willicks nodded, gaze immediately drawn to where his wife sat quiet, to all appearances deep-engaged with her knitting, though her own eyes skipped hither and yon whenever she seemed to think they weren't looking. "How long a ride, you figure?"

Jenkins made calculations. "Ten days' hard slog, just about. I've been moving slower myself, but that's on account of fanning to cover the most ground and knowin' what I tracked went on foot; go straight and we'll get there quick as weather allows, if the horses don't wear out."

Later still, as he sat dozing by the fire, heaped with rugs, Jenkins listened to Willicks cozying the missus around. Given the few words she'd let drop at table, the two of 'em had met by correspondence with her an old maid already (though she hardly looked it) and Willicks well aware that his choice of job made for slim feminine pickings, entering into alliance long-distance with little hope of much more than mutual compromise. Yet by what he'd witnessed, their gamble seemed to have paid off in spades. He hated to part such a meeting of true minds, 'specially with Willicks' wife in her gravid state and no doctor handy. So he'd all but made his mind up to beg off by morning, only to have Missus W. herself shake her head no at him, adamant—hair high-piled yet sleek, brown as Willicks' own, with only a thread here and there of silver.

"I knew what Fred took on before I met him, Sheriff," she said, packing both their bags with tucker. "Sacrifice is sweet to my Lord, so the Good Book says; if Jeptha gave his own daughter over for righteousness's sake, who am I to retain my man, when similarly called upon?"

"You're a strong woman, Missus."

"It's God's strength only, Sheriff, as all true strength is. And I'll look to see you later, both of you, when this charge of yours is fulfilled."

Jenkins tipped his hat to her prediction, sending up a brief sketch of a prayer himself—perhaps useful, perhaps not, depending on who might be listening—that the next few days wouldn't disprove it.

What might've been Reese's first foothold out the grave had already been mostly dead when Jenkins surveyed it, those months past. Now it was entirely empty, broken like eggshell, a slack rind of itself sucked dry and left open to the wind; dust and weeds had made the streets their home, sand blowing in through shattered shop windows and doors left careless-open in its few surviving residents' headlong scramble to vacate the premises, to eddy 'cross the floors in an aimless devils' dance.

Jenkins slipped down and went to tether his horse, expecting Willicks to follow him. But the marshal-by-self-election stayed obdurately mounted, hands slipping to hips as he swung his head, eyeing the place up and down. "Where-all'd they hang this One-Shot Reese of yours, exactly?" he inquired. "Don't see any trees handy..."

Jenkins wracked his brain. "Uh...from the saloon's roof-tree, if I recall a'right. Had to haul him up with five volunteers pulling, then wait for him to go slack before the doc had the town smith jerk on his legs a few times, make sure his neck was good and broke."

"He must've complained though, surely, when he realized what they had in mind as regards his ending—raved some, or cursed, or both. Maybe tried to turn tail, to flee? For it's a truly heart-breaking sight, when the gallows you're being drawn to is made by amateurs."

"No," Jenkins said, not thinking to wonder how Willicks came by this particular intelligence. "I don't think so; never heard Sartain Reese to've acted the coward, neither behind a gun or in front of one. They told me they found him stone, mostly, right up to the drop...same as in every other place."

He had his back to Willicks now, still looking up at the building in question, head perfect cocked in memory. Which is why he couldn't know exactly what might've accompanied the little sigh Willicks gave in answer, be it shrug or grimace, contempt or sorrow—an admixture of both, perhaps, those hazel eyes taking on a momentary shine. Yet he did hear the sound of iron clearing leather, if too late, half-turning on the hammer's cock, so the bullet took him not neatly in the spine (as must've been Willicks' intention) but messily in the side, punching through and through with such force it spun him to fall at his own mount's hooves. The pain was ferocious, so bad he could barely breathe, let alone speak; he lay there looking up, and saw his traveling companion—

(*friend, my dearest*)

(*never thought to see you here, Sergeant*)

—slip from the saddle at last, graceful as sin, to stand there re-loading, unhurriedly, with the sun behind him dimming his face to a merest silhouette: Pleasant, well-spoken Fred Willicks simply all at once gone, his wife's joy and his young son's pride extinguished, with nothing left behind but a ruthless, calculating liar, thief, and murderer—candle-snuffed as though he'd never existed, though Jenkins could only assume he *had*, at least up 'til this son-of-a-bitch had played much the same trick on him.

"That does sound like him," the man who'd taken Willicks' place at some point admitted, chambering a fresh bullet, before spinning the replenished cylinder with a showman's flair. "For Sartain's a gentleman first and foremost, you see, immured through long tradition with the idea of striking honour's pose under even the severest sort of duress—to stand fast and take your medicine, setting an example for the rest, no matter how fools around you rage and squall, or let their stupidity-aiding hatred present you with opportunities of escape. Not like me, sad to say."

Jenkins coughed up blood, then almost strangled on it going back down. "No," he agreed, finally, once he'd retched his air-pipe clear again. "Not like *you* at all, from what I heard...Bartram Haugh."

At this, Haugh really did shrug. Pointing out: "And I agree. Yet, you might well notice—'tween the two've us, chivalrous Mister Reese and me, I'm the only one that's still alive."

"So you...do believe he's the revenant I...painted him, at least."

"Oh, stranger things've happened, I suppose. Hell, who would have ever thought I'd find some nonentity such as Fred Willicks' ridiculous little life a fair enough fit to shape myself to? Then again, it was Phyllida who did the trick on that one, really, turning up on the next stage after like she did, all fresh and ready for love; had stars in her eyes the moment she heard his name come out my mouth, so who was I to disappoint?"

"U'huh," Jenkins managed, unintentionally imitating verbally-truncated storekeep Mister Mahershah-whatsit. "N...then, there's hers and your...son, too..."

"Simon, yes—he's mine sure enough, poor mite, no matter his last name. May he never have need to discover his own in-born capacities, in future."

Haugh put just enough resonant tone of emotion into this last that Jenkins could almost think he meant it, 'til he remembered who he was talking to.

"Truth to tell, I thought you knew already," he continued, conversationally. "That this quest of yours was some ruse, a protracted wild goose chase, calculated to get *me* out where you could pull a gun and collect the Union's money. But it took a bare half-day's ride with you for me to see how lamentably honest a fellow you really are, Sheriff, and that's when I decided to let our trip here play itself to the full—further away you took me, after all, the less likely anybody'd be to prevent me covering your corpse over, once our business was done."

"Always meant t'...kill me, then...is what you're sayin'."

"Well, *yes*. You'd've wrecked what I've built, otherwise, and I can't have that."

Jenkins coughed yet once more, and murmured something wetly in on top of it—

Haugh leant in, waiting for him to repeat it.

"I...pity you," Jenkins said, finally, drawing a snort. He rolled his eyes far enough to glimpse something both sudden and surprising, though horribly familiar. And closer by far to boot than he would've ever expected, given the softness of its approach—

Haugh, however, noticed none of the above, continuing to muse aloud:

"Well, that's your choice, little good as it'll do you, or me... for you see, Sheriff, I'm no firm believer in God at all, let alone his mercy, or his judgment either. Christ knows what it was you thought you saw, back there in—Esther, was it?—but Sartain Reese had about as little to do with it as grace has with error. I shot him down, saw the front of his heart pop out from under his breast-bone in a spray, and I've killed more than enough men in my time to know the way they fall. Reese could tell you the same, if he was here."

To this, and with gross effort, Jenkins could conjure only a dull creaking noise—something he himself was surprised to recognize, eventually, as laughter.

"Hysteria, eh? That's one way to salve the sting. But we've chatted long enough, for my money, so...damn, what *are* you lookin' at, anyhow?"

Said a voice from behind, preternaturally calm: "Always did please you to think me a fool, Bart, just as it pleased me to let you. But that's over with, now."

131

(Much like all else.)

These few words—or just the sound of 'em, Jenkins didn't won-der—were enough to turn outlaw Bart Haugh, a man with more sins on his soul than Judas good and three thousand-odd dollars on his head, sheet-white. He turned towards their speaker, slow as river weed current-caught, perhaps unaware he was even doing so; blanched yet further when he saw who stood there, making all the tiny, charm-crinkled lines on his face stand out like scars.

For: yes, it was the man himself, of course—though "man" might no longer be the most accurate term, Jenkins thought, giv-en. "One-Shot" Reese, in whatever he used for flesh, corporeal enough to touch yet inhumanly mutable under pressure; Sartain Stannard Reese, his sandy locks slicked down with the same phan-tom blood still sticky-coating him from head to toe, skull topped in a buzzing black crown of flies. He cocked his head, regarding Haugh narrowly through almost yellow eyes, and watched that anything-but-gentleman go suddenly all a-tremble, shook juice-less, same as some storm-withered leaf.

"Been quite the spell, Bart," Reese told him, unhurriedly, like they were chatting over supper. "Yes, I did have myself some rare difficulty finding you. But then, you always did know how to make us both scarce, when it suited your plans best."

Haugh gulped, straining for even the smallest measure of his usual sanguine humour. "Sartain—" he began, only to find himself cut off when Reese waved him silent.

"The sheriff here has a fair idea how long I've been at it," he continued, indicating Jenkins, "not to mention the cost of my quest, to me, and others. Oh, but I walked *so* far and found so *very* little, 'sides from a grinding sameness! Delivering judgment on others, yet finding no respite of my own...it was enough, frankly, to drive me to despair. Until, just the other day, I received pos-sible word of my imminent respite, and from the most unlikely of sources—that still, small voice above I catch just a whisper of, I only strain hard enough, letting slip how after all this time, *you* were finally comin' to meet *me*."

Haugh shook his head frantically, shoulders hiked like he wanted to back away but couldn't gather the necessary steam. In-stead he stayed fear-rooted while Reese stepped closer, stained boot-soles leaving reddish clumps of print on the street beneath;

looked back Jenkins' way as he did so, watching him spit up a pint or so more of his own blood to keep his airways open, and sighed at the sight.

"Should've kept to your own place, Sheriff, 'specially after I worked so hard to clear it out for you—but I guess you know that, already. Who'd you leave in charge?"

"Good men," Jenkins half-retched, in reply. "Not...too many left t'make...trouble for 'em, after you was...done with us."

"Well. S'pose you can take some consolation, then, knowing they won't need to rely on your return." To Haugh: "And what about *you*, Sergeant? For I do hear you made a place for yourself on the other side of things, putting your skill at preying on your own kind to good use."

"I was a marshal, or close as makes no never-mind. Took a wife, made a son. Got another coming."

Reese nodded, with just a hint of sympathy. "It's a hard world for those abandoned, and that's the truth. But it's hardly their fault the man they call father and husband can't be trusted to recall how he made his true troth-pledge years back, to *me*."

"That, between us—that was boys' foolery, Sartain. Spartan fun, best kept for Army days."

"Was that all? No, I don't think so; much as I pity this gal you tricked into bed with you, least she'll make your child a home and pray for you after, little as you deserve any such thing. You and I, though—we're shield-brothers sworn, blooded together in battle, now and hereafter. Remember the song you taught me, riding away from Lincoln? That was prophecy, 'friend,' disguised in tune. Don't believe I've ever let it out of my mind since."

And here he tipped his gory head back, conjuring a low and moaning refrain—some dour Appalachian holler slowed 'til its verses stuck fast in the mid's crevasses, harmfully catching, like lines from a Satan-inspired hymnal.

Oh the owl, the owl
Is a lonesome bird
It chills my heart
With dread and terror
That's someone's blood
There on its wing

That's someone's blood
There on its feather...

A pause, followed by this conclusion, with a mindful glance Haugh's way—

But now I know
That time has come
When you and I
Shall be as one.

"*Not* now," Bart Haugh denied it, in return, his voice like dust. "Oh God, no. Not now, not *now*..."

"As well now as any other time, don't you think—for given all you've done, did you really believe there'd be no consequences to come?" Reese gave a cold sketch of a smile. "If so, consider yourself schooled, for here I stand, a walking object lesson; your destiny's sketch, guilty on every charge, with only the barest fraction of my due payment yet rendered. And I did nothing at all, Bart, that you hadn't done first, or told me to."

"My job, it began as a jest, yes—but I was *good* at it. I've got a *boy*." Hopeless: "Doesn't that count for anything?"

Reese shrugged. "Should it?"

Maybe not, Jenkins thought, too exhausted to stay even minimally upright. And fell face-down before he could hope to stop it, filling his bloody mouth with dust—dry dust turning pink, then red, becoming mud.

He choked himself to sleep, in fullest expectation of never waking again.

Much later, after he *did* revive, laid up convalescent in what had been Bart Haugh's bed—or Fred Willicks', rather, a notion he never could bring himself to disabuse the Widow Willicks of, even once she'd finally agreed to swap her lost spouse's name for Jenkins' own—Jenkins made sure to tell her how "Willicks" had gone down fighting, bravely managing to transpose himself 'tween Jenkins and their supernatural foe, and paying the price for his heroism. He slathered detail on detail, 'til by the fourth repetition, the story ended with "Willicks" throwing his life away gladly by all but grabbing "One-Shot" Reese and dragging that troubled creature single-handed good down to whatever cell awaited him in the Infernal realms, instead of...the opposite, basically.

T'was Phyllida he had to thank for his life, it turned out—said she'd had a dream, or been sent one, and used her God-lent strength to trace his and "Willicks'" trail at as high a speed as the ox-cart would support, with little Simon riding literal shot-gun. They'd picked up a doctor in one of the towns Reese's route had barely grazed and found Jenkins in dire straits, his wound miraculously glued shut by a fortuitous chemical coincidence of blood-mud trapped 'neath Jenkins' flopped trunk forming a loose poultice which unseasonably fierce overnight frost turned to ice, plugging things deep enough to prevent further infection; he'd suffered through fever and bronchitis before mending yet emerged hale, regaining his strength with surprising rapidity.

Miraculous, his eventual wife called it, and Jenkins didn't dis-agree, since if there really was nobody up there looking out for him, it seemed bad form to throw that sort of happy synchrony back in the universe's face.

Then again, might be it was less gratitude he felt than respect, reverence, or simple fear. Because, as Phyllida liked to point out, Reese had been an instrument of judgment, though a singularly rough and contrary one—which meant that the same force Jen-kins credited with his recovery had probably set Reese in his path in the first place. Why? To teach a lesson, prove a point?

Reese, who was indubitably gone—laid back down, if not to rest, with Haugh surely traveling alongside him in proverbial double-harness, wherever their eventual destination. Which was probably all the conclusion that dreadful figure'd ever really want-ed, in Jenkins' own estimation.

Impossible to discern which of the images he occasionally found himself summoning at odd moments, caught between dream and memory, were actually based in hard experience. Yet sometimes the former sheriff turned let's-call-him-marshal heard voices and shivered to recognize their tones—one wildly pleading, the other sure/coolly certain yet somewhat dead, too tired even for anger. Saying:

Moral deeds mean nothing, when the heart's not in it. That's a good man, right there, with your bullet through his chest—God only knows I'd do my best to save him, if I weren't made for other work entirely. You and I, though...for all that's passed, we're just the same as we ever were.

All I'm asking for's a little mercy, Sartain. Just that.

Oh, but this is a little mercy, Bart. You really don't want to see what no mercy looks like.

What then? Jenkins sometimes wondered. Had Reese pulled Haugh into an embrace and begun to decay? Had the dirt sucked them both down like a sink-hole, then, while heavy rains and flash-floods—no longer sanguine yet hardly natural, given the way things had gone those last few months weather-wise—scoured it all clean overtop, leaving no trace at all to show they'd ever been there?

One way or t'other, if Reese's misfortunes and Haugh's come-uppance formed any sort of sermon, Jenkins might as well account himself converted. For though in continuing contact with bad men (and some women) doing evil things, he fought hard to keep himself un-blooded, at least by the standards that'd cost Esther Township's previous sheriff his life and—possibly—his salvation. In a world where invisible principalities and harsh recompense were no longer in doubt, in other words, Jenkins thought it better by far to keep his soul's immortality intact, safe, at all costs that didn't endanger the same in others...and let his body, in the main, take care of itself.

Haugh's second child was born as summer turned to fall, a girl, blithe, kind and fair. They named her for Jenkins' former home, and loved her as best life's vicissitudes would allow for.

DRAWN UP FROM DEEP PLACES

Ofttimes Jerusalem Parry dreamed of the noise—that one snap, so small yet final—which his mother's neck had made giving way, or the creak of her body swaying from a Cornish gallows-tree; other times he dreamed that Solomon Rusk lay beside him in the bed that'd once been his, long rogue's body pressed so close that he near to crushed the breath from Parry's lungs and slipped a thigh 'tween his knees to force them open, so their weapons might joust for precedence. From the former visions Parry woke with cheeks wet and throat restricted, while from the latter he woke with teeth all a-grind and trousers shamefully tight, for he well-knew that that great bastard's ghost still lingered somewhere nearby, smirking invisibly at how easy his murderer was to discomfit.

Less often yet, however, he dreamed of the storm whose fury had first disclosed him, both to others and to himself—seen him bloom up a wizard under its tumult, little though that black apotheosis had seemed to benefit him, at the time. This night, it seemed, had been such a night, borne back on a rush of wind and thunder: a downpour alternately salty and sweet, great swells and breakers tipping the Navy ship he'd signed onto at Portsmouth like a child's bath-toy while cold rain dashed straight in the crew's faces, stinging all their eyes half-blind.

Parry found himself handing his way up the deck, clinging to the guide-rope while those around him reeled and shrieked like Bacchantes, busy as any half-drowned ant-hill. Wherever he tried to help they scurried from him, averted their gaze and threw out signs to ward him off as though he were Satan or the plague; called out as soon as they recognized his face, bawling the same idiot warning from stem to stern, no matter their more pressing distractions—

"'Tis him, the Jonah... Ensign Parry's a Jonah sure, cursed by God, so's any ship carries him will flounder! It's he our Saviour hates, and we who suffer for it!"

"You rave, sir," he recalled telling the bo'sun's mate, whom he'd seized by the collar—pulling him close as circumstance would allow for and channeling every jot of cold authority the Church had taught him into it, as he did. "Superstitious rot. There's no such thing, you fool!"

"So *you'd* say!" the man had thrown back, not quite brave enough to strike at him with aught but words. "Now give me room, you curst damned creature—let me to my work, that real men not perish on your sins' account!"

It cut him, enough to make him let go with a shove, feeling a cruel jolt of pleasure to see his accuser slip to bruise both knees and tear his palms in the scuppers' white backwash. Hearing himself roar, at the same time: "Then go, you scum, and good riddance! May the Sea take your bones and Hell itself tear your black heart in half, likewise!"

(That mate *had* died later on, Parry only now remembered, for which they'd blamed him too. But then, he had never held as short a bridle on his own tongue as he might have wished, under pressure; it was a fault his masters had tried to cure him of, and his back still bore the scars of their tutelage now, 'neath his current captain's coat.)

Aye, so I recall, Solomon Rusk's hated voice told him, here. *For I saw those many a time, when you and I were in our sin. But then, ye'd've made a terrible parson, my Jerusha, no matter had they managed to beat every last scrap of pride from you, having no great talent for forgiveness—as ye must surely know, if you're any sort of honest.*

But there was no point in answering, for conversation with Rusk was the most blatant of traps, now more than ever. So Parry only shrugged to himself instead, thinking in reply: *Well, we'll never have proof of it now, will we? And whose fault is that, pray tell?*

(God's surely. His, or the bloody Devil's.)

Then, in the way of dreams, he found himself standing several feet above-deck, as those who'd taken his name in vain stared upwards, faces blank and gaping: a moment of purest ecstasy, surer than any proof of the Divine love he'd chased after all his life—so immediate, so *real*. Ablaze from top to toe with blue-green Saint Elmo's fire, Parry watched the storm peel back 'round his presence as his will plunged upwards, parting the weather's knot, and felt himself lit so bright that all his store of gall was burnt away at once.

I did this, he remembered thinking. *This is my work.*

Such joy as he'd never known, before, or after. Yet it lasted only until the ship's witch-finder withdrew a heavy iron cross from his belt and flung it, cracking Parry 'cross the temple so hard that he hit the deck already unconscious.

Here he felt himself bolt awake once more, iron-made collar scar 'round his neck puffed worse than usual, so choking-stiff he could hardly breathe. Whilst through the cabin door, his own bo'sun hammered hard and called to him, a cringing note of apology in his voice: "Cap'n, sorry t' disturb ye, but you're wanted on deck, soon as possible. Ye know we'd not rouse ye but 'twas necessary, given your orders...Cap'n Parry, sir?"

"I hear you, man," he managed, at last, voice a bare rasp. "What is it?"

"That creature of yours, Mister Dolomance—he's found somethin' as has an air of...supernature about it, such that we thought it best ye take a look."

"I'll be up soon as modesty permits, then. Tell them to leave it be, 'til I get there."

"Yes sir," the bo'sun replied, gratefully. "There were no great plans otherwise, believe me."

Oh, I do, Parry thought, darkly. And levered himself upright, cracking his neck gingerly side to side, to loosen the scar's hold on his wind.

Ignoring Captain Rusk's phantom gaze, he refused to be hurried in his customary toilet; gathered his hair back in a neat tail and took care to re-order his linen, wrapping his cravat doubly high, brushing his coat 'til he was satisfied with the way it shone. At last, he pulled his boots on and strode forth, flicking the lock to behind him with a blue-green whip of sparks. For though the door would not keep his evil angel confined, it pleased him to keep it closed between them, nevertheless, as proof of their division.

You are dead, sir, if not gone; stubborn as ever, and greedy of this bond you still claim we share, for all I never wished one. Yet much as I will one day break this curse you laid on me, I will see you learn, eventually, to leave me be.

Rusk would have laughed at this last, and maybe did, since Parry couldn't hear it outside of dream, or drunkenness—a state to which Parry had seldom been used to abandon himself, even before he knew doing so would put him once more within reach of his former slavemaster's growling voice and wandering hands. It was a different sort of skill to speak with the dead, one Parry was glad to know he did not share, unlike Rusk's half-sister in Porte Macoute, the sorceress known as Tante Ankolee. God alone knew that if he could have somehow banished Rusk back to her side, he would have, without delay...but given the man had met his well-merited end aboard-ship—*under* it, any road—that did not seem an option.

Bitch of Hell, Rusk had called her, then, this craft which became his grave, for he'd been a coarse man, loose of impulse and restricted in vocabulary. But Parry had put paid to that, overseeing her masthead's re-painting himself, which now read *Salina Resurrecta*: a salt-borne lady, cobbled from shipwrecks. Since the curse Rusk had laid upon him in dying rendered her both home and prison to him now, he shaped her to his likes, which varied by occasion; stiff as he outwardly seemed, he could be mercurial when the fit was on him, or when the pain land's touch now bred in him reached up through however many fathoms of ocean to curl 'round every limb, setting his blood a-boil in its most infinitesimal vessels.

A steep price to pay for his freedom, or so it sometimes seemed— yet they had always agreed on this, Captain Rusk and he, if little else: nothing came for nothing in this world; payment was always required, usually in whatever capital seemed most expensive.

On deck, Parry found Mister Dolomance lurking by the anchor-line with head down-hung far as his lack of neck allowed for, flat black eyes kept fixed on the salt-swollen boards beneath his nail-less grey feet. He looked barely human, and Parry had made him so intentionally, that his presence would disturb those around him, rather than smooth the way. The creature was a born weapon, after all, birthed to roam and kill and eat without rest; to render him otherwise would have been to betray his true nature and leave the spells which kept him above-water prone to unravel at the slightest mis-step.

Wizardry was intuitive, in the main—none had tutored Parry at his craft, not since Tante Ankolee had so briefly quizzed him before sending him on his way, with a beginner's hex-bag and a borrowed fetish to grow it on from. The same hung at his belt even now, dangling with all sorts of fresh ammunition; the witch he glimpsed now and then in dreams, like Rusk himself, seldom telling him anything useful. And he remained alone, as he always had been.

Still, better to it, without delay. Parry drew himself full height, staring down this monstrosity he'd wrought as scornfully as possible. "They say you've a gift for me, sir," he said. "Well, bring it out—I must have some recompense, to pay fee on my interrupted slumber."

Sheer rhetoric, of course, for the crew's benefit—Dolomance did not "speak" save for the occasional squeal and grumble, though if Parry cared to press him he could conjure a crude alignment of their thoughts, picking squeamishly through the nasty rush of hatred and hunger which resulted. Such proved unnecessary, however; instead, Dolomance flapped one four-fingered hand over the side, inviting the captain's gaze to follow after. On the waves below, a longboat floated—debris from some wreck or another brig's overthrow, since its sides bore the smudged marks of fire from swift passage through lit oil. Its sole occupant, wrapped to the eyes 'gainst the sun's depredations, raised the portion Parry took to be its head and blinked at him incuriously, offering no greeting.

"Towed it 'ere, 'e did, with its rope in 'is teeth," offered a nearby salt Parry vaguely recalled having sworn the Articles after their last prize was taken, some verminous sot claiming skill in carpentry but yet to give much proof of it. "We was just waitin' on you to bring it closer, Cap'n...or not."

Great bunch of milksops. "Do so, then."

A haul and heave-ho commenced, and Parry stood frowning, arms crossed, as the boat drew near. The figure did not stir; he might almost believe it asleep save it sat upright, swaying slightly. When the boat's prow struck the *Salina*'s, however, its passenger seemed to rouse, looking up again, sharply—its cerements fell away, disclosing a face that made all men present gasp, seeing it proved both female and of an undeniable attractiveness.

Pale skin, a red mouth, long black hair in ringlets to the waist. And blue-grey eyes almost light as Parry's own, with their odd silver cast, yet stormier—more mutable and opaque as well, unreadable, even for him. Mercury, caught beneath a glaze of stone.

"Where am I?" this lady demanded. "It has been days...are you men, or dreams, only?"

"Surely, madam," said Parry, "most dreams smell far less ill than my crew; only sniff the wind to find yourself assured of our existence."

She shook her head. "Nay, but there was a thing that seized me, brought me here. Like a shark, if sharks had legs."

Parry shrugged, waving Dolomance forward, and watched her start again as the shark-were grimaced down, fixed teeth a smile's bare parody. "My servant, madam. And you?"

"I am...they call me Clione, sir. My father was Haelam Attesee, who doctored on the *Nymph*."

"And I am Jerusalem Parry—once of Cornwall, and the Navy. Pirate now, though not entirely by choice."

She obviously recognized the name. "A magician too, as your *servant* proves. And a cursed man, if other rumours be believed."

"Yes, though not so long as I stand on water. Still, 'tis true enough we are about no good business, by merest definition—so if you'd prefer to wait for less outlaw transport, I'm sure we can accommodate your scruples..."

The woman—Miss Attesee, he should call her—furled her lip out prettily, thinking the matter over: elegant in every way, with her black-winged brows and a high spot of colour on each smooth cheek, lush as any Spanish grandee's. "Clione" was one of Poseidon's conquests, if Parry recalled a'right, ocean-swept and transformed for his pleasure, which did seem to fit. At closer quarters, her viperous mane took on the shade of black shared by grapes grown on Veritay Island, seat of Captain's Rusk's familial holdings; her soft hands were two doves, and that mouth a bitten pomegranate. And though his experience in such matters was woefully narrow, he had seldom seen anyone who pulled at him so, thus far...aside from one, and him only intermittently.

"I'll come up," she said, at last, so surlily Parry might almost believe he'd forced her to it. As though there might really be some other choice to make.

A fine-made baggage, he could almost hear Rusk's ghost observe, as hands hauled her over the rail. *And aren't ye taken wi' her, too, my cold young gentleman...should I be jealous?*

Of what? Parry might have snapped, had he found himself alone. But even as the words formed, he saw those eyes of hers widen, as though she'd suddenly glimpsed something—some very *tall* thing—just over his shoulder, where Rusk had been all too wont to loom, in life.

I will not turn, he told himself. *'Tis some ruse. Who is the wizard here, she or I?*

And before he could think better of it he'd already reached out, slipping his gaze inside her own through some maneuver he could barely parse, the better to see what she saw: a man rearing up behind Parry, blotting out the sun—Black Scots, dark-tanned and leonine, with his King Charles hair and his single eye, the other a scar-messed socket. Captain Solomon Rusk, larger than life even in the utter lack of such, regarding her with a crooked smile and growling, in a voice like self-satisfied thunder: *So she can see me, eh? You as well, through her. What a to-do!*

Miss Attesee put one hand up, as though about to swoon; in anticipation, Parry withdrew himself perhaps quicker than was wise, for it made her give a hopeless little cry and all-over tremble, as though he'd felt up under her skirts. The crew exchanged glances, all equal-baffled. But Solomon Rusk's ghost threw back his half-there head and guffawed, with so little sympathy it made Parry long to kill him all over again.

Welcome aboard, Madame Seer, Rusk said, finally. *This will be quite the long voyage for you, I'm thinkin'. Though you and Master Parry may comfort each other against my presence, I s'pose, if ye've a mind to.*

Then vanished, leaving she who termed herself Clione Attesee to roll her wave-coloured eyes up and faint—and it was only Jerusalem Parry's memory of what deck hitting skull felt like, along with the speed it leant him in catching her, that saved her from a similar fate.

She hung in his arms, soft and limp, rounded in highly intriguing places; he stared down at her, baffled, wondering what came next.

What am I to do with you? Parry thought. *Whatever are we to do, with each other?*

No reply came, however. So he toted her back to his cabin and laid her in his bed, as Rusk had once done with him—then withdrew, unlike that rapine-inclined picaroon, so she might sleep her fear-trance off alone.

Parry walked the deck until morning, disturbing his crew, a fact he took pride in. Through a process of trial and error, he had found it best to allow them to make a fear-object of him, if only to prevent them destroying themselves in useless attempts to take his place. In the time since Rusk's demise, he had put down three mutinies already, for though the memory of their former master's passing was enough to dissuade most of the older generation from underestimating their new one's power, the steady shifting of balance between those hands engaged under Rusk and those he'd signed on himself seemed doomed to eventually oblige Parry to prove himself once again whenever they began to see him an obstacle to their own upwards passage.

What none of them understood was that although he had never coveted his current position, now that Rusk's curse was in place, Parry would kill without a second thought to keep it—a man barred from shore needed to keep himself afloat, after all, and he had no compunctions over harshness where treason was involved. One early fool, idiot enough to fall upon him in his repose, he'd accidentally atomized with an undirected blast—the touch of a stranger's hands on his neck-scar had been enough to catapult him back into unhappier days, and he'd struck out without thinking. Others he'd given to the shark-were's kin or swung from the yard-arm in Navy style, as a tribute to past training.

None had joined Rusk under-hull, however, for Parry did not care to risk populating his entire ship with dour phantoms, not when the company here was already so uncongenial. So things continued, with Parry knowing himself despised and avoided by all except Captain Rusk's leering fragment, of whom he could well-stand not to be reminded on quite so regular a basis.

(Miss Attesee, now: she did not fear him, not as yet. Though time might teach her otherwise.)

At length, Parry sat down on the fo'c'sle cross-legged and laid a protective circle 'round himself before sending out his spirit, that his body be left undisturbed. Then, reaching deep into the hex-bag, he ended up winding his dead witch-mother's hair in its frail red braid 'round one hand like a rosary, while at the same time rolling Rusk's false ivory eye 'tween two fingers of the other—victory's spoils turned fetish, sweet as any battlefield prize.

Power, Parry had learned (the hard way; he knew no other), was nothing at all without self-governance; a cracked gun-barrel, apt to explode when fired. It must be ordered, aligned properly with the secret lines of force that ran this sphere along its celestial track...and here those came now, blazing up at every compass-point, illumining a different world. A waking dream, wherein all things—however unlikely—became possible.

Was this what his mother had felt? he sometimes wondered, though he doubted it, given she'd had so little faith in her own powers as to shop him to the black-coat God-botherers the minute he proved educable. Then again, illiterate herself, Arranz Parry set great store by book-learning, and the Cornwall Church certainly had books enough to spare. At the time, however, he would have fought tooth and claw to stay with her, running barefoot through the marsh—did so, ably enough for his size, 'til some bull-sized farmhand-turned-sexton carted him away, screaming. And he had never seen her again, not before the day they pulled him from his studies to see her swung, telling him his blood put the lie to his vocation. How he had resented and denied her, all those intervening years, in his pursuit of a parson's collar—cursed her, even, a thing he now sorely regretted.

On the one hand, she was his mother, and he would always love her fiercely, no matter how he tried to do otherwise; on the other, she *did* worship the Lord of Horns, and made no claim to the contrary. But in a witch-hanging country, perhaps that had been as much effect as cause.

Up through the holes of his own skull Parry boiled, fine as smoke, to spread himself from bow to stern. Saw the silver cord that bound him to that meat-sack he normally wore stretch out behind, infinite extensible; saw the spark-knit chains linking him to the *Salina*, as well as those linking Mister Dolomance—unseen below-decks, lurking somewhere in the ship's guts, just as he would once have ridden the ocean floor's murky currents—to him. Not to mention the gross mechanics of Rusk's curse, twining in and out of his shucked flesh like a swarm of soot-worms, blackening his coronal light with limitation: fatally incurable, the same as life itself.

Inevitably, however, widening his perceptions thus showed him what he'd rather not see, as well as what he sought: Solomon bloody Rusk himself, leant up against the mast with arms crossed, staring down at Parry's back as though he yearned to lay one hand between its shoulder blades.

Be off with you, sir, Parry told him, lips unmoving. *Take yourself elsewhere. Your presence is neither required, nor welcomed.*

Ah, ye're a hard one, Jerusha. Surely I might do ye some small service in this enterprise, given it ensues we're of similar make?

How so, pray? What I know I learned, through hard study; you never dreamed you might share your family's gift for sorcery, not 'til you saw the Salina's *hull at close range.*

Yet your Salina *was my* Bitch *once, Master Parry, and I know she has not forgotten me. What keeps me from resuming my post, if you leave her behind?*

That not a man aboard could hear your orders, even were they inclined to obey?

Well, there is that. I'll attend your return, then, shall I?

As you please.

Raising hand to forelock, the ghost turned away, upon which Parry closed his eyes and sank downwards through dark fathoms, great blooms of fish wheeling like starlings from his path on every side—seeking for some trace of Miss Attesee's vanished vessel, the *Nymph.* And soon found it, as though some lodestone charge pulled him there, currents drawing him on both swift and steady, imbrued with a briny musk that made his theoretical nostrils twitch.

Time soon fell away under-ocean, so Parry had no true sense of exactly when he finally saw a mass of drifting scraps before him resolve into a scuttled brig, open-broke and upturned. Part of the prow still remained, blazoned in gold with what looked from this angle like H-P-M-Y-N, deformed to reverse through water's heavy lens. Around him, the blue-black swam with drifting corpses, torn and bleached, many entangled as though fighting; at his left hand, two men had their teeth sunk deep as fight-pit dogs' in each other, purple-haloed in blood too cold to dissipate.

Had it been battle that had done this, he wondered, or a mutiny? Some ship-wide outbreak of madness, or another sort of infection entirely?

Parry saw no craft in it, one way or the other, just as he'd seen none in Miss Attesee herself—nothing beyond that vague flutter of power that some without witch-blood seemed to carry unawares, developing through various schemes to scry palms and dowse water, or the like. But he had been fooled before in such matters, as Ankolee Rusk had remarked during his first bout of curse-made land-fever, her spirit hanging over him as he sweated a sickbed-full of bloody sheets.

Amazing, how ya can know so much and so pitiful little, all at the same time, she'd scoffed, when he voiced his doubt against her diagnosis. *But then, ya never do trust nothing an' no one, even 'fore Solomon's curse take hold.*

I've not had much cause to, madam. Least of all where that half-brother of yours is concerned.

Nah even that White-Christ God o' yours, eh, who you was t' serve an' praise your whole life long? But the Sea herself be my goddess, Cap'n *Parry; far more our kin than yours, both we Rusks. So perhaps it follow we might know more'n you about some t'ings, whether ya like t'think so or nah...*

Parry shook what he presently called his head, impatient to clear it of such trash. And sent out an imperious call, demanding, of any whose souls might linger close enough to be listening—

All they who made up the Nymph's complement, I know you perceive my power; come now to my command, swiftly, and with courtesy. Which of you, in life, was Doctor Haelam Attesee?

At last, he heard the reply, weak and warped, issuing from somewhere inside that murky cloud of wrack and decay—

I...sir, 'tis I, I think. Who, once, was...he...

Squinting harder still, Parry was just able to make out one more drowned man—Attesee—clawing towards him through his fellows' detritus, a clumsy crawl executed with stiff limbs. He was torn at the throat and the chest, skull perforated with at least two close-quarters shots and bruised all over as well, as though every man aboard had wanted a crack at him by his life's sorry end. Floated upright, he appeared barely five-and-thirty, nothing like old enough to have a

147

child Miss Clione's age...and nothing like her in other ways, either, with his puzzled brown eyes and his once-florid, now-peeling skin; upswept in the current, his wig-shorn hair was a green-tinged shade of blond rather than black, holding not a jot of her snaky, luscious curl.

Yet nevertheless: *Sir,* Parry addressed him, *your daughter has found shelter on my ship. I would know what passed here. Tell me, if you can.*

A salt-logged sigh. *Oh, my Clione...poor girl. Poor girl.*

Yes, 'tis she I mean. I have put her under my protection, and will see to her comfort as well as I may, 'til we can put her ashore. Now—what trouble cut your vessel down, that I may avoid the same?

The corpse shook his head, neck-bones grating, perhaps severing something; his skull fell sidelong, throat bulging unpleasantly.

Poor girl, he repeated. *Not...her fault. She does not, cannot...cannot know. 'Twas I who...erred, terribly. And all paid the price...*

Parry frowned. *'Not her fault'* the ship sank? *But why would it be, Doctor?*

Another shake: now Attesee's jaw flapped open, one grind away from swinging free. A fish had made its home inside his throat, blinking out at Parry's "face." *Cannot...* the doctor managed, voice a mere mucky groan. *Oh, my poor creature! These men, too...so many. 'Tis all my...if I had...only...*

—But even as Parry thought to press him harder, the man Clione Attesee claimed as parent gave way, resolving into a quick-unravelling scum of bones. The fish darted off, no doubt headed to seek out less unstable shelter. And now there was a new voice beating down through the water, reeling Parry back in, pulling him up to the Salina's decks once more, where he wrenched back inside his body just in time to find the bo'sun (whose Christian name he never could recall) leaning in over him close as the protective circle's flames would allow, repeating—

"—Must have words wi' ye, Cap'n, on a matter of some urgency... do ye hear me, Cap'n Parry? I said, do ye—"

"I *hear* you, sir, yes; one could not fail to, really. Now give me some room, and bloody well wait your turn."

It took a sad amount of concentration to snuff the circle, pry his stiff legs apart and lever himself up gingerly—shins to knees, knees to feet—without causing injury; the bo'sun tried to help, but Parry waved him aside. "I am still capable of standing without aid, thank you. Now: what matter do you bring me, that it must be put with such urgency?"

"Sir, ye gave orders that the woman, the passenger—"

"Miss Attesee is her name."

"—that she not be disturbed, and set your...Dolomance to watch on her, 'fore ye bent to whatever you was just engaged in. Now there's two hands bit and one stabbed, all for a-knockin' on your cabin door wi'out permission."

"I gave Mister Dolomance no such task. As to the other—why would they trouble her?" The bo'sun shot him a look. "Well, for *one* reason, of course, and more fool they, for thinking I would not learn of it. But otherwise."

"Word is, there's some thinks she'll bring the ship t' grief. That she's some sort of, uh—"

"*Jonah*," Parry said, the word ill-tasting yet, memory-poisoned. "God damn them all."

A rage kindled, draining the ocean's chill; Parry stood straight, eyes sparking—possibly literally—and was coldly pleased to watch the bo'sun cringe back. "She is under my protection," he confirmed. "Who moves against her moves against *me*, with all that entails. What more need be said?"

This would have cowed better men, which the bo'sun most certainly was not. Yet he stood fast.

"I understand that, sir," he replied, carefully. "Truly. But...there's some others don't, an' that's a problem."

In which he had the right of it, of course. Annoying, contemptible man!

Aye, a good sailor, that. You'd do well t' keep him close, my Jerusha.

Parry hissed. *You do realize your very opinion of the man makes me disinclined to.*

Naturally. Now go and see what that creature of yours is up to, before—

I had planned to!

Ridiculous, how Rusk (or what little was left of him) could still disturb. It annoyed Parry enough to make him turn on his heel, striding off cabin-wards at such a pace he left the ghost in his wake, if only momentarily.

He had expected to find the shark-were posted outside, not in-, and certainly not crouched at Miss Attesee's feet with its receding chin almost in her lap, stolid-worshipful as any sandpaper-skinned dog. Let alone for it to look up as he entered and dare to bare its teeth—begin to, any rate, 'til he fixed the damned thing with a stare that made it drop its lidless eyes and crawl away, groaning.

At the movement, Miss Attesee looked up as well, recalled to herself; her gaze widened prettily, to find him standing before her. "Oh, Captain Parry! I did not hear you...your servant was keeping me company, as you see. Thank you for lending me him."

"Is that what you think I did, madam?"

"Did you not? He frightened me at first, but—when alone, he is surprisingly well-behaved. And..." She paused here, as if feeling her way. "...useful, in some circumstances."

"So I have found." He furled a dismissive little lick of sparks Dolomance's way, urging it to remove itself, which it did, though not without a mournful glance Miss Attesee's way. She gestured for Parry to sit down beside her, which he did, even though there was no place other than the bed to do so. "Now...my bo'sun tells me you were disturbed, for which I tender my apologies. Those involved will be spoken to, harshly."

"Oh sir, it was nothing so bad, really."

"Bad enough to require Mister Dolomance's interjection, or so I'm told. And believe me, madam, mercy is not looked on favourably, when dealing with sea-scum such as the *Salina*'s complement. They are men sworn to do ill and profit from it, if they may."

"Yes, I suppose this is true. Though the men of the *Nymph* did not seem so evil, in the main; not before that last night. And then..."

And then? Parry longed to ask. *Please, elucidate; I have seen the fruits of it, heard your father struggle to give warnings. Yet I cannot hope to understand, without your testimony...*

All this fell away, however, when her distress prompted him to lay a comforting hand on her sleeve, only to have her fold herself into his side and press her head beneath his jawline, shuddering slightly. It was a moment of such force he found he had pitifully few words to describe it: a jolt, a spark—what *was* that, exactly, raising the hairs and ruffling his spine?

(Rusk would know, damn him.)

At that, the man himself came fading through the wall, as if summoned. Leant down over them both, remarking: *Hmmm, she works fast, this drab of yours. Not that you seem all too happy wi' the results.*

Parry shook his head, gulping. *Nay, I mislike this...cannot order my thoughts, calm my pulse. Some enchantment, perhaps; was that what Attesee warned of? But I sense no real magic about her, beyond her ability to see such phantasms as you—*

Rusk all but rolled his eye, sardonically. *Oh, certain,* he agreed. *Or perhaps she likes your looks, had ye never thought of that? Can it be ye've had no dealings with females at all, before?*

Parry cast his mind back. There'd been no girls for him in Cornwall, since all knew his Church-bound intentions—besides which, he was hardly the sort of young spark that mother-in-laws found suitable, being too lean, too reserved, too haughty by far to tempt most happy buxom village misses. *You are naught but a mire-bred witch-get brat, 'Master' Parry,* he remembered one good-wife shouting after him in the street, *who think yourself so far above us all!* And later on, those clots of women who clustered 'round Navy ships like rats after cheese, scouting for sailors on leave—they'd been a positive horror to him. Not to mention they wanted a man with money who'd drink enough to splash some of it out, then grow quick-fuddled enough not to be able to tell in the dark who might be poxed, after...

Ha! So I did pluck your flower, as I'd suspected. Lucky me.

Say your piece, you filthy bloody lump of—

She likes you, is all. So allow her t' show ye t'other side of things, and see if it suits ye better.

It could hardly suit him worse, Parry supposed. But: *As I said, your counsel's enough to turn me elsewhere, from any subject. Besides, given how oft I've had it practiced on me, I've developed no particular taste for outragement.*

Rusk shrugged. *Cheat the both of ye, then, for all I care. 'Tis obvious she wants ye t' pay court to her, wi' no ravishing involved—her choice, her will. You have only to bend to it. What can it cost?*

He didn't know, Parry realized. Which disquieted him all the more.

"I am sorry indeed, to inconvenience you so," Miss Attesee—might he call her Clione now, at least in his mind?—said, into his

151

clavicle. "The shock, you see...I can still see my poor father, pushing me into that boat, setting the waters alight. How they fell on him when they perceived I was gone, like animals. And I had known each and every one of them, growing up. I thought them my *friends*."

"What changed?"

"Oh, if I only knew!" She drew back a bit, seeking his eyes. "I lived my whole childhood on the *Nymph*, sir—indeed, I cannot ever recall being *not* a-sea. That must be odd, surely."

"I...find it somewhat hard to know what is odd myself, madam, living as I have."

"Yes, I can see that." She stared, as though committing him to memory. Then added, softer: "You are not as I had supposed you."

"Less piratical?"

"Younger. More gentlemanly. And kind, too."

"Not by most standards, I think."

"No, you are; far more civil than I'd thought you'd be, also, given your reputation. And handsome, as well. Those eyes of yours, they shine, like...fish-scales."

"A pretty compliment." Adding, as she looked away: "Beg pardon, madam. I am saturnine by nature and unused to company, particularly of the female kind." He paused. "You know my limitations, but so long as we navigate carefully, we might come close enough to shore to put you off at Port Macoute. 'Tis a rough place, yet there's a woman there would surely take you in, if I but asked her..."

"Oh, then my estimation is confirmed, sir," she replied, impulsively laying her hand upon his arm, and Parry felt it again—that sensation he could not easily name, nor explain. "If I can only find some way to repay this fresh courtesy of yours..."

"Madam, any man would do the same."

(*Not* any *man*, Rusk piped up. *Precious few, in fact. Oh, my poor innocent!*)

Miss Attesee frowned in the ghost's direction, brow wrinkling prettily. "Who *is* that man, Captain Parry? Must he be always here?"

How oft have I asked myself the same thing.

"'Tis Captain Rusk, who had this ship before me," Parry told her shortly. "I took it from him, and was obliged to kill him over it."

(*Only over that, Jerusha?*)

"Did you want it so very much, then?"

He sighed. "Not...as such, no. It is a complicated question."

(*Ah, but explain it her anyhow, will ye—what we fell out over, and why. I do long t' see you try.*)

Reaching for the words, carefully: "Captain Rusk did me a good turn, by saving me from a Navy ship's hold and breaking my witch-collar—but he expected to be paid, and his idea of due recompense went far past what seemed fair, by my tallying. Eventually, I grew beyond his ability to halter, and then..." He spread his hands wide, fingers grasping at air, a blue-green flutter linking them briefly together, then passing away in a flourish. "...as you see."

"He was a bad sort."

"Undeniably, given his occupation. But considering I now share it, it might be more accurately said he proved himself untrustworthy."

(*How so, man?*)

How not, you great ape? You gave me your word, then broke it. You forced me—

(*But how could I, Jerusha, beyond that first time? You, wi' all your powers? You could've burnt my parts away, if you'd a mind to—and why not, if I so offended you? Unless they were giving you too much joy, entirely...*)

Your "parts" are gone now, sir, along with the rest of you. Put them by.

(*My point stands: You could've unmanned me, with a second's thought. Yet ye did not.*)

You...distracted me.

(*As she does now, I'll warrant.*)

Cease your prattle! She is speaking again, and I want to hear her.

"Was there no peace to be made between you, then?" Clione asked. "Not ever?"

"No. He was a man of odd humours, and took pleasure in being hated. We had both had our fill of the other, I think, by the end."

"I would think it would not be so easy to have one's fill of you, Captain," she said, seriously. And cupped his chin in both her hands, studying his sharp-planed face closely, before sealing his half-open mouth with a kiss that tasted, as only befitted, of the deepest, darkest parts of the sea.

So different, this sport, from any he'd experienced thus far: Clione Attesee was God's own gift, a lady born, all-observing, passionate and discreet, whose hungers and interests matched his own. Though surely innocent as he'd once been, she had no modesty, and no seeming need of any. Parry felt himself swept away, fast and sure as he'd ever been while pinned in Rusk's arms, but without the sour accompanying tang of defeat, the total ruinous overthrow. Instead, he was allowed to set his pace in tidal fashion, their joining never quite complete and never entirely over. Great waves crashed then split apart, gathering themselves for a fresh crescendo, with everything in between rendered hot and salt and sweet, so all-encompassing he could never be entirely sure whether he had actually *spent* at any point, or no. Though neither did it truly seem to matter, overmuch...

"So many books, Captain Parry," she observed, leaning in from above, so that her hair fell to curtain them both. "Have you really read them all?"

"Many times. For there is always far too much gold and jewelry on these ships we take, and never enough new literary matter."

"Ah, is your hold quite stuffed with treasure, then?"

"Like as much. I do not concern myself with its reckoning—that job goes to my ship's purser, with the bo'sun watching over. But I somewhat doubt these bastards would resign themselves to my command if they were not paid for it, and plentifully."

"I do not see how anyone could hate you, Captain, for all your prickliness, or the terror of your reputation. Though I *can* well see now why Captain Rusk wanted you kept chained to him, beyond mere utility."

This was a note he'd not heard in her voice, before—coolly assessing, older than she seemed—and Parry stiffened at the sound of it, eyes skittering to where Rusk's ghost leant against the wall, alternately watchful and sulking, but increasingly frustrated by his own inability to join in.

"You...know? What passed between us?"

"Yes, of course." She touched his scar, lightly stroking balm into the contorted tissues. "I can see it, the closer we draw together.

What you feel, when you think on him—and what he feels, too, thinking on you."

"But *how?*"

She shook her head. "I cannot tell. A voice seems to whisper it from the walls, or the planks below."

At that very moment, the *Salina* juddered under them, for all the world like some great creature twitching in its sleep, a dog whose back legs kick when it senses its name being uttered. Parry looked at her, a bit wonderingly, and asked: "Are you a witch, too, then? Like my mother, or myself?"

"They called you wizard whenever I was told your tale, previously."

"'Tis all the same, or almost so. 'Man-witch,' Rusk called me, whenever he wished to tweak my pride—but there is no insult in truth. Cold iron burns me, and I bear the scars to prove it."

"Yes," she said, gently touching his collar's print once more—then leant in, impulsively, to lay a small kiss upon it also, so sweet it set his sore head ringing. "Did she have such eyes as yours, your mother?"

"Aye, these I get from her, along with my craft. Of the rest, I know not exactly who to credit—only that the man I should, by rights, call father was some 'man of parts' who could not think of paying for my upkeep, or saving her the noose."

"To see your mother hanged...oh, Captain. I am sorry."

"Most witches end so, madam, at least where England reigns. Had she been Scots instead of Cornish, 'twould have been the fire before, not after."

"And yet she named you for the City of God."

Parry paused, breath shortening. "She was...not an educated woman, by any means," he said, finally. And counted himself grateful when Clione pulled him down with her, rolling them both so that he could take the upper hand, drowning himself in her again.

They were sweating hard by the time they pulled apart once more, panting, and Parry saw her eyes travel back to where Rusk lurked. "How he scowls at us, now!" she exclaimed, with a sort of triumph. "Yet it only serves him right, and he knows it; he lost whatever chance he might have had to turn your hate to something softer long before you used him to scrape the ship clean. What an infamous fellow! He burns to have you still, were it only possible. But we shall confound him of that base desire, you and I—shall we not, Captain Parry?"

"Yes, with the world's best will. And you may make free to call me Jerusalem, Miss Attesee—*Clione*—if it please you."

"Oh, it does, Jerusalem...yes, there, please! It does, very much, indeed."

Fireworks came and went behind his eyes, then, a shower of red-tinged silver bright as his own gaze's reflection when briefly glimpsed in hers. Midst-caught, Parry thought he saw those eyes change—their pupils slide sidelong, opening like a cuttlefish's, even as her hips slipped, knees gone triple-jointed, twining 'round his legs like two fishtail tentacles. While the inside of her grew scaled and stringent, scraping him tip to root, leaving her mark forever.

Mine, he thought, incoherently. All blissful-unaware, at the time, how he'd traded ownership of one kind for one of another.

What followed in this maelstrom's spindrift, however, was pleasure piled on pleasure: laxity, satiation, a deep and pleasant slumber, and for once blessedly dreamless...

...but only to a point.

As the ship's bells rang midnight, Parry came to, opening his mind's eyes only to find himself already meshed tight in memory's toils: later in that first bout of "sport" after his initial defilement, with Rusk still at him like a rat with cheese. Tugging at the man's mane hard enough to rip scalp and hoping it hurt, as he complained: "Christ, leave off—leave *off*, did you hear me? What possible pleasure could you get from—"

Rusk laughed then, dark and growling as ever, be he man or ghost. "The pleasure of *your* pleasure, fool. To watch you work yourself up 'til you're fair panting for it, 'til you beg and weep for an end..."

"Sir! You go too far, entirely!"

"Aye, and would go further still, as I damn well know ye'd love t'allow me, much though you prate th' opposite. Come now, Jerusha, must I really bend the knee? What gestures must I play out, t'bring us both what we seek?"

"Ask—ask my permission, for once. Not that I dream you would."

"Like some puling schoolboy, some mother-may-I? Nay, doesn't sound much like me at all...and yet, very well: Jerusalem Parry, will ye grant me the honour of you? Might I be let to breach that strait-laced gate, and make us both the happier for it?"

Settling back onto him before Parry could object, 'til Parry fell limp at the feel, unable to do more than punch the air and gasp. Then heard himself answer, much against his better judgment—

"...You may."

At this, Rusk gave a satisfied sort of snarl, a hungry lion's half-cough, and heaved himself up, re-settling in. Smiling in triumph, as he crowed: "Ah, my Jerusha, you marvel, my poor sweetheart! My nice divine, pretty little parson-to-be, aspirant soul-saver; *you*, who hate everybody and everything, yourself included..."

"Do not mistake me for some—Navy slug, sir! I know *my* sins, at least, instead of...*revelling* in them..."

Yet here he lost the thread, every part of him buzzing, raked and itching from the inside-out. Rusk laughed again to see it, dropping his face in the crook of Parry's neck and keeping unmercifully on, voice flesh-muffled—

"Aye, as I do mine, 'revelling' aside. Which makes you no better than me, for all your airs! Or perhaps 'tis that we're neither of us *so* good, let alone so bad..."

"The one thing we're alike in's damnation!" Parry made to snarl, but groaned instead, knowing it far too late to stop his own disgrace. While the coda to this stew came, as ever, in a rush of heat and mess and awfulness, a dreadful coring joy. Parry tried to turn from it, but Rusk seized him fast and forced his gaze forward again. "Nay, none o' that," he growled. "Stay wi' me 'til the throes are done at least, if no further."

"Leave me my *shame*, man, for Christ's own love!"

"Ah, but 'tis a foolish habit of yours, my Jerusha, that same shame. I aim t' cure ye of it, if it takes me 'til Doomsday."

Parry cursed him roundly, to the very limits of his knowledge and invention, before invective at last turned silent. Then, exhausted, he lay awhile in Rusk's arms, too tired to fight on, and was forced to accept the unhappy benefit of his ravisher's cold comfort.

Yes, 'twas a brave bloody night, by Christ, Rusk's ghost said from somewhere nearby, a trifle sadly. *I think on't often, who have little enough left to distract me, for all I'm sure you don't do the same. But then again, the pleasures of the dead are few, as you'll eventually discover.*

It was another of those contortionate dream-moments, twisting Parry free and fading the past in a single wink, so he sat once more upright next to Clione in their nest of sheets, staring Rusk's full-dressed spectre down with all his hairs upright and his frame rage-rigid.

Why would you? Parry demanded, insult of it burning in the nose, like blood. *Bad enough in life, but to come to me thus in dream! You amaze me, sir.*

Oh, I doubt that. Rusk gave a sigh. *Yet how else am I to gain your attention, Jerusha, with you so enmeshed?*

Parry huffed. *Aye, on your advice, as I recall—and why not, since it ensues she does indeed find me pleasant, after all? I have little enough to make me happy in my waking life, forever confined by this curse you worked on me...*

Yes, well: about that. Might be I was...inaccurate in my estimation, when first I pushed you t'wards her arms. For there are things in her I glimpse that I can only assume you don't, still bein' locked in your fleshly state—

Oh, do tell—or don't, *rather, for I have no patience for it! Might be you shouldn't've played through my life's most humiliating night as preface, if you truly wished my attention on the matter!*

Ye damned contrary creature! Are you a sailor born, now, to know the ocean's store of uncanniness better than myself? For if 'twas me, I'd've thrown her back in the sea to sink or swim as she pleased, days agone. As there were many said I should have done with you, by Christ!

Indeed, sir? I confess myself unsurprised.

I did not mean—Jerusha, only listen t'me, for your own profit! She is not what ye think her—

Nor you, I warrant, when you seemed to mean me well, 'til you showed your true colours! When you broke your oath and treated me as no host would an honoured guest, unless perhaps that host be Satan himself, welcoming damned souls into Hell—

But: *Be still,* a third voice intruded, cutting through their wrangle like Alexander's blade. *Enough o' this muddle. We must put yah house in order, Cap'n Parry, 'fore ya sink yourself through foolishness, and all else along wi' you.*

Parry did not even have to turn to know who it was who spoke, though he had not had the pleasure since his first attack. Merely inclined his head her way, all at once on best behaviour, and acknowledged, with as great a courtesy as he might muster—

...Miss Rusk, the inestimable Tante Ankolee. What is't brings you here, madam?

As this *fool says, an' in support o' his arguments: because that yah done brung trouble on yaself, Jerusalem Parry—terrible trouble indeed, drawn up from deep places, for all it treat ya sweet and look on you wi' love. More than she herself know, even, poor creature...not that ignorance ever any excuse for ill-doin', as we all three o' us well-know.*

Doctor Attesee's corpse swum into view once more, mouthing its curious warning fragments: *Oh, my poor girl...not her fault. Clione, my poor creature.* And Parry found it easier by far to read between the lines of that palimpsest now, with the fit of love no longer immediately upon him. Staring down upon the too-fluid curve of his sleeping lover's spine, vertebrae sharp-raised as if poised to tear free and form a sea-trench eel's dorsal fin, and knowing in his heart how it would have had to have been this way, all along. For who could ever feel pulled to him, in all his Cain-marked glory, who did not themselves bear such a taint in turn?

Clione, taming Dolomance without intent and tracing the lines of power linked between Parry and his ship, all ignorant of their import, before laying a cooling hand on Parry's sorest spots and folding him in, giving him so much delight he thought himself healed. Just like Rusk, in his way—so Devil-sure he could bend Parry to where he'd accept this bond he saw between 'em, without even a pennyworth of proof to that premise. Dying still so unconvinced, in fact, that the grim manner of his execution freed the power he didn't know he owned in one great burst of ill-wishing, a reel of spellwork which proved both first and last.

She is not human at all, then, Parry said, sadly. *Is she?*

Nah as such, no.

There she sat, the shade of her anyhow, all decked out in her pagan finery—locked hair hung with bells, a bone through her blue-rimmed lip, and daring somehow to feel sorry for *him*, who'd once stood to take the pulpit, shepherd of every soul in the district! Who'd studied Greek and Latin, writ on holy things...by God, it was insupportable. Her with her green eyes and her tea-coloured slave-girl's skin, the set of her nose so much like Rusk's own it made Parry want to break it with a single slap—

(*You are being ridiculous, Jerusalem,* mabyn *mine,* his mother would have said, though, whenever some passion made him stamp and scream. *Things are as they are; the world has its order, much as we may rue it. Not even magic can ever make it otherwise.*)

Prideful as always, therefore, he drew himself up, made himself cold and still. And put out a hand, demanding that he might be the one ordering, rather than the reverse—

So show me the truth of it, madam; I will believe it from you, if not from that "cousin" of yours. Show me it all.

That one time, Haelam Attesee, on th' bounding main—surgeon o' the Nymph, *who study hard on nature for his own reward, an' seek t' steal the Sea's own secrets from Her t' gain him passin' land-locked fame an' fortune. That one time, he.*

Dredging the ocean wi' a scoop-net of his own design, sent down along o' the Nymph's *great anchor, in an uncharted corner of Her ever-changin' waters. An' one day, along wi' all the usual muck an' trash, he find something else entirely, drawn up from dark places: an egg made from jelly wi' a skin—nah, a shell—which he raise up towards the light, feelin' it warm in his hands. An' as he do, he see something deep inside start t' move, to change...to grow.*

One day more an' that tiny thing a baby, whole an' perfect-formed, hoverin' inside the egg in its glass bottle, as it set on Doctor Attesee's cabin desk. An' the egg get bigger as the baby do, growing 'til it fill the glass so full Doctor Attesee take an' break the glass over an old hip-bath, pouring seawater in 'til the egg float up unbroken yet an' the baby open its eyes, blinking, making faces like it nah know whether it want to cry or nah— an' smile at him, too, like it recognize his face.

By the time a week gone, the egg split an' a child come out, a little girl-baby. Two month later, that girl-baby a girl for true, tall up to Doctor Attesee's waist. An' so she keep on, growin' and growin', 'til she as you see her now: a siren sure, made ta bend men to her will. Made ta tempt men to their death an' take 'em down with her, deep under, to that airless place from whence she born.

The crew think her a sweet child when she still look like one, an' treat her like they would have treated one of their own. But the minute she gain her maiden form an' commence ta bleed, they perk up they heads, like sniffin' dogs. First they start ta fight amongst 'emselves, an' then they turn on Doctor Attesee to get ta her, ta fill her full of their seed an' see whah may grow of it—how can they help it, when she fillin' th' very air wi' heat an' botheration? An' she, she know no better, bein' lied to all her short life. For Doctor Attesee never want to tell her the truth, nah an' risk him lose her love...

An' when the end come, how could he know where the Sea take her on to, once he commit her once more to Her own bosom? How Her currents would carry her on, ceaseless, 'til that creature o' yours recognize her an' pledge her his fealty—pull her on through wrack an' ruin ta where he know she best be welcomed—an' lay her at last at your feet, Jerusalem Parry. You with your craft, powerful enough ta protect her 'gainst all comers...not ta mention your ill-fatedness when it come ta such matters overall, forever doomed to be loved by those ya never can, or love them who never love you th' exact same way in return...

At these words, even in sleep's tight grip, Parry gave his head one fierce rejecting shake, thinking: *Who are* you *to say that, witch? Do you know my whole life, planned out beforehand? Perhaps I will never love at all, never having loved thus far, aside from she who bore me...*

But: *Oh, little wizard,* Tante Ankolee's now very far away spell-voice told him, softly, sadly—water-warped, as though filtered through every watery mile between them. *Be it here a-Sea, or on Veritay Isle where that half-me-blood brother o' mine first saw light, or them Cornwall marshes you an' ya mother call home, cunning-folk go only ever one o' two ways. Others we can make love for, but ourselves...to such as we, love is dangerous; worse than iron's kiss, an' far more lastin'.*

An' as for you—you damn well know you love this sea-girl already, fast an' hard enough to drown in. You nah the triflin' sort, worse luck. If ya had been, well...

(*...if so, I still have a "cousin," 'stead of his ghost. An' you nah be stuck afloat for the rest of ya life, just 'cause ya too proud ta bear the proof of someone else's love, true though it might be, so long as you nah share it.*)

Almost a whisper now, yet still he fought to rail against it, twisting in his sleep...'til another voice again intruded, equal-familiar, if far more unwelcome. Commanding, in its turn—

Jerusha, rouse yourself! Jerusha! Spring up and don your breeches, man, lest ye crave t' put down a full mutiny bare-arsed!

What—?

That hammering at the cabin door, tweaking him sharply up from slumber into immediate waking danger—less like flesh than wood and metal, staves and mattocks, grappling hooks. The din of many feet and the blabber of many voices, all of them calling for

161

his blood...or hers. Clione's.

His Clione's.

Rusk's ghost stood by the door, gesticulating peremptorily. *There, out there! Arm yourself, fool, for they come in force, and will not be long denied entry!*

"Those damnable dogs," Parry exclaimed, torn between shock and rage, as he fumbled at his buttons; flame bloomed all 'round him, a blue-green protective conflagration, and by its prompting light Clione Attesee arose likewise, stumbling to her feet whilst still in a sweet state of nature, with only her long black hair for clothing. Grasped for his arm with one hand, her soft fingers now slightly webbed between with crepey folds of skin, and asked: "Jerusalem, what is it? Has the madness come upon this ship, too? Are we safe?"

"While I yet have strength to make it thus, my dear, yes. But perhaps you should cover yourself, before we find ourselves in slightly less agreeable—"

'Company,' he might have meant, before the door gave way at last, rendering the point moot. Men spilled in over the threshold, howling various obscenities and execrations, but Parry did not pay them much heed. Instead, he let loose at them full-force, much as he had with that earliest attacker—but doing so intentionally cost him more than he'd bargained for, causing blood to gush from his nose as though punched. The resultant blue-green wave bore the two closest hands away entirely, reducing them to fragments, and flayed the wall itself away behind them a good ten feet on either side, leaving the doorway's frame to wobble a moment in the wreckage before falling backwards, resolving to splinters. Other men took it in their eyes or across their half-turned faces and thrown-up hands, like vitriol, before it finally broke over the railing; the deck was awash with dissipating force, rising screams punctuated by general discharge of pistols, and a ball had struck Parry's upper shoulder before he could shield himself, spinning him Clione's way.

"No!" she cried, face white with horror. Then: "To *me*, sir!"

Who can she mean? Parry wondered, queasily; he wavered, grabbing his wound and pumping yet more magic into it to push the lead forth and speed its healing, weeping bloody tears with the effort. At the same time, however, the question answered itself—

Mister Dolomance came threshing into the back of the crowd, summoned by Clione's cry like a dog to his whistle, and made wholesale bloody work of two more men before getting his teeth stuck into a third, slowing his slaughterhouse passage to a standstill.

Up on the fo'c'sle, Parry glimpsed the bo'sun waving his arms like some carnival mountebank, trying to shout his damage-bent brethren down; when this had no effect, he seized the next one rushing to offer violence and fetched him a buffet that almost pitched him over the side. So perhaps Parry had, indeed, underestimated him—annoying to think Rusk might have been right on that score, or any—

—but that hardly mattered right now, not with Clione hissing beside him, teeth bared, and the shark-were finally pulling his head free with a wet red *crack*. Not with one more fool (a master's mate, he thought) pointing his blade at her while snarling, in Parry's direction: "You're leakin' power, man-witch. So call yer beast off, an' quick-smart, or I'll slit this wet bitch's throat!"

Parry felt his eyes narrow, blood-clogged lids slow and sticky. "You *will not touch her*," he heard himself grind out, barely recognizing his own voice. "She is *mine*."

The closest on scoffed. "Don't think ye'll lose yer whole crew over some skirt, *Cap'n*."

"Then *don't* think, I pray—you're none of you good at it, since you've failed to grasp that every man here stays aboard only at my sufferance. I can run this ship myself, if needs be."

"Aye, ye talk a good game! But we're many, you one. What can ye do, if we attack all at once?"

Parry smiled, grim as a blade. "*This*."

For: his stores *were* running dry, true enough—but there was yet something else to call upon, in worst circumstances; a force he only seldom felt stir against his presence, stroking itself on him and purring, like some great spectral cat. It lurked all 'round him in the very wood and weight of the ship itself, Rusk's *Bitch* turned his *Salina*, and if Parry did not pretend to understand it (being no sailor, as Rusk had pointed out on so many different occasions), he nevertheless knew it ever faithful to his touch, eager to do his bidding and willing to lend him its connivance in all sorts of mischief, no matter the cost to others...or itself.

I will have to hurt you now, he told it, soundlessly, this invisible daimon, *and I am sorry for it, truly. I wish there was some other way.*

I understand, something seemed to reply, meanwhile—but no, not so clearly. More consent as a twinge, at the very edge of consciousness, as he reached out with the next-to-last of everything in him and scooped a great chunk from the ship's own side, planks spraying everywhere. The hull cracked, deck tipping to slide the bulk of the troublemakers brine-wards, below the water-line, which Parry proceeded to suture over their screaming heads with a solid blue-green seal like ice or glass, two feet at least in depth. They hammered at it, desperate, but got no relief; he saw their lungs empty out, bubbles rising, and smiled through his bloody flux, straining to not cough up his guts.

Give me a moment, he thought. *Only a moment...I can recoup. Can move the ship's parts back in place, fit nails to holes, trust in motion to keep us from taking on too much water...*

(Dolomance had made short work of those remaining, all but the bo'sun, who'd wisely gone aloft, taking refuge in the rigging. Those stubby fin-hands Parry had fashioned were not made for climbing, so the man was safe enough, for now. Parry would have to calm the creature's blood-lust to make sure that stayed true, later on—)

Oh God, it hurt. It hurt so magnificently, all over. But 'twas almost worth it to see Clione gaze on him with worship, for all he could now clearly see the lines of gills fluttering open along her neck, neat-frilled as Mechlin lace.

And now ye've gutted your own ship, Rusk's ghost observed, from where the cabin had once stood, as though it were some great insight.

How fortunate *I am, to have you to note such things for me!* Parry snapped back, using a blue-green thread-net to fold the planks—haphazardly yet finally, all the same—back over the bulk of his thrashing, swearing, blood-maddened crew's heads.

"There," he said. "We are done, now. It is resolved."

"I knew you would save us, Jerusalem. Ah, but yet..."

"But yet?"

Turning to her, seeing her shake her head, fine eyes already growing bleached and transparent-lidded. The tentacle-sway of her naked body, dorsal-raised spine barely concealed by hair. The Dolomance, snuffling to his knees, keen to lay that terrible head at her similarly-webbed feet.

"I cannot stay," she said, sadly. "My air is almost gone—I know it. Come with me."

"Where?"

"Down. Down. Oh, my magician...only come below, and we will rule together; you will be king of a dark place, beyond all their reaches. Dark, and deep, and shining."

(Her sea-coloured eyes, her weed-thick hair, her skin green-tinting. Oh, how he longed to change along with her, to rip his own skin off and take his chances with whatever he found beneath—or didn't.)

"The land does not love you, Jerusalem Parry; it never has, and never will. But I do."

"Clione...madam. We...barely know each other."

"Call it what it is, then. Call it magic."

Rusk at his shoulder one more time, a buzzing bloody gnat: *No, my Jerusha, no. She's not for you, nor you for her. Do not try to make yourself over in her image, I pray, lest you lose your grip on life entirely—*

Reaching out a hand to stop him and failing to take hold, miserably; how it made Parry crow to watch the bastard's grip slip straight through, his living flesh a mere ghost's ghost. And think, crazily—

Why not? I could make myself breathe water, I'm certain. I can do... most anything.

The storm again, but only in his head. And weak as they were, he hated Rusk's efforts to detain him worse than he ever had the cold iron tether, the spectral keloid burn 'round his neck which tightened halter-tight as he heard the bastard yell:

Jerusha, behind ye—'ware, damn you, contrary man! The shark!

For here was Clione, damp hand slipping from his with a pitiful look, stepping backward towards the gap's scooped-out rim, gravity already taking hold—in another second she would arc backwards and down, hit water, be gone in a trice. And here was Mister Dolomance, thick legs already bent, poised to follow—

'Til Parry reached out one more time, with a single massive frozen shout of *no!*, and stopped him.

He came to expecting to find himself dead, torn to pieces by the monster he'd made—he knew it would happen, eventually. The spell itself required such a sacrifice. Instead, Parry found Dolomance fast-tethered once more, staring his usual sullen hatred at him; the deck was cleared, stuck back together at all angles, blood from Dolomance's kills dried under the same sun that had tanned Parry's hide almost to burning. And Rusk's ghost leant nearby, inevitably, his arms once again crossed, with an odd look on his one-eyed face—was that satisfaction, or sympathy? Did it matter?

Not to me.

No. For Clione was long gone, down deep, into that impossible darkness. And he had only the man he'd murdered left for company, along with the foolish-loyal bo'sun, unless one also took Dolomance into account.

"I would not let this creature of mine go," he said, out loud, meeting the shark-were's black doll-eyes head on. "That's why. If I had, I'd be with her still."

And drowned as well, belike, Rusk pointed out. For I've never known ye t'go without air overlong, wi' all your craft.

Parry did not seem to hear. "To keep him with me...make sure our bond stayed unbroken. Because, in the end—I wanted power, more than love."

False love, man. She was not for you, or any upright creature. A thing apart, only.

At these words, a great wrench pulled hard at Parry's heart, shivering it so sharp he almost thought he felt the organ itself (which he'd otherwise supposed merely vestigial, given how little it normally troubled him) shake apart entirely.

"Then what am *I?*" he cried out, in a tone that made Rusk's ghost wince before replying, gently as that gentleman knew how—

That too, I s'pose, in the end. But better here than down there, surely.

A frost fell on Parry then, hardening him within and without, thinning his voice to bitterest poison as he replied: "Yes, that would suit you best to have me think, I warrant."

Oh, Jerusalem. Yes, tell it yourself thus, if ye will—for I am culpable in much that brought ye to this pass, and can easily bear th'extra burden. But think on this, and know it true, Hell-priest: we cannot help our natures. Not she, nor you, nor I...

Do not speak to me, sir! Parry broke out at last, internally, all his other words leaving him in a rush, blood-hot and galling. *Never speak to me, ever again, 'til we both be fleshless and Hell-bound alike. For I have more than done with you, along with all the rest.*

Though Parry expected protest, perhaps Clione had passed so far below already that Rusk truly could not, for the bastard only shook his head at him, an egregious look of sympathy on his face. And faded from his sight, leaving Parry blessedly alone at last, at least to all appearances.

Mister Dolomance turned, mulish and still with his cold blood up, only to cringe away from the heat of Parry's glare. "*Get from me, you lump,*" Parry told him, hoarse, every breath agony. "Do as you please with those in the water, but do not let me see you 'til I call."

He stared the creature down until it turned those lidless eyes away, stumping to the side, where it disappeared without a splash. Then let himself sit down, panting, too exhausted even to weep.

He glimpsed the bo'sun peeping down at him through the rigging, half-hid behind a foremast, where he'd held on for dear life against his fellows' punishment. The man would come in handy later, of that Parry had no doubt, but for now he did not acknowledge him. Only looked at his own hands, flexing and unflexing of what seemed like their own accord, studying his fingernails for any trace of hidden claws.

Ensign Parry's a Jonah, he thought, without rancour. *A monster amongst monsters, loved by them alone...this is what I'll always be. My very blood foretold it.*

Yet: *If you'd gone in you'd have lost hold of the spell for sure,* another voice told him, insinuatingly, coldly logical—and was that voice his own, finally? The only one left in all his hollow aching head? *Beneath-waves, Dolomance becomes truly shark once more; neither you nor she could have hoped to stand before him, then. You* saved *her, thusly, and yourself as well. She will live on because of you...if that anything matters.*

Was that enough?

Well, it would have to be.

Later, he would bring those of the crew left yet intact by Dolomance's hunger back up, salt-cured and only slightly rotten, to pilot the *Salina* towards its next prize. Those who survived the attack he would offer the Articles, after dealing with whatever witch-finders might prove to be hidden amongst them in such a fashion as to honour his poor dead mother. Of Clione Attesee, or the thing that had once called herself by that name, he was careful not to think; his mind he sent skipping from her, forming a habit that would eventually wipe her from him entirely. Until, one day, he closed his eyes to find he could barely recall the lines of the woman who he would have killed himself protecting's face, let alone her touch, or the sweetness of their time together. Not even the scent her dark, thick masses of hair had seemed to give off, when dragged across tender human skin.

And in the background, Rusk's dark form, always watching. *He have his hand ever on ya heart,* Tante Ankolee had told him, once...a thing Parry knew for nothing but uncomfortable truth, much though he might pretend otherwise.

"Do not speak to me," he repeated one more time, out loud—knowing himself bereft, yet somehow knowing also that it would not be long at all before he forgot his present wounds entirely. Then buried his face in his hands, shoulders shaking, 'til he raised it again with an exclamation over the odd clamminess of his cheeks, unable to remember why he had been crying.

HELL FRIEND

You could make paste for Hell stuff from flour in a pinch, but it didn't burn as well and customers didn't like the smell, which even incense wouldn't cover. Jin-li Song bought three unmixed boxes for five bucks at the Dollar Store—just add water—and negotiated her way back out, threading a narrow path between teetering wicker receptacles of every given size stuffed haphazardly in/on top of each other and piles of open boxes packed full of Fung's Gold Rosette sandalwood-, rose-, or jasmine-scented soap.

Outside, the air reeked like smeared goose-shit, pressing down with a palpable weight. It almost hurt to breathe as Jin drifted back slowly, through Chinatown's sluggish, skipping heart. The smells of home were everywhere, thick enough to slice: Dhurrian and fireworks gunpowder, dried persimmon, pickled ginger, red bean jelly. The stiff stock and vinegary dyes of Hell money. The sweet stink of joss-sticks. Kuan Yin and the Monkey King staring down, smiling and glaring. The zodiac's animals, rat to pig and back again, contorted in red lacquer poses.

And since it was the last week of *Zhongyuan Jie*, after all, getai were indeed everywhere, just as her Ah-Ma had warned her—

blooming in every doorway, on every porch and corner: little shrines, wilting plates of food, smoking joss-sticks. Passersby whose ages ranged from roughly eight to eighty swirled carelessly around them, wearing brightly-colored clothes designed to insulate their chi against the streets' death-heavy atmosphere; everywhere Jin looked, people (maybe tourists, maybe not) could be seen laughing, dancing and singing to entertain whatever ghosts might be lurking—resentfully, implacably, invisibly—in their immediate vicinity.

Step lightly, Jin, Ah-Ma would say if she was here, and even if she wasn't. *This is a time of confusion, in which every decision—no matter how well-intentioned—may bring harm...less a celebration than an inconvenience, even to we who honor it. The doors of Hell stand open, letting the dead back up onto the earth. And so, though we may make money from Hungry Ghost Month, it is Hell money only...*

Yeah: Hell cash, thick and crisp and useless; only fit to spend *in* Hell, by those who lived there—or rather, who didn't. And this was what Jin's ma spent her days cobbling into commissions, stuff made expressly to burn, falling down through the fire to give some lucky ancestor's ghost a big surprise—Hell cars, Hell fridges, Hell air conditioners. Hell cellphones.

While up here above, there was no buying a new house, no renovating the old one, no going on vacation or hanging at the beach, for fear of ghosts luring you down into the water...

Jin stopped short in front of the Empress' Noodle restaurant, between its flanking totem dragons, and bent over for a minute, rummaging for her inhaler. Inside, framed by the front window's fever-red rows of halved pigs and Peking duck-flesh, Mrs. Yau— the Empress' owner—sat alone at her usual table near the back, playing mah-jongg with herself. A cup of green tea steaming at one elbow.

Her name is Yau Yan-er, was all Ah-Ma had said the first time she'd caught Jin studying her, out of the corner of one eye. *You don't ever go in there, wei? Don't speak to her, don't look at her...*

Why not, Ah-Ma?

Ah-Ma had sighed. *Because. People like us—we don't want people like her to even know we're here. It's safer that way.*

Sometimes, like now, Jin wondered exactly what Mrs. Yau must have done—what she must *be*—to have become "people like her," in Ah-Ma's eyes. From the outside-in, at least, she seemed perfection itself, a T'ang Dynasty screen-painting come to graceful life—regally slim, black hair tamed into an elaborate, chopstick-skewered crown of knots, veins showing faintly green as milky jade beneath the pale skin of her long-fingered hands...

...and her eyes, black stones, raising suddenly from a cast-down fistful of Plum Blossom, Knot, the Centre, White...to meet with Jin's own, through the glass. Faint twitch at the temples, those high, nude arcs where her eyebrows ought to be; she raised one palm slightly, a subtle yet unmistakable gesture of beckoning. Jin coughed on the draw, tucked her inhaler away again, and stared: *You mean me?* Now?

Apparently, yes.

But: *Don't look. Don't speak.* never *go in.*

Waaah, Jin thought; *I'm thirteen, for God's sake. I'll do what I want, this one time. If not now, when?*

Jin straightened, touched her hair lightly, then gave up on getting it to look any better than it already did. Shrugged Ah-Ma's voice away, like a horse switching flies—

—and opened the door.

Though the summer job she'd lined up to start a week from now would officially be her "first," Jin'd been an unpaid worker in Ah-Ma's Gods Material Shop pretty much ever since she, Ba and Ma had come over from Taiwan, when Jin was five. Which meant she could reckon federal and provincial tax in her head, make chit-chat in enough other dialects to deal with people who didn't speak Cantonese (or English), and locate back-stock items without checking the book (mostly).

But none of this impressed Ah-Ma enough to stop her from taking Jin—and Ma—off the floor whenever she could; though she often said it was because Jin's Ma was "so good!" in the workshop that she wanted Jin to pick up her skills, Jin suspected different.

"Ma," Jin had overheard her Ba saying that afternoon, quietly, as she let herself in by the delivery door, "you have to stop. Eun-Joo is Asian as you or me..."

"*Not* like you and I, and you know it. What good does it do to pretend?"

"That's just...*insanely* racist, even for you. Besides which, you do get that if my wife is unacceptable, that makes Jin at least *half*-unacceptable, right?"

"*Ai-yaaah*! You know I love Jin, but things will be hard enough for her, without drawing attention. How can she ever make a good marriage? So tall, with so much color in her skin? And her face, so long—like a melon!"

At this, Ba had huffed, and fell straight back into Cantonese: "*Wan jun, Ma! Dim gai lay gum saw?*" Which would surely have brought on an exchange too quick for Jin to completely follow, given how red Ah-Ma's face went, if they hadn't both suddenly spotted Jin where she stood, rooted to the spot by throat-roughening embarassment.

Ba coughed, looking down. "Uh...Ma's not back yet, *ah bee*. You could start setting up, I guess..."

Ah-Ma nodded. "Best, yes. Do you have enough paste?"

"I think I forgot," Jin said. "I could...go and get some." As Ba reached for his wallet: "No, I can...I've got it. No problem."

And: "Watch out for *getai*," Ah-Ma told her, as she turned. "Remember, mind where you step. Don't get in any ghosts' way. It's their time—they expect politeness."

Jin's mind raced, a thousand replies suggesting themselves: *Wish I was a ghost*, uppermost. But it wasn't even vaguely worth the trouble, considering that come tomorrow, they'd all still have to live together.

So she nodded instead, avoiding Ba's sad eyes: "*Wei*, Ah-Ma." Bowing her too-long melon head, pulling in her too-long limbs, crushing down her too-tall half-Korean self in general—almost to "normal" height, or close as she could get—as she went.

Inside the Empress' Noodle, meanwhile, everything was cool and dim. Mrs. Yau flicked the same hand she'd used to entice Jin closer shut once more, a five-fingered fan, and nodded to the chair at her left elbow; as she did, red-shaded lantern-light glinted off nails grown just a half-inch longer than anyone Jin had ever seen before wore theirs. Jin nodded back without thinking twice, and found herself already sitting.

"*Ni hao, mei mei*," Mrs. Yau said, her Cantonese softened by a wind-through-willows shading of Mandarin. "What is your name, please?"

"Jin-Li Song."

Mrs. Yau pursed her soft lips, disapprovingly. "Song Jin-Li-ah, *ai-yaaah*. Don't your parents know enough to teach you how to properly say your own name?"

"Well, uh…that's how we say it at school, so…"

Another nod. "So. How *they* say it, the long-noses. But *mei shi*, never mind. Perhaps this is only proper, given the age we live in: two names for two different worlds—one for use amongst the *gweilo*, the barbarians, and one to use here, amongst ourselves. Still, one cannot live in two places at the same time, *wei*?"

"…No?"

"No." She peered closer at Jin then, eyes narrowing further. "You must be Song Pei-Pei's granddaughter, I think."

At the sound of Ah-Ma's "real" name, Jin lowered her head, blushing once more. "*Wei*, Mrs. Yau."

"And how does her business flourish? Very well, I'm sure, this time of year."

Jin didn't know what to say, so she said nothing. It was true that Gods Material Shop often stayed open around the clock during Hungry Ghost Month; only a year ago, when Ah-Ba was still alive, they'd probably have set money aside to hire extra help. Now it was just them—Ba and Ah-Ma out front, Ma and Jin in the back. And she was wasting time dawdling here, under Mrs. Yau's unreflective gaze—her eyes that took everything in, gave back nothing…

A small nod, as though Jin's silence constituted a valid answer. Mrs. Yau tapped the tablecloth between them, just once. Asking—

"Do you know this design, Song Jin-Li-ah?"

"Sure: *Yin-yang*. Right?"

"Yes. See how it is: one here, one there. They twine around each other, mix together—a little spot of *yin* in *yang*, a little spot of *yang* in *yin*. *Yin* is female, dark, cool; *yang* is light, hot, male. *Yang* acts. *Yin* is. Both are necessary. The building blocks of the world—without both working at once, in harmony, the mechanism no longer functions cleanly. But there is another thing too, something you don't see here…it may be inside, or outside, or invisible. *Yomi*. Hell. Ten thousand kinds of Hell. Another thing to thank the long-noses for. *Yomi* is what's hidden, what lies beneath. It is not for you. Not for anyone, unless…what time is it now, Jin-ah?"

"5:45…oh, I'm sorry. Hungry Ghost Month."

"Yes. So be careful, *mei mei*—little sister. Careful of what you see, and what you don't. Because this month, what is hidden becomes revealed; what was obscure becomes obvious, without warning. Consider this my gift to you, and come back later on, perhaps, once my advice has been of some use. You may even call me Grandmother, if you wish."

Jin frowned, studying the odd curl of Mrs. Yau's tiny pink smile across her pale, pale face, and feeling as though the dim red world around her had somehow begun—almost imperceptibly—to swim.

With effort: "But—you're not old enough to be anybody's grandmother."

The smile widened, pink deepening. And: "Oh, I am old enough to be your grandmother's grandmother, child," said Mrs. Yau, without much emphasis. "Old enough to be *everyone's* grandmother."

"You're not a ghost, are you?"

"Ah, no." But here Mrs. Yau bent her beautiful head, and took a single sip of tea from her thumbnail bone-china cup, adding—

"I am *far* worse than that."

Read the Ullambana Sutra, was all Ah-Ma said, when Jin first asked her where the idea for Hungry Ghost Month came from, exactly. But Ba, knowing she never would, had been the one to paraphrase: How one time, long ago, there was a guy who ran away from home to hang with Buddha and become a monk—Maudgalyayana, that was his name. After he attained enlightenment, he looked around to see what his parents had been doing in the meantime, and found his father in heaven. His mother, though…

She didn't approve of Maudgalyayana's choices, Ba said, his eyes on Ah-Ma's scrupulously turned back, where she stood at the till sorting money. *So because she was stingy and unforgiving, the gods condemned her to Hell, where she turned into a hungry ghost.*

The sutra says her skin was like that of a golden pheasant when its feathers have been plucked, Ah-Ma seemed unable to resist adding, without turning around. *Her bones like round stones, placed one beside the other. Her head was big as a ball, her neck thin as a thread, and because her throat was too narrow to eat or drink, her belly swelled out in front of her as though she was pregnant. So she went terribly hungry, but when her son tried to feed her, the rice and water he gave her caught fire inside her, and choked her throat with smoke...*

That's the story, anyways, ah bee, Ba put in, quickly. *And that's why we spend Hungry Ghost Month being nice not just to our ancestors—we're nice to THEM all year 'round—but to HUNGRY ghosts, ghosts of people we maybe don't even know, they're the ones with no one left to take care of them, wandering between earth and heaven. So we pray for them and leave them food, put on shows for them, burn Hell money to help them buy a happier life in the afterworld—*

So they won't stay up here, and make trouble, Ah-Ma said. *So they won't scare us, and feed off our fear.*

So they'll be at peace, Ba corrected. *So they can—*

Ah-Ma snapped the drawer back in, with a sharp rattle of change. Saying, as she did—

So they'll leave us alone. Everything else is—

(A quick glance at the shop's front display, here—two whole tiers of magical fengshui items arranged to best advantage, under hot lights and gaily-painted banners. Male and female Fu dog pairs, Seven Stars Swords and Elliptical Coins, the Universal Cosmic Tortoise with a Buddhist mandala stenciled on its back, a whole dish full of Hum pendants strung on neon "silk" thread. Images of Kwan Kung standing at fierce attention, pointed towards the front door—once a mere human general, now simultaneous Taoist God of War and Wealth. At his side, more deities: La Zha, most potent of all the gods. Chung Kwei, the "ghost catcher," festooned with bats, as symbols of abundant good luck and great continued happiness...)

—*"window dressing,"* Ah-Ma concluded, finally. *Nothing more. Or less.*

Whatever *that* was supposed to mean.

But maybe, Jin mused, as she paused to wait for the crosswalk to change—maybe what it meant was that ghosts (hungry or otherwise) didn't *have* to look like that guy's mom in the story, after all. Maybe it meant they could look like whatever they wanted to...like anything. Anyone.

Which meant, in turn, that half the "people" she saw every day could not be people at all, and she wouldn't even know: that crazy dude on the other side, crab-walking along, arguing out loud with himself. That little girl with the massive Hello Kitty plushie, trailing along behind a couple who might be her parents, but pointedly not holding either of their hands. Jin's own wavery reflection in the Bank of Macau's frosted window, rendered suddenly sketchy enough to seem eyeless, alien.

(*Ah, no. I am* far *worse than that.*)

(*mei mei*)

"Ma. What's worse than a ghost?"

"What?" Ma looked up from her last few finishing touches on the Po family's Hell house, blinking short-sightedly; as ever, she'd taken her glasses off for the close work. Claimed they made her eyes cross. "Did you get the paste Ah-Ma sent you out for?"

"Right here." Jin sat down next to Ma. "What I meant was... if somebody said something was *worse* than being a ghost, what would they be talking about?"

Ma's voice dropped, conspiratorially. "You know I don't believe in ghosts, *ah bee.*"

"You better not say that where Ah-Ma can hear you."

"I know. She thinks we'd lose half our customers." Ma smiled, wearily. "It's good to see you, Jin. Ah-Ma gives you long hours, doesn't she?"

Jin shrugged. "I don't mind. Want me to paint anything?"

"Hmm...no, I think everything's done, actually. Just in time, too."

"In time for what?"

Ah-Ma gave a disapproving sniff, from somewhere near the workshop door—how long had she been there, anyways? "Don't you listen, Jin-ah? Po family *getai* is tonight—they need this Hell house for their daughter, dry and ready to burn." She stepped in, wiping her hands on her skirt, eyes skipping over Ma like she was something hot. "Why are you so late back, huh?"

"I, uh, got held up." Adding, reluctantly, as Ah-Ma's raised eyebrows made it clear she wouldn't take vague for an answer: "Talking...at the Empress' Noodle. To Mrs. Yau."

"You *spoke* to Yau Yan-er? *Ai-yaaah!* What did I *tell* you, girl?"

Jin flushed resentfully, thinking: *Uh, get good grades...don't talk to boys... gweilo* may run the world right now, but that won't last, and they don't know everything, either. They're all just long-nosed bar- barians, at heart...

"Always be polite to older people if you can, because they're closer to the ancestors?" she ventured, at last.

"Don't be smart!" And then—wow, this really must be bad, be- cause Ah-Ma actually turned to Ma directly, barking: "Eun-Joo, I need to talk with you. Come with me, please."

"Oh, Ah-Ma, I don't think—"

"Right now. *Alone.*"

Ah-Ma cast a single, significant glance back Jin's way; Ma sighed and bowed her head. "Yes, all right," she said. To Jin: "We'll be back in a minute, *ah bee.* Don't touch the Po house, all right? I think it might still be a little tacky."

The door closed behind them, with a definitive click. But Jin could hear the thrum of their voices anyhow—Ah-Ma's rising, thinning, dumping tense and conjunctions as annoyance sent her grammar sliding back towards Cantonese. While Ma's stayed carefully quiet, deferential, respectful—not rising to the bait no matter how vigorously Ah-Ma might fish for a penultimate blow- up, the argument which would finally force Ba to choose sides (badly-selected *farang* wife vs. good Chinese mother, mother of his melon-faced halfbreed child vs. wife of his own dead, much- beloved father), forever.

And if, maybe, at the beginning, there had been some note oth- er than anger in Ah-Ma's voice—something like fear, a shadow of genuine dread, at the name of Yau Yan-er—it was forgotten now, like Jin herself, in that endless, pointless hostility, that grudge- match negative feedback loop.

Jin shut her eyes, wishing it all away—*them* all, even Ba and Ma, in this one painful moment.

And heard Wu Mingshi speak up from behind her at the exact same moment, as though in answer to her pain—his light voice soothing-soft, liquid as a Cantopop ballad, welcome beyond all words—

"Are they both gone, flower?"

Jin's heart shivered inside her at the mere smell of him, flopping like a fish. "Yes," she whispered.

"Good. Then it can be just you and I."

So she turned, and there he was: right *there*, like always, wrapping her in his arms. Enfolding her completely. Mingshi, with his perfect almond-flesh skin, his liquorice eyes as smoothly shaped as pumpkin-seeds, his whole face symmetrically stunning: shiny, shining, lambent and airbrushed, like any given Disney Studios' multiracial hunk-of-the-month.

"I die so much when you're not here with me," he murmured, with perfect sincerity; "Me too," she whispered back, thinking: *It's like a soap opera, isn't it? So corny. So glorious. Oh God, it's like a dream...*

Could it really only be two weeks since she'd met him? When he'd told her he lived inside the Po family Hell house, she'd just laughed—until he'd shown her. *Taken* her. In through the same door she saw her Ma paint on, to a room whose nude grey cardboard walls were hung with bright red marriage-bed silk. And under those billowing curtains, on a genie-in-the-bottle bed made from folded Hell bank-notes and crumpled paper wads of Hell cash, he'd laid her down and climbed on top of her, fitting himself to her like a velvet-lined glove. Gave her her very first kiss, in super-slow step-print stop-motion—and now just looking at him made her delirious, hot-and-cold shaky, like malaria. Like love.

But: How could he possibly fit in there? Let alone make *her* fit in there?

(Didn't matter.)

Of course not, no. But...how did he even know English? Or was that Cantonese—Mandarin?—they were both speaking?

(Didn't matter.)

Yes, but how—

Didn't *matter*, any of it: It was like *Twilight*, like *Titanic*, like *High School Musical 1, 2* and *3*. He was Edward, she was Bella; she was Claire Danes and he was Leonardo DiCaprio, before he grew that grody beard. It was *Romeo + Juliet*, but without the dying part. Fate.

Say it Jin-Li Song or Song Jin-Li, the facts stayed the same either way: she was so ugly, so insignificant, belonging nowhere, to no one. But Mingshi, her Hell friend, he chose *her*—

(*This month, you should be careful of what you see...and of what you don't.*)

And: "Come with me," he said, tugging her back towards the

house; Jin came, of course. Willingly. Without question. Stammering, as she did—

"I brought you some food, Mingshi—stole it from the corner. Ghost-food…my Ah-Ma'd have a cow, if she knew…"

"Oh, I don't care about that. Kiss me, Jin. I'm cold; just lie with me a bit, will you? Kiss me. Keep me warm."

Into the Hell house again, wrapped tight in Mingshi's arms—and vaguely, as if seeping down through slow fathoms, she thought she could hear her Ba calling from outside, her Ma, her Ah-Ma: *Jin—where is that girl? Jin? Jin, we have to go…just load it up, the Po family won't wait, the getai for their daughter is tonight…she'll be fine, she has keys…*

After which came a rocking, a heave and a lifting, a slam followed by rumbling, a pulling away. And throughout it, Mingshi just kept on holding her—close, closer, closest; tighter than she'd ever been held before, by anybody. So tight, she never wanted him to stop.

Yet Jin could still hear Mrs. Yau's voice as well, buzzing always in one ear, dragonfly-insistent—the voice which never quite dimmed enough to become unintelligible, never *quite* went away. Mrs. Yau's susurrant murmur, *yin*-tinged like every other Mandarin accent, even Mingshi's own. Saying, over and over:

Remember, what's hidden, what lies beneath…is not for you, little sister. Not for anyone. Unless…

Snatches glimpsed through the Hell house's windows, fragments of sorrowful revelry: the Po family's *getai*, already at its halfway point. Jin caught flashes of light and moving color, a community centre banquet hall full of neighbours, relatives, tourists all clustered around tables set with lazy Susans, stuffing themselves with Taoist Association food offerings the ghosts had supposedly already "fed" on. Earlier in the evening, there would have been an auction of auspicious items—more feng shui stuff, some donated by Ah-Ma, some by other Gods Material shopkeepers—with all the proceeds collected in one common public purse, to cover next Hungry Ghost Month's expenses.

Ghosts like a party, Ah-Ma told Jin, this time last year. *So we use that, to bribe them to stay out of our affairs—we get to eat and dance, they get to watch. Not such a good bargain, on their part. But—*

(better than Hell)

The red silk hangings flapped, as Mingshi pulled her ever-further into his warm, strong, inescapable embrace; apparently, it was opera time now, the classic aria from *Bawang Bie Ji* rising and falling in mournful ecstasy, as Yu Ji expressed her fatal loyalty to the king of the state of Chu…and yet this too was already dying away, somehow, time skipping a beat to admit a steady stream of ringing gongs, droning scripture, Mrs. Po's weeping. Even clutched to Mingshi's chest, his heart pounding quick in her ear, Jin could hear the Taoist master praying out loud as he waved a fistful of lit joss, his other hand simultaneously touching an open flame to the sheaves of Hell money which fringed the Hell house's roof and walls: *May this house be a home for Po Ching-hsia, her life continue uninterrupted, may she live there happily, with her new friend, and never again be lonely…*

(*She took her own life, that girl, you know,* Ah-Ma whispered, in Jin's brain. *Ai-yaaah, the shame—such a pity, for one so young, so rich, so full of promise. Her poor family! She was only just your own age, Jin-ah…*)

But: "Don't listen, Jin-ah," Mingshi said, at the same time—a sudden catch in his too-beautiful voice, like he'd been crying. "Don't look, not at them. They don't have anything you need. Look only at me, at *me*…"

The smoke filled her nose, her throat, her eyes, making her cough and weep. Had the Hell house always been so *small*? She couldn't remember. Couldn't think.

Look away, mei mei, Mrs. Yau's tiny buzzing voice said then, quiet, yet loud enough to drown out everything else. *Look back outside, no matter how he begs you. See how things* really *are.*

Jin listened; she couldn't help it. She looked—

(*only at ME, oh no*)

—and saw the whole first row of chairs, seating strictly reserved for ghosts, occupied by the same people her eyes had scudded over all day, along with many more she'd never seen before: the little girl with her plushie, the crazy man—a woman her Ah-Ma's age, in a flowered dress with yellow sweat-stains down both sides from armpit to waist, who scowled hatefully at Jin as she hugged a double load of tattered plastic shopping bags crammed with rags to her breasts, balancing them on her ample lap. A perfect anime-character teenager in private school uniform and Japanese loose socks, violet-streaked hair in two bouncy pigtails, who held up her spectral cellphone to snap a photo of the Hell house as it brightened, blackened, began to crisp and fold. All sat there staring, rapt and ravenous, waiting to see her burn.

They want me dead, like them, Jin thought, horrified. Then looked Mingshi straight in the eyes, equally appalled by what she'd finally caught looking back at her, and blurted out loud—

"*You* want me dead, too. Don't you?"

Mingshi shook his head. "No, never. I love you, flower."

"But…you're not even real. You're…"

(His perfect teeth shifting askew in that kissable mouth, even as she watched; perfect hair already fire-touched, sending up sparks. His face, far too gorgeous to be true, a mere compilation of every Clearasil ad, every music video, every doll Jin'd ever owned, or coveted.)

"…made of paper."

His face crumpled, literally. He knew she knew, and she knew it. Pleading with her shamelessly, in that dreadful, broken voice—

"Oh no, oh please…stay with me, Jin…*come* with me. I don't know that girl, Po Chin-hsia. She's nothing to me; we're nothing to each other. Hell is such a dreadful place—I don't want to go there alone, not after having met you. I'm afraid…"

Which was good to hear, Jin supposed, given everything he'd put her through, but not quite good enough. Not nearly.

So: "I'm sorry," was all Jin could find to say, as she stood up—

—only to find herself abruptly full-size again, bigger than the Hell house itself, ripping back out of it in one not-so-smooth move: a shattered plaster cast, a husk, a shell—a burning birthday cake, and her some soot-covered stripper. The pain was immediate, all over, fifty torn Band-Aids at once; she could see half of her own hair already hanging chunk-charred, one arm of her shirt still smoldering, as she stumbled off the stage, cleared the front row (ghosts melting back from her on every side in a wave of angry regret, hissing like rainy night arson) and ran straight into her shell-shocked parents' open arms.

Weirdly, Ah-Ma was the only one who thought to grab a pitcher from the nearest table and soak her with it. Ma just hugged

181

Jin tight, holding on for dear life, while Ba just stood there, mouth open.

"*Wo cao!*" he blurted, finally. Ah-Ma immediately rapped him hard on the side of the head, snapping—

"*Waaah, on gau,* filthy-mouth man! Look at the house, ruined, totally useless—the Po family will run us out of town." She turned to Jin, voice full of a mixture of worry and anger. "And you, what were you *doing* in there? Playing a silly trick in the middle of Ghost Month? *Mahn chun yoh yeuk yee!* You think we're made of money? Who's going to pay for all this?"

"I think we should probably go, while they're still distracted," said Ma. Adding, pointedly, to Ah-Ma: "Unless you want it to be *you.*"

Ah-Ma looked at Ba, who nodded; Ah-Ma snorted, and rolled her eyes.

"You are all against me," she said, with great, despairing dignity. And suddenly hugged Jin as well, without any warning—so hard, so fiercely, Jin almost thought both their arms were going to break.

Afterward, once the entire strange tale had been told and—wonder of wonders—digested, Ma apologized to Jin for not telling her Mrs. Po had commissioned her to make Po Ching-hsia a Hell friend to go with her Hell house, because she'd thought Jin would think it was creepy. "*I* thought it was creepy," Ma admitted.

"I...don't know how we could have possibly known..." Jin began to say, then trailed away. Everyone nodded; exactly.

"You said his name was Wu Mingshi?" Ba asked, a few minutes later. When Jin nodded: "*Ai-yaaah, ah bee,* that's like calling somebody Mister—Nobody No-Name, or something. John Doe."

"Huh. Weird."

But no weirder than anything else, really.

The next week, Ah-Ma announced she and Ba were selling the shop to the Po family, for a hefty price. Now Ah-Ma would be able to retire the way she'd always wanted—perhaps to Australia, where there were many other "good Chinese"—while Jin, Ba and Ma could move to Vancouver, where Ma's family ran a computer store.

That Friday, however, Jin found herself once more inside the

Empress' Noodle, sitting across from its owner as the lanterns shone overhead like dim red moons, casting barely enough light to see how little there was to see by.

"*Ni hao*, Song Jin-Li."

"*Ni hao*, Mrs. Yau."

Mrs. Yau laughed, a throat-sung trill of touched-glass music. "I said you might feel free to call me Grandmother, child," she reminded Jin, softly.

"*Wei*, I remember, and thank you, very much. But…I don't. Feel free."

Again, that one-eyebrow/no-eyebrow twitch, twinned with a delicate quirk of lip. "Ah. So you are finally becoming wise, *mei mei*—or wiser, at the very least. How it gladdens my heart to see this."

Jin swallowed. "Did you know? About…him?"

"Your little paper husband? Not directly, no. Though I did see some sort of influence trailing behind you when you first passed my window—something foul with too much *yin*, like a snail's track, leaving a stain. And seeing how you shone with *yang*, I thought that if that stain were to be removed from you, you might be better off."

"That stain." Jin's first love. A cold and lonely thing, made only to be burnt, which had reached out blindly, grabbing at the first warm hand it found; a liar and a thief, perfectly happy to get Jin killed as long as he got something out of it, Mr. Nobody No-Name Nothing…

But beautiful, nevertheless. More so, Jin feared—late at night, when she had nothing else left to think about—than anyone else she was ever likely to meet for the rest of her boringly normal life.

"Well, anyways," she said, at last. "Looks like you saved me."

Mrs. Yau shook her head. "No. Because you trusted in everything you saw, I simply showed you what it really was you trusted—after which you saved yourself, as I'd hoped you might. Very impressive, Song Jin-Li-ah."

"If you say so." Jin cracked a small smile. "Definitely lost me my summer job, though."

"Then for that I am sorry. Would you like another, perhaps?"

"What, work here? For you? I…can't cook, or anything."

"Ah. *Mei shi*, little sister—never mind, no matter, not to worry. A restaurant holds many different jobs. Besides which, this is hardly the only business I own."

Jin nodded. "Uh, um—no offense, but—I don't know you very well."

"True enough." A beat. "Would you like to?"

"...What do you mean?"

Another beat, held longer, like a drawn breath. And: "Hmm," Mrs. Yau asked, musingly, of no one in particular. "What *do* I?"

Jin felt herself trembling on some kind of precipice, with no real idea of how she might have gotten up there in the first place— so high, so exposed. So very much in danger.

"Look closer, *mei mei*," said Mrs. Yau, her lips barely seeming to move. "*Look*, and see. *See me*, now..."

...Fully revealed, reigning Empress of all the New World's *hsi-hsue-kuei*—suck-blood devils, half-souled Chinese vampires, worse indeed than any ghost who ever lived once (but doesn't anymore). Enthroned in her antipathic Dragon-boned Lady glory, and terrible as an army with banners; her unbound mass of hair floating up and away like drowning weed, tendrils seeking delicately in every direction for any scent of blood on the air, with her porcelain mask-face the one seed of light still left in this whole black velvet poison-flower. Lotus feet in tiny jade-green slippers, curled and atrophied like mushrooms; nine-inch nails girt with golden sheaths so long, so sharp they scratched the tablecloth beneath as she gestured, cut the air around her, made it bleed. And worst of all, what might be a train or even a tail switching drily under the table, its jewel-scales rustling along the floor like toxic leaves...

Best to leave Yau Yan-er alone, Jin-ah—it's safer. She's NOT like us. Not like—

(*anyone*)

My Hell friend, Jin thought, unable to stop herself. *My REAL Hell friend.*

"And now, as the old tale goes, you have seen the witch in her true ornament," Grandmother Yau Yan-er said, softly. "For we are seldom any of us what we seem, Song Jin-Li-ah, as you will always do well to remember. Perhaps you too will be something other than you seem, in time."

A ghost; the idea came to her, numbly—maybe that, yes. Everyone would be a ghost, eventually, after all.

Everyone but Mrs. Yau.

"Thank you," Jin said again, bowing her head. As was only polite.

"You are most welcome. And remember this, too: You *may* still return to see me yet—when you are older, perhaps, and have come into your full power. Whenever—if ever—you feel most...comfortable."

"And how will you be then, Grandmother, if I do?" Jin-Li Song was unable to stop herself from asking, no matter how she tried—lips tight around the question, mouth dry and strained, as though the word itself were carved from salt.

But Grandmother Yau Yan-er just inclined her beautiful head further, obviously seeing no insult was intended. And murmured, so softly it might only have been to herself—

"Oh, me? As to that, I will probably be..."

...*much the same.*

SATAN'S JEWEL CROWN

I walked into Satan's Jewel Crown, having no horse, then stopped a while at the town pump to order myself before going any further, taking time to splash my face and beat the dust from my brother's old coat. As I did, a little girl playing by the saloon door looked up when my shadow fell across her, gawping—maybe at my height, which has always been noticeable, or the bandage 'round my throat, which I suspected might have commenced to bleed through once more, during the last and hardest phase of my travels.

I had a rifle across my back and a knife in my belt plus another, smaller knife in my boot, all donations; my pack was full of dead things' heads, well-wrapped, which I'd heard some towns were now paying good money for, then turning in themselves later on for government bounty. I hoped to at least be able to swap these for a few nights' room and board, and perhaps (if I was lucky) a fresh pair of boots, since the ones I was wearing were both down at the heel and slightly too tight, as my blisters could testify.

So I smiled down at the girl, hoping to make a better impression. But: "Are you a lady?" was all she asked, at which my heart lurched, thudding traitor against my ribs, where I'd wrapped myself to bind those poor things I'd once called breasts down far enough to imply their lack. Yet I trusted in my voice—that awful rasp, made worse by thirst and rough weather—to give that very idea the lie.

"I look like a lady to you?" I inquired of her, therefore, in return. And on hearing me, she shook her head, falling properly silent... though to be frank, she still did not seem *entirely* convinced.

Such an odd little thing, all eyes, in a solemn, peaky face. We stood there admiring each other a moment, while I studied on what to say next. Luckily, it was at this very point that her mother came out, dressed in low-cut muslin, hair gold-glinting in the last of the sun. Saying, as she did—

"My daughter's touched, sir—has been ever since the War, the night her father died. It's these times, y'see; they weigh particular hard on small things, and the soft."

I nodded at that, honestly enough—I'd certainly found them so, after all—then smiled again, to which she gave me just the slightest sketch of a smile back, both faint and weary: something worth cultivating, even in that state, polishing up and finding its full shine, so you could admire it at closer quarters. And I knew I was lost.

"Have t'keep my eye on her from now on, I s'pose," I told the woman—Anthea, her name was, and is. The girl's was Esmee, called Meem, for reasons I never thought to ask. She I let go, at her own request. Yet Anthea, my lovely wife, I hold to still.

And thus it began, the tale I'm calling on you to pen. Take it down at my direction, leaving nothing out, but I warn you, do not think to elaborate, either—for though my handwriting may be disreputable, I can cipher with the best of them.

"I have a secret wound," I told Anthea, on our wedding night, several months from that same day. "From the War—don't like to speak of how it happened, as I'm sure you can understand. So let me do for you, my darling, please. Tell me what you like, and let me do my best to supply it."

"You're the only man I've ever known who talks like that," she said. "Sometimes..."

"Sometimes?"

"...you talk like you're not one at all. A man, I mean. But only sometimes," she hastened to add, for she did not wish to offend me. And hid her face in my shoulder, embarrassed.

"Perish the thought," I said.

It was a good choice, in hindsight, though I mostly do not count myself philosophical. For what is life but a series of secret wounds, as well as what those wounds leave behind? Our scars hold us together, more than anything else. Wouldn't you agree?

Well. It's a thought, only; an opinion, whatever that's worth. Even in my current position as mayor, not to mention this cursed place's sole surviving citizen, I surely can't legislate you share it.

Now, we all know that the bodies of the dead had commenced to rise long before I ever got into the "business" of killing such creatures again. Some people date this turn of events back to the War Between States, or even to slightly before it, claiming it a sign of God's impending judgment on America for harbouring hexation. For those slightly more well-read, however, it's easy enough to prove how the first *true* incidences had far more to do with the influence of two heathen Mex demons who called themselves gods allied with a passel of dueling hexes than to anything the Good Book ever predicted.

To begin with, in the wake of the Mexico City earthquake, there was a springing up of what would come to be called Red Weed all across Arizona and New Mexico—pernicious stuff, well-known to infest livestock, causing them to move about long after they'd been drained of all true life. And it's true that the first dead things I killed, back on my family's farmland, were definitely Weed-infested, staggering here and there with little scarlet flowers a-bloom from all their orifices—they'd twist their vines as I approached, snapping and creaking, juicy with anticipation of seeding my flesh and mulching my remains. These I took down from a distance when I could, popping their knees, then stamped on their heads and jointed them as they lay twitching, stacking the remains up afterwards to burn.

But then came the Hex War, in which those old Mex demon-gods met their downfall, along with plenty of others. By its end, mages who'd never before been able to meddle formed compacts and founded whole cities, the Pinkerton Agency gave way to the Thiels, and a crack opened halfway down to Hell itself, some said, releasing all manner of bad things into this world: horse-sized spiders, bone-dust monsters, dogs with human hands. Was only after that when the dead we know today began to make 'emselves evident, either clawing up out of graves or fresh-turned, with no trace of Weed to be seen. They spread their sickness through biting and ate all in their path, which was why the government fixed so high a bounty on evidence of their destruction.

Thus the era we now live in was formed, so far as I can reckon: a place of black miracles where towns feed their Weed-banks blood in exchange for fertile soil, where hexes can finally be diagnosed through arcanistry and expressed at their own request, either emigrating to Hexicas to live with their own folk or joining up with the Thiels to fight the unnatural with yet more unnaturalness, after. And we poor unmagicals are mainly left to flounder, finding our own way through darkness, with corpses nipping at our heels.

I had left Caxton, back Georgia way, as a too-tall, ugly woman with no prospects, monetary or otherwise. But by the time I crossed the border into Tennessee, circumstances had conspired in such a way that I now passed for a towering, raw-boned man, my general lack of beauty suddenly rendered "noble" and "distinctive" by a mere change from skirts to trousers. Which is how I eventually came to stride these streets like Lincoln reborn, though by necessity rendered beardless.

It was nothing to me to alter my sex in such a manner, since I have been treated as a workhorse all my life, which may well be why I've grown to look it. I was not raised gently, nor am I gentle by nature, and thus it ever seemed to me I was probably not made for gentle things, long before later experiences managed to prove that thesis well beyond a shadow of a doubt.

My family claimed to have been of some stature at one point, long before the War (though that conflagration might be, and often was, credited with marking the utter end of their fortune's downwards turn), and as is often the case, they had long pinned all hopes of social resurrection on my brother, sole heir to what tiny fortune we retained. Unfortunately for them, as is equally often the case, Philip turned out to be both completely uninterested in and woefully inadequate to the task at hand; instead of delivering on his supposed promise, he instead chose to use the Hex War's final spasms as an excuse to betray them by taking whatever he believed himself entitled to and running off, never to return...one of those things, as it ensued, being me.

I suppose I could have fought him on this point, but given I had no great interest in helping to redeem my family's name either, it was easier by far to leave with him than to do so alone. We did not long stay in company, at any rate, only reaching so far as it took Philip to find a low groggery, some fools to try and cheat at cards, and enough drink to get him in the mood to do so.

I fell asleep in the corner and woke to find myself alone, aside from the man I'd previously seen pouring drinks the night before. His friends were outside, hooting and hollering. When I asked him as to Philip's whereabouts, he all but rubbed his hands together at the prospect of shocking me with a revelation that proved no great surprise at all, before commencing in on whatever else he might've had in mind.

"Left you to us in trade, that brother of yours," he said. And: "Oh really?" was all I replied, reaching for the slim-ground paring knife I'd secreted in my sleeve.

Though thus disappointed in his intentions, he nevertheless approached me without any sort of fear, perhaps assuming me as stupid as I was ugly, or that I had some sort of investment in thinking myself a frail flower in need of rescue. Whilst I, on the other hand, simply waited for him to draw close enough, then drove my blade deep into his eye.

He had a belt with a gun on one hip, and I buckled it 'round me, though I knew it unlikely to do me much good; indeed, there was barely enough time to do so before his friends kicked the door open and saw me all over bloody, their leader at my feet. They made their threats and I listened, then laughed. "Little pleasure to be had from a corpse," I told them, palming the knife's hilt once more, "but you're welcome enough to it, I suppose."

A second later, I'd already drawn its still-sticky edge 'cross that place where my Adam's apple should have been, quick as a wink, and lay there watching them dissolve into darkness even as they stood looking down on me, cursing. Yet I woke later, alone, surrounded by fresh carnage. The place was silent, bloodier still than I'd left it. By the marks left behind, I took it that a herd of dead things had passed through, coming and going, leaving ruin in their wake. That they had left me untouched was indeed an oddity, but my throat hurt far too much for me to ponder on it long. Like them, therefore, I rose again, albeit in a very different way.

The rest of the man's clothes fit me as well, to a point. I covered up my wound, cut my hair. And so I became myself, at last, leaving the creature once called Myrtella in the dust behind me; I was "Mister Phillips" from thence on, with no real need of a first name, seeing how I'd already reclaimed my brother's and thrown away my father's.

Looking back, I now see that much of what I've accomplished since has been in the service of turning myself *into* him, only better—becoming in truth the man he only professed to be, between the big talk and the sister-selling. One way or the other, I know beyond a shadow of a doubt how in my own odd way, I've done more for others than he ever would have looked to do, and ten times more effectively. This whole town stands testament to that, as I believe you'd agree...

...if nothing else.

I well-knew I should've left Satan's Jewel Crown right after I turned in my haul and got my coin, but the plain fact is, I just didn't want to. Instead, I felt a new and aching need to stay 'round Anthea for as long as I could, to follow this hook she'd set in my heart, and see where it might lead. It posed a puzzle, since to be near other folks was usually never much more than trouble, or so I'd always found: they soon enough started to want to know me, to ask after where I'd come from, where I'd been. What-all I might—or might not—have done.

Anthea's boss, Mister Colquitt, who ran the saloon she worked in, thought paying her was tantamount to owning her. She'd been able to cry him off thus far by citing her widowhood, but when he saw her look to me, that all fell by the wayside. He was high up in the town council and commenced to whisper in ears, making them wonder what it was I was after, 'sides from what *he* already wanted.

"You're looking to marry my mama, ain't you, Mister Phillips?" Meem asked me. "Why?"

"To look after her, 'course. Don't you want that?"

"I guess. She does need looking after."

"You too, I bet."

"...Maybe."

That very same night, the first of the dead came in, and while others ran and screamed, I stood and fought. I'd already been noticed, but that got me some credit. Was enough so that three nights on—once we'd dug the trenches I suggested, and filled 'em with pitch against new incursions—I slipped into saloon-keeper Colquitt's rooms with a particular head I kept deep in my pack, too rotted up to sell but still straining to bite, whenever I set my hand on it. In the morning, he came staggering down with his eyes rolled back and his teeth all a-snap, so I drew Anthea out of his way and let him get far enough outside anyone near could see, before pocking him through the forehead.

The verdict came in he'd died in the night of wounds he'd kept hid, then risen back up. And I was good and in after that, clung fast, dug deep as a tick…so close to the town's beating heart I could not only feel its pulse but taste its blood as well, sipping it down like finest victory wine.

Meem saw me bury the head, later on; made certain I saw her see me, too. But she never said anything, so I gathered it must've suited her I stay, as well as the rest. Strange little girl.

I'd been one of those myself, once.

"*Are* you a man?" she asked me, whilst Anthea was elsewhere.

"I am now," I said.

"You *were* a girl, though. Like me."

I paused, thought hard about it for a moment. Then allowed: "They did call me so at home, for all I don't think they treated me much different than they would've a boy, so long as he wasn't their favourite. But I never really thought about it, one way or t'other—not 'til I needed folks to assume I was somebody your mother could love, and feel comfortable doing it. Which would *you* prefer I be, honey?"

"Well, I already have a mama."

"You could call me Papa, then. If it suits you."

And I guess it did, because *she* did, from then on. Right up until the day she died.

That night, I looked in on Anthea watching Meem sleep, and thought: *I want to stay here, to do what I can to keep you both safe. I want to be the man you think I am. Want to kill anything that threatens us, same as I'd kill anyone who'd even try to prevent me from doing so.*

And—I will. Oh yes.
You best be very damn sure, I will.

By that winter, I'd been less elected mayor than acclaimed so, for the dead things kept on coming, and I was the best they had at knowing how to protect ourselves. Wouldn't've thought the earth held so many, but that it always seems to be the most unwelcome creatures which seem limitless—they flocked in from miles around, when they weren't propagating by the usual methods. As each day was increasingly given over to clean-up and every evening to funeral pyres, we were also struck with corpse-fever, which thinned our numbers somewhat, while consolidating my own base of power—for it was the nay-sayers who tended to drop hardest, and those who acknowledged me as best choice for role of wartime leader to recover.

But in and between these misfortunes, we did see the first instances of something no one else had, thus far: an apparent cure for infection, as mysterious as it soon proved (thankfully) complete. There were those who lived, for once, after having been caught in the dead's jaws—fell silent a few hours, suffering bad, yet got back up the very next morning, apparently unscathed. And amongst these was Anthea, who'd already put two bullets from her little gambler's derringer through the thing that had hold of her before I could rush over and shear its head off, even though it'd already buried its teeth so far in her shoulder that they stayed there, lodged fast, when I finally pulled it off.

I spent the whole night crying over her, with Meem's solemn little hand on my bent head, stroking away at my shorn hair. At last, worn out, I fell asleep beside the bed—then woke to find her down in the kitchen, making flapjacks.

Beautiful Anthea, her long curls gold in the morning sun. Smiling. Talking. Better.

"You all right?" I asked her, to which she answered, brightly: "Oh, 'course. Shouldn't I be? Did something happen?"

I studied her a moment, unsure what-all to say, given her wrap had just slipped far enough to let me see how those two raw holes in her flesh were still visible—not bleeding, not anymore, but not exactly healing, either. Much like that wound at my throat.

She noticed, started a bit, and covered them up again. Gave me the same smile I'd sold my soul for, sweet enough to stop my breath.

And: "No," I said, "nothing like that, darlin.' Just had a bad dream, is all."

"Oh? Well, you're awake now—so sit down and eat these, Mister Mayor, 'fore they get cold. Given they sell my cooking 'cross the street, it's not everybody gets their own private sample."

"But Papa," Meem said, once Anthea'd gone back upstairs to freshen herself, in anticipation of opening up the saloon. "She *isn't* really better, not at all. She just isn't done, yet."

I swallowed. "What do you mean, honey?"

"That she's still here," she told me, sadly, "though she shouldn't be. 'Cause you love her so much, you just won't let her go."

And did I notice, looking back, how all those who survived their brushes with the dead were people I had use for, while those I disliked failed outright and rose back up, necessitating a second destruction? No more than I ever traced the seemingly endless wave of plague-bearing, Weedless dead we now fought back almost daily not to the Hex War at all, but to one very particular instance of the chaos following in its wake.

My neck remained tetchy, never entirely sealed over. Sometimes it wept blood. Anthea would soothe it with compresses, brew me sweet tea, then bandage it anew. I used whiskey to treat it too, increasingly—medicated myself from the inside, so to speak. No one thought any ill of me for that, since I ran myself so ragged in service of this town, and its folks.

My town, now. *My* folks.

"Papa," Meem said, a little further on that winter, "you really should let Mister Corcoran move on, at least."

"Oh, but I couldn't do without old Corcoran, honey. He's my right hand."

"Well, then Missus Yee—let *her* leave, while you still can. Her girls, too."

"Now, but where would they go *to*, exactly, with all the dead things out there sharpening their teeth for 'em? Think, Meem. I have a responsibility to Missus Yee, just like t'everyone else."

"But Papa..."

"You don't want me to lose my job, now, do you? Where would

your mother and I live, then? Or you, either?"

I was only teasing her, gently, or at least I thought I'd been. But she looked down right then, and by God, I almost thought she was about to cry. I'd've done about anything in this world, at that same moment, to take my clumsy mockery back.

"Just don't bring *me* back, please," she told me, at last, soft enough I had to cock my head to catch it. "When it comes to me, at last, I mean. I know why you kept Mama, but I see how it is, for her...for *all* of them...and all things considered, I'd really rather not."

"You have my word," I swore, though I still didn't really know—wouldn't allow myself to see, more like—what it was, exactly, I was swearing to. And I've kept that promise, as it happens...thus far.

Can't say what may happen in future, for loneliness is a curse. Yet so long's I have Anthea, I believe my sweet Meem can continue to sleep easy, unlike the rest of this town's citizenry. Her presence, though sorely missed, is no longer required.

I do owe her that much, given all she did for me.

Right about here, meanwhile, is where *you* came in, with your shiny Thiel Agency badge and your cunning arcanistric instrumentation: Agent Lucas K. Law, at my service, or so you claimed. I remember you standing in my office, sipping the whiskey I'd poured you, while down in the street below, I could see my people going to and fro, doing their jobs; by the saloon door sat Meem, as ever, playing with her doll in the dust, which set me to thinking about that first day, and all that'd followed after. Listening with only half an ear as you told me why you'd come—that Doc Asbury's measurements reckoned Satan's Jewel Crown as close as made no never-mind to "the very epicentre" of this latest outbreak of (possibly) hexation-created unnaturalness. How it was part of your rubric to investigate, and that you hoped I'd give you every sort of aid in your quest to discover exactly why the dead seemed to find this area—the place, even—so damnably attractive.

"People do say Satan's Jewel Crown's prospered under your rule, Mister Phillips."

"I'm only a mayor, sir. We don't elect any kings, 'round here."

"Of course not. Still, to brave such continual incursions from these, eh, graveyard emissaries and survive—no, more than just that, surely. To *thrive*..."

"We've been fortunate, that's true, though we've suffered our share of losses: corpse-fever, brawls, the regular range of insults, as well as gettin' bit. But as to that, we do seem to have an amazing survival rate, even amongst those took down in battle."

"Excuse me?"

"Oh, a good third of our folks've shook it off, thus far, even once the poison's took hold. My own wife, for example—"

You blinked. "I'd...like to meet that good lady, if so."

"Well, sure. She's just over thataway, if you care to cross the street."

As we walked out together, you casting your eyes 'round in obvious curiosity, something began to mount in me that I barely recognized, so long had it been since I'd last felt it—anxiety, doubt. *Fear*, not only on my own behalf, but on behalf of all.

My town, my people, my family—I, me, mine. All I'd built up and kept safe even in the besieging face of death, and so much worse.

"Those fortifications look military-grade," you said. "You have soldiering experience, I'd wager."

"No, sir," I replied, pulse starting to stutter. "Learned it all from books, or veterans' tales. My brother—"

"No? But you *must*'ve fought the risen before, somewhere—back along the original line of infection, perhaps."

I nodded. "In Georgia, when the Weed first came up, we got our share of infestation: live animals, dead bodies. We soon learned how to deal with 'em."

"But nothing like this new strain, exactly."

"No, t'be sure. Wasn't 'til just before I crossed the border I first saw ones like these-all, and then only their tracks—before the bounty laws came down, and I started in to hunting."

You paused in your step, a spark of sudden interest lighting your eyes. "Really. You know, Mister Phillips, our investigations while back-tracking the herd's migration eventually uncovered tales of a certain long-burnt-out watering-hole—so close between states, apparently, it almost didn't matter exactly which side it lay, while the place still existed—that might've witnessed this country's very first mass conjunction of plague-bearing dead. We examined its

ruins a month ago, and found evidence of great hexational discharge still resonating; its foundations gave off an Asbury Scale
reading of 68.5 even after several months' inactivity, seemingly
collected 'round a bloodstain on what was left of the bar-room's
floor..."

"I did pass through that area," I admitted, feeling my throat
contract, "and it's a hard road to travel, full to the brim with all
manner of untrustworthies, or was. Don't ever recall hearing much
about any hexes, though."

"Well, they do exist almost everywhere, inherently—everywhere I've been, anyhow, since joining up. By the by, if I may ask
you about that wound you bear, under your neckerchief...is that
from your recent toils, or did you sustain it earlier?"

My hand went to the offending bandage. "Some time ago, thank
you kindly. I hardly notice it now, given all my other distractions."

"Really? It looks quite painful."

"Oh, once, yes—but these days, it's nothing I can't deal with.
Just can't seem to get it to seal up, not completely."

"I'd think that would make things...very difficult."

"I'm not sure I take your meaning."

"No? Let me rephrase, then: that does not, in fact, seem like a
wound it would be possible for a man *to* survive, no more than it's
usually possible to survive a revenant's attack where the bite breaks
skin, everyplace else but here. Would that be your wife I glimpse
there through those doors, the lovely woman tending bar?"

I bristled. "It would."

"Well, well! She, too, looks in remarkably good health, given
what you say she's been through."

"You think I'm lyin' 'bout her getting better, is that it? Just like
Mister Corcoran did, over there, or Missus Yee and her girls, down
at the wash-house? What possible reason would I have to misrep-
resent our triumphs, small's they might be, when the losses we've
had remain so much greater?"

"None at all."

"Then why're you quizzing me on all these whys and hows, exactly? I'm no arcanologist, not like your bosses, or yourself."

"Well, this *is* your town, isn't it? Who else should I think to
ask?"

We stood there glaring a moment, eyes locked, like we were

about to draw down; you reached into your fancy waistcoat, and I fairly twitched. But instead of a shooter, you instead brought out one of old Doc Asbury's famous hexation-measuring manifolds, the latest model; it could drain spellwork too, as I recalled, though I think you somewhat forgot about that part, once things'd gone fully to perdition. At any rate, you held it outstretched my way like a dowsing rod, attempting to explain how the spinning of its various dials revealed there was far more to me than I'd hitherto suspected.

"You see, sir," you said, "I believe that *you* are *causa generis* of this infestation—unintentionally and all unaware, I can only guess. As most new-turned hexes are, concerning the damage they do."

"A hex. *Me.*"

"Can't see any other explanation, really. There are those who've shown similar powers, already, upon expression...what the witch-hunters of old once called necromancy, whether demonstrated by bringing the dead back to life, or keeping those already on the cusp from, uh—going any further. That said, of course, I frankly can't think there's been a case before recorded in which one man did both at once, spreading revivification in his wake like typhus... or re-ordered an entire town to his personal liking, either, using a threat *he himself* was author of to keep its populace under his rule..."

God, the pure shock of it. Though it *did* fit, I had to admit, if only to myself; if I couldn't recall having had anything like magical powers previous to that truncated attempt to cut my own throat, things certainly had gone to my benefit ever since, albeit in odd and awful ways. Even the idea that I should have made my change in the manner a man usually does, rather than a woman—for I'd received my monthly gift years ago, and never made much of it, aside from an excuse to change trousers more frequently—that, too, seemed right, when placed in context. As right as any of it could be.

The way you regarded me, though, when you thought I wasn't looking; it was like you thought I'd done it deliberately. And the rage rose, kindling me from head to toe, pumping me full of poison and fire admixed—up, and up, and up. My fingers itched, longing to form fists.

Yet at that very instant, I heard my sweet little Meem yell out, from behind: "Papa, don't! Papa, they're coming—they're almost here—you just *got* to stop them, Papa, *please*—"

We turned as one, then, you and I, Agent Law. Just in time to see a fresh passel of rotten, reaching dead come charging down the street as though summoned, all sunken eyes and moaning, open mouths.

How'd they get past my barriers? I remember wondering as I whipped out my knife, fast enough it must've looked like I was fixing to juggle it. *My sentries? The catch-pits? Christ's sake, how damn deep we got to dig those trenches, anyways, 'fore they finally start to do the trick?*

Then I saw the whole range of their faces, just as the first wave broke against us—those intact and fresh as well as grave-kissed, same ones I'd called out greetings to that morning, on my daybreak stroll from one end of Satan's Jewel Crown to the other.

And I knew, finally. At last, that was when I knew.

You should let them all go, Papa—let them leave, let them move on. While you still can.

Before...

...the crush was on us, and everything turned to carnage, with you and me back-to-back against the horde. I saw you put down six, a round for each, before you were forced to throw your gun away and grab whatever came to hand, instead—first a good, solid length of log, snatched off the nearest pyre pile, followed by the Cavalry sabre old Mister Hudgens no longer seemed to know how to use. I found myself trying to thrust aside those I recognized while taking down those I didn't, but that went by the wayside soon enough, once the berserker-fit was on me. And at some point I stood gasping, glancing down, only to realize that the figure crouched beside me was Anthea—Anthea, her long hair blood-dabbled, hugging Meem to her like some awful Madonna and munching away on the side of her neck all the while, like it was the world's best slice of watermelon.

I groaned out loud, then, and punched my wife full in her beautiful face—knocked her sidelong, slapping her down further, so I could wrest what was left of the only child I'd ever be likely to call my own from her still-grasping arms. Saw you from the corner of my eye, Agent, watching me do it, even as Missus Yee's eldest took a chunk out of your nicely-dressed calf. But I didn't have time to note what happened next, let alone to care.

Oh, but I held Meem tight, tight. Gripped her like she was salvation. And then—

"You all *stop*, goddamnit!" I cried, cradling that poor girl close. "All of you, just...*stop*."

Which, without further ado—they did.

So...here we are.

Even after that wonderfully useful explanation of yours, I've no doubt you were startled when I roused you up once more and burnt the fever from your veins, sealing that ragged wound with a touch (just like my own throat, at last. Like Anthea's pale shoulder, under her muslin gown.) And saying, as I did, in true Galilean style: *Awake, O sleeper—Lazarus, I command you, roll away the stone. Come out. Come back.*

I am not done with you, Agent...no, not yet.

Maybe not ever.

Here you are again, though, after all that—made almost good as new, barring some ill-usage. And it's thus I'll send you back to your masters, to Doc Asbury himself, who I reckon may well wish to study you for years: a living dead man, walking and talking, to demonstrate the untapped depth of my powers. But one way or the other, I'll trust you to warn them to leave me alone, from now on—not because Satan's Jewel Crown is far too small a place for them to trouble with, so much, but because if they do not, far worse things may...hell, *will*...happen.

Think about it this way, Agent Law, and inform others accordingly. When *I* die, whether by natural means or otherwise, I expect the town will go with me—fall silent forever, like a stopped clock. That's what I hope. But there's always the alternative: a general exodus in the wake of my passing, these people I've sacrificed so much for streaming out across the land like locusts, rotten and hungry, to spread their awful sickness everywhere they turn...

And why should this be my legacy, anyhow? Well, we know that all hexes' power centres around what they know best, the thing most familiar to 'em: Chess Pargeter with his guns, Reverend Rook his Bible. The Chinee and Indian hexes have their traditions. I once heard of a woman burnt back in Caxton who'd used embroidery, sewing her desires onto the world around her. So is there something in me that's equal-hungry and cold and rotten, at my core? Or is it just that when it came upon me, when I cut my own throat and first made sacrifice to myself, I had already given myself up for dead?

Little enough pleasure to be had in a corpse. Yet I will take what I can, and call myself thankful for it.

You see, I know what I am, now, for which I really do thank you—my true nature, what I've *been* capable of, thus far. Yet I don't think I know the extent of what I might still achieve, if I'm given reason enough to push things further. Which is why it's better for all concerned that I not be—you, most especially.

If (when) I die, *you* die, too—finally, fully. It's a foregone conclusion.

Better to leave me alone, again, from now on: here on my throne, king of all I survey, danced attendance on by my dead wife's body and my dead daughter's ghost. A lost, uncertain thing no more, though forever damned to wear what my town's named after; if the shoe fits, as they say. And after this, all who meet me—thanks to you—will surely know it does.

(Meem knew already, it occurs to me. Perhaps because she was as I am, or might have been; another hex, potentially—a friend, a companion, far more than her mother is, or can be. But still I let her lie, as she asked me to.)

Mister Phillips, Myrtella; it's all the same. I'm both, and neither. I'm what I am, only—nothing ever seen before, and nothing to be trifled with. And this much is certain, either way...

...even if I don't want anything more than what I already have, I will *never* settle for anything less.

THE SALT WEDDING

Oh the bodies rise and fall in slow motion,
As the flesh gives way to coral and her charms.
If you listen hard, you'll hear the sea is breathing,
And she's waiting there to hold you in her arms.
—Robyn Hitchcock & the Egyptians

That one time in Porte Macoute, Tante Ankolee: A wise woman, cunning sorceress. Who buy she-self out-bondage wit' her own money, make she livin' wit' her charm, who owe no debt and leave no insult unpaid. Who all men fear an' all women come to, 'specially in them time o' worst need. Whose magic like the sea itself, so dreadful-strong and changeable, much deeper still than any grave. That one time, she.

Ta she door one day a Navy man come, upright-stiff an' white in him great blue coat. Him who take him hat off t'address her, same as if she na wear a bone t'rough she lip or bells in she hair. Captain Collyer, that him name, an' he come ta tell her strange news only she might know how ta deal wit', offerin' the king's penny for she trouble. Need her help, him say, but she know she got no choice, nah really—for even there on the very edge o'things, it nah good form ta turn what that old, cold England-King send ya away.

Tante Ankolee, our ancestress, who no man never make slave, not even when she wear him chain; hush nah, child, an' listen. For 'tis always useful ta hear of she doin's, no matter how long time agone, if only ta know what might be possible, under similar circumstance. Ta see proof how a woman of this family can seize hold o' fate like a damn horse and ride, if only she know how. Thus, and so: The tale commence, and go now 'til 'tis done.

The Navy man sweated hard in Porte Macoute's heat, being no doubt unused to such temperatures. Or perhaps it was Tante Ankolee's presence alone made him so strained and shiny—she liked to think so, for he himself was not ill-looking, for a white man. But from her own experience the better policy by far, if one wished to 'scape danger, was always to assume nothing.

"You are kin of a sort to the Rusks of Veritay Island, I hear," he said, one hand at his high-buttoned collar, to which she nodded. Then, studying her closer, seemingly bent on mapping the spray of freckles 'cross both her tea-colored cheeks: "Some...*distant* kin, perhaps?"

"Nah quite so distant as them make it sound, no, if it they the ones y'ask. Old Carson Rusk, him buy me maman at that same market outside me door here an' get me on her whilst him wife sick wit' child-bed fever, then keep her an' me both ta raise him full children while still sowin' bastards aplenty, wit' her an' otherwise. Yet lucky for us, Aphra-Maîtresse an' Maman cleave together as firm friends once they get t'know each other, much ta Old Rusk's confoundation."

Here she gifted him with her favorite brand of smile—sharp-curved lips rimmed in tattoo-blue, with a dull line of teeth just showing, in between—and watched him blush awhile at the way it made him feel, let alone in what region.

"Well, be that as it may," he replied, at last, once he'd managed to re-order his thoughts accordingly. "I have here in my hand a letter drawn straight from the Admiralty itself, the king's own seal affixed, that bears your name and requests your aid in a matter of some small urgency and delicacy, both. 'That the woman known as Angelique Rusk be petitioned to lend her aid in matters magical, for the betterment of all men under the Crown, and the restoration of trade-lines betwixt these waters, the ports of old England and their holdings,' etcetera and etcetera, 'as here writ...'"

"*Ankolee*, that me name, my pretty young man, an' don't ya forget it. Though ya may call me 'Tante,' if ya so inclined."

"'Auntie,' as the degenerate French would have it? Madam, I believe I will decline."

"As ya please, then." And with this, she lifted her skirts to show bare feet, their painted nails like claws, before settling down into a nearby chair and crossing her legs at the ankles, delicate as any lady. "But since y'come so far, 'tis only proper I might as well hear y'out, after so many mile an' difficulty. So tell me these so-bad troubles o' yours, Cap'n Collyer, an' I'll tell ya how 'tis I can help, if indeed there's help t'be had for 'em at all."

Thus invited, the Navy man sighed, crossed his arms, and did.

His tale was an odd one indeed, to say the least, though—the sea being what it was, so infinitely brim-full of all sorts of awfulness and delight—Tante Ankolee might honestly say she'd heard odder. It began with a low-laden ship of the line, set sail with a cargo of various necessaries from out of the Seychelles and headed towards Port Royal. This vessel never reached its destination, though a pair of survivors were later plucked from the ocean, clinging to a spar...*not* one originating with that same ship, as it turned out, but salvage from another entirely, not to mention so well-encrusted with barnacle-overgrown corals 'twas a wonder the thing could even float, looking as it did as though it had spent much time underwater.

These survivors told a story of their own, which their rescuers dismissed as mere raving: Said they'd been approached mid-voyage by a spectral three-master massive enough as any four ships slapped haphazardly together—the which, on closer inspection, it seemingly proved to be. Blown forth on burning sails from the darkness, this looming, lurching hulk's ill-cobbled upper deck was back-lit by an unnatural corona blue-green as the horizon's sunset flash, and on it stood two equal-phantom figures, a careful distance kept between 'em: one a single-eyed rogue done up in piratical finery, so large he made the other (tall enough, by most standards) seem small by comparison, while his mate stood slim and upright with silver-pale eyes in an even paler face, clad head-to-toe in parsimonious black.

With a contemptuous little hand-flourish, knuckles a-dance with sorcerous sparks, this second apparition caused the ship's frontispiece to split straight down the center, bowsprit dividing, the hull itself appearing to swing open like a stove-in casque. Through the spray of this division, the survivors could glimpse a dank interior cavern festooned with weeds and barnacles, garden-stocked with all manner of slimy life most usually found only within the sea's much deeper reaches. Towards this their own vessel made a sudden little leap, as though hooked, and commenced to plunge straight for what proved to be a veritable graveyard of marine detritus, possibly compiled from the shattered remains of other travelers along the same route—masts and hulls, nets and rigging and wet sails hung slack like popped bellies amongst the corpses of barques, cogs, carracks, plus what looked to be half an entire East-Indiaman torn stem-to-stern as though by some kraken's beak and tentacles.

Overhead, the first ghost-pirate strode out onto the bowsprit's right-hand outcropping as though walking the proverbial plank, so uncaring of his own safety he couldn't possibly be any living man. Roaring, as he did: *Them as swears the Articles may stay on, whilst them as feels un-inclined may throw 'emselves over-side and swim—for we'll have no slackers on board this ill-starred beast, my fellow captain and meself! Ye must serve one of us in our endeavors, no great matter which, or take your chances wi' She Below, resigning yourself to Her cold mercy!*

"And did them choose t'stay?" Tante Ankolee asked, out loud. Answering herself, before Collyer could try to: "But no, couldn't be, or they nah be here t'tell them tale to *you*, who tell it me. So them must've took t'other option, instead—plunge back out into the waves, clingin' fast to whatever come t'hand: this spar ya talk of, whah bear 'em back out into darkness."

"Exactly, yes. Which, when examined, proved to bear a name of both notoriety and ill-repute, for all common rumor brands the ship it's attached to as having sunk a good ten months ago."

"An' what be this name, exactly?"

"Uh...*Salina Resurrecta*, those were the words found when we scraped it clean. Though it has, on occasion, borne another title, too—one I hesitate to mention, before a female."

Leaning forward, her eyes suddenly a-flash: "*Bitch of Hell?*"

"That would be it, yes. Do you know her?"

"'Twas the name me half-brother give *him* ship, who sail a pirate 'long the trade-routes from Seychelles to Jamaica an' back again—Cap'n Solomon Rusk, Old Maître's youngest, who I call 'cousin' when I nurse him up, even though we close enough linked by blood t'see just by lookin' if ya stood us both together. Or so '*twas* called, 'til the man who kill him take it, and sail her on himself: Jerusalem Parry, who me brother find collared in some Navyship hold, bound out for wizardry an' marked t'swing."

"Yes, I do seem to recall both those names now, from reports. Yet Captain Parry died too, did he not? Or must have, if he now pilots this monstrosity..."

"Oh my, yes; dead almost this whole year gone for all him considerable power, by fightin' the curse Solomon lay on him in dyin' so hard, he finally bring 'bout him own comeuppance. For Parry had me brother keel-hauled, y'see, an' from that day on couldn't set foot ashore wit'out he commence t'bleed; spent a good ten year roamin' ocean to ocean, searchin' for a place more sea than land yet firm enough t'lay his head on, before doom fall on him at last. As, doubtless, him always knew it would."

"Ah yes, now it comes back to me. Made a man into a shark, too, didn't he, with devil-magic?"

"Nah, was t'other way 'round: made a *shark* take on *man*-shape just t'guard him from any who might think t'avenge Cap'n Rusk, or imitate him—bid him wear clothes, walk upright, call he-self 'Mister Dolomance'; fah, pure foolishness, and cruel, too! But they was cruel men both in them own ways, thus makin' 'em perfect fah each other's downfall. Since like do call ta like, or so all say..."

"I'm...not sure I take your meaning, madam."

Tante Ankolee arched a brow at Collyer, skeptical he could choose to miss the point so wide. "An' you call yaself a sailor," was all she said—then laughed, long and loud, to see how he flushed once more.

How well she still recalled her first meeting with Jerusalem Parry—*my sweet Jerusha*, Solomon had called him, probably 'cause he damn well knew how the doing of it made that former blue-coat twitch. For that brother of hers was always a one apt to be over-happy with his own bad behavior, pitch-black in his heart if not elsewhere, yet gifted with such a store of dark good looks and animal high spirits as to make people call him charming, even after they'd already felt the brunt of his thoughtlessness. Parry, however, had just cold self-possession enough to remain unaffected from the neck up, no matter how his traitor nethers might've welcomed Solomon's attentions; never having lived slave before, he was determined to win free, at any cost—to break rather than bend, scorning the softer path, and crush all before him like an earthquake wave, destroying everything for a mile on either side just to make sure Rusk went down along with it.

Lucky how Solomon's curse made him have ta stay afloat ever after, then, when ya think on't, she thought. *For most, if not all.*

"Be easy enough t'make things go smoother 'tween you two, Master Parry," she'd suggested, gently, as they sat at her table together, Solomon a-lurk in the background with his long body leant up 'gainst the wall and his blind eye turned their way, pretending not to wonder what secrets they might be whispering in each other's ears. Him who she still somewhat saw, without wanting to, as the baby who'd delighted in tugging at her plaits or that man-size boy who'd thought to make her his first adventure—holding her fast to that same brickwork with both hands snuck up under her skirts, while she just nipped at his ear and laughed, reminding him she'd once changed his nappy. "For the cap'n a man of simple tastes, well-apt t'lose interest swifter than he seem like, you only give 'im time..."

"I have *given* him quite enough thus far, I think, by any civilized measure. So much so that he will simply have to count himself satisfied already, from this point on."

Such clean lines to that devil-stubborn man's sharp face, profile cut like a coin, even turned 'way with his odd silver-penny eyes cast down and frowning; Tante Ankolee could well-enough see what it was drew her "cousin" to him, beyond the obvious. A rich vein of magic ran through this one, clear as any needle in quartz—felt it cry out to her equal-strong, almost as hard to pay no heed to, for all *she* at least both knew what she was hearin', and was canny enough to keep from trying to answer.

"Where is't ya get your witch-blood from?" she asked him, as a distraction. To which he shrugged, and answered: "They called my mother such, and hanged her for it; I suppose I saw evidence enough to support the charge, of a kind, before the Church took me in and paid for my education. Yet...I never thought it anything but slander myself, ill-will towards one far too young and sharp for safety, from those who were no longer either."

"Hmmm. An' who was it got ya on her, in the first place? What man's name should ya wear, if him care enough t'lay claim?"

Here Parry looked back up, gaze sudden-lit like light off a blade, to show him less than happy with her bluntness—yet quick enough to take offence for most things as she'd seen him proved already, this was an old wound she prodded at now, one he obviously rated not worth the unstitching.

"'A man of quality,' was all she'd say," he replied, at last. "Some squire sowing his oats, more like, content enough to dress up Satan-suited at Sabbat and lay down in the graveyard with a pretty marsh-girl, but not to meet her bastard-price after; same fat scum who signed her warrant, perhaps, little as I could do about it. Let him keep his secret to his grave, and be damned for it."

"Still think that Good Book-writin' God o' yours makes sure o' such, after all you seen, and done?"

Parry gave a thin variety of smile, cold as Cornwall Christmas. "'Tis exactly what He's best at, or so I've heard it rumored."

And: *Aye, true enough,* she thought, yet did not say. *An' perhaps that's what you thinkin' on even now, havin' made ya mind up t'stay insulted over somethin' there no earthly help at all for, seein' it already done and gone wi' no recall...*

Watching close, Tante Ankolee saw Jerusalem Parry cock his fine-made head like a whistled dog, those same words inside her skull obviously equal-resonant in his, and sighed—for he was a puissant one, worse luck, as most wizards never proved.

"So she never teach you *nothin'*, this maman of yours?" she asked, aloud. "Leave ya unprotected in this world, knowin' herself how them wit' cunning end at the hand of them wit'out, most often?"

"Little enough, in all, and that the Church soon had out of me, or so they thought. I can only suppose she hoped not to have to..."

...and yet, she heard him add, interiorly. To which she chimed back, proving what he knew already: *Aye, 'tis true; I nah wish the*

same on my child either, boy or girl. That bein' why I go wit'out, for the instant.

They shared a meaningful stare, capped with a tandem nod. And he paused, gathering himself visibly, before continuing—

"I chose *none* of this, madam, I will have you note. Not magic, like my mother; not the Navy, when I was always to be a parson— small and quiet, *useful*, in my own place. Certainly not to be called out by my own people for something I cannot help, to have hot iron put 'round my neck and squeezed shut 'til I was forced to expend all my power in healing its touch, or be made some pirate's... plaything, as a consequence."

"'Course not, no. Still, we nah t'know where She bound t'take us in the end, the sea, wit' all Her deep currents. Nah ever."

An' even ya stay in that marsh ya maman call home all y'life, whah guarantee but ya still end up right where y'are? You never made t'serve God, not you—made different, to follow where your magic pull ya, whether you will it or no. Who know but that this ain't where you should be, right here, with—?

(him?)

Though she felt a rage that beggared description well up in him at the very notion, Parry kept fast hold of those courtesies her brother claimed he never forgot; simply shook his head, polite and calm, while at the same time thinking: *Madam, no. I will not countenance it.*

Never.

Solomon behind them, unwitting and arms crossed, with all ten fingers briskly a-drum on their tanned hide; never could stand to wait for long, that one, no more'n a stallion to be haltered. And smiling ownership-proud down at the back of Parry's head at the self-same time, like he was thinking how sweet it'd feel to kiss the frown from that rigid mouth. Yet never even guessing on the touch of him sickening Parry just as much as it stirred him, and what a terrible harvest he might reap himself, eventually, for choosing not to understand the inside of someone else's skull could be such a damn different place, no matter *how* good the rest of him might feel to lay down atop of.

"I *would* take it as great kindness, nonetheless, were you to teach me what your conscience allows you," Parry added, soft enough, almost into the highest fold of his neat-tied cravat. "To gift me with whatever you might, that my power continue to grow and I to master it, enough to defend myself against...all manner of dangers."

Should've told him no, she knew that now; *had* known, at the time—and yet. For blood did trump magic, or ought to, if most were asked—but when blood and magic both came equal-tied, on either side, what then? What remedy, in such a case?

None, surely.

"One way or the other, this I maintain: If he truly wished anything from me but contempt, then he has gone about it in the least effective manner possible," Parry had told her later that day, before turning on his heel and stalking off, looking anywhere but in Rusk's direction. To which she'd merely shook her head, and murmured—

"True that, yes. As him almost always do."

Less than a half-year on, Tante Ankolee woke suddenly, knowing in her heart how Solomon Rusk had at last found the death he'd so assiduously courted. And a month after that, when word came that the *Bitch of Hell*'d been sighted off Porte Macoute's shores, she went down to meet its longboat, thinking to question Parry directly on how this had finally come about, only to watch him taken short as he stepped but a single foot to sand—saw blood bloom up all over like red pox, flooding his pale skin 'til his eyes rolled back, dulling in an instant from silver to mere muddy gray. That sad shark-creature he'd fashioned had him well in hand, however, begrudgingly saving his life by swimming back with him to the *Bitch* before he could quite exsanguinate.

So she sent her soul out instead, to save effort, coming to Parry in a dream while he still lay recovering, shrouded head-to-toe in a healing calyx of power—and found Solomon's ghost sitting beside him, stroking the sorcerer's sweaty hair with a hand whose coldly insubstantial touch made him flinch only slightly, never knowing why.

Her, though, Parry could see well enough; he raised his head at her approach, haughty as ever, to demand: "Did you...do this t'me, madam? As...payment, for your 'cousin's' end?"

"Nay, fool. For though all our acquaintanceship nah so long, I think y'already know me workings ain't too hard to recognize—so if *I'd* any part in ya current condition, you'd nah need t'ask."

"I...can only suppose this to be true, yes." He took a struggling breath. "And yet—though I do feel myself cursed, I wonder...how? By *who*?"

Tante Ankolee shrugged, leaning closer, various draperies seeming to pool as she took a figurative seat by Parry's bedside, warning Rusk's too-attentive specter away from them both with a bare, brief finger-flutter. "T'best answer that, let me now tell ya how I come on *my* witch-blood, *Captain* Parry, since ya never before think t'inquire—from *both* side, as it happen. The which be why that brother o' mine able t'lay the very last of him ill-will on you by instinct alone, wit'out knowin' he even could..."

So she gave Parry the tale, same as Aphra-Maîtresse had told it to her maman, and her maman to her. How there had been three witches once found each other back in Old Scotland, swelled similar-full with talent and wickedness, who formed up a compact to do evil together and passed through the countryside like a foul wind, keeping the Devil's sole commandment wherever they lighted: *Revenge yourselves, or die.*

"All manner o' bad work they bring to conclusion, these sworn-sisters three—kill an' eat them enemies' unchristened babes, then boil the remnants down for flyin' ointment; ride a man in him sleep or a girl in hers, stealin' seed from both ta birth monsters; raise storms, sink ships, curse wit' a touch; blast who them will an' slave the ghosts t'do their biddin', after. Yet wit' one mistake only, all three find 'emselves caught an' clapped in the Witch-House at Eye, to wait on King James' Burnin' Court."

"Which was?"

"Them trust the wrong person, o'course. Like we all apt to, most 'specially when affection enter into things..."

(And here she cast a glance back Solomon's way, only to see him turn his head, no doubt not much liking to be reminded of his own folly, let alone the depths it'd sunk him to. *But whah can ya do 'bout it now, you great murrain?* she found herself thinking, while Parry tilted his head at her once more, shrewd gaze narrowed, as though he might pry out the truth of what so amused her simply by staring closer.)

"Oh, they all roast in the end, sure enough; stake-tied and screamin', in a lit bucket o' pitch. But wit' one, bein' as fair and fancy as she was, the guards an' tormentors take them time, which

211

is why she able t'live far longer than either of her two gossips, since she have that big belly o' hers t'plead on. So twelve month on, her son born just like you, Jerusalem Parry—Judas Rusk, first of the line who make Veritay Island them home, wit' craft in him veins an' no name t'wear out into the world but hers, no matter how many fathers him have t'choose from."

"Is that tale designed to make me feel more...*understanding* towards Captain Rusk's memory?"

"Nah, 'course not. But 'tis true enough you'd have burned th'exact way she did, if the twice son's son of Alizoun Rusk's boy'd not found ya so damn good t'look on, he throw his own soul away just t'put you on ya back the once...or more than once, if I know him."

Parry looked down, lips quirking: *Far more*, she saw, in the resentful shadow of his eyes. Yet he said nothing.

"As for the cap'n, meanwhile," she continued, "don't surprise me all too much how he end like our ancestress, since he a fool in many ways, an' greedy wi' his wants, too. Yet I do think there was more than he ever suspect 'twixt the two o' ya, an' more than *you* suspect, likewise. Think him lust could have turn t'love, eventually, if only you was to've seen ya way towards lettin' it."

That same bitter smile, sharp as when she'd last seen it, twisted his mouth yet further. "I have never had any great interest in being *loved*, by him most particularly."

"Ah, ya disdainful creature! Would ya truly t'row such a gift away wi' both hand just 'cause it come wit'out ya beckon it, an' never ya mind from who?"

"Why, yes indeed, madam. To my dying breath."

Which, for all she knew any better, had most probably held true 'til Parry himself was laid down likewise, in the end.

They had sat there a moment more, then, with Parry visibly willing himself calmer, both the rustle of breath in his iron-scarred throat and the high pulse that drove it dimming; Tante Ankolee gave a sigh, and gathered herself to go. Only to hear him ask, as she did—

"He is here, though, still—even now. I am correct in thinking so, am I not?"

She looked to Rusk's ghost, and saw it shrug: *No more secrets, big sis, not that I was ever good at keepin' 'em. Ye may speak as ye please.* So she nodded, replying: "Aye. He be sittin' right there beside ya, him hand on ya heart...an' you can't even go nowhere t'rid yourself of him now, either, can you? Nah wit' that touch-o'-land-make-ya-bleed curse on ya."

Parry gave a shudder of what seemed like pantomime disgust, as though eel-touched; what was left of Rusk turned his face away again at the sight, perhaps annoyed by such cheap dramatics. While Tante Ankolee simply snorted, similarly unimpressed; shouldn't've killed a man on board his own ship, if you *didn't* want his ghost hanging forevermore over your shoulder. Even those with no craft at all knew as much, most-times.

An' you the man-witch thought joinin' the Navy a good idea, as I recall, when the Admiralty assign one witch-finder at least t'a ship. What was't they did teach you 'bout the way things are in that Cornwall marsh church of yours, anyhow?

"If so, I can only assume he does not actually plan to exact vengeance unto death on me," Parry observed, once the fit had passed, "since, though wounded, I remain still alive."

"Do seem unlikely. So you've years yet t'torment each other, I'm sure, given ya both seem so bent on't."

"Well. We will not see each other again, then, in all likelihood— for which reason I will bid you my farewell now, madam. You have been...kind to me, in your way; more so than I deserve, probably."

He gave her that carved-ivory profile of his once more, still blood-besmeared under its healing-spell's glow, all unknowing how doing so angled him straight into Solomon Rusk's view, putting him exactly where the man he'd killed could look his fill, yet never be entirely satisfied. So the man he'd murdered for violated honor's sake might forever study him in the same hungry way others might some religious book, the far horizon, or their own newborn child.

Thinking only to herself, since speaking it aloud would do no earthly good at all: *Fah shame. What-all you two done t'each other, wi' your ridiculousness an' botheration? What-all ya done to yourselves?*

Turned the coolly assessing eyes of her soul on devil-proud Jerusalem Parry a last time, before replying—

"P'raps. For as much harm been done t'you, 'tis undeniable how ya done equal-much harm, in return—just like me poor Solomon, in that way. So, in the end, might be what you two most deserve..."

(you *and* him, both)

"...is each other."

213

The next morning brought another survivor, a ship's carpenter named Mipps who claimed to have both taken Rusk's fabled Articles and spent almost a month aboard what Tante Ankolee had begun to call (in her own mind only, thus sparing poor Captain Collyer's feelings) the *Bitch Resurrecta*. His allegiance had gone to Parry rather than Rusk, a decision he did not regret even though it'd ended badly, at least for him.

"'Twas hardly the cap'n's fault the ship sank," he claimed, eyes darting like a hat-maker's. "For magic be no fit or adequate substance t'build worthy vessels with, not at sea, no matter *how* powerful the wizard what wields it—"

Collyer shook his head, baffled. "Speak plainly, man. The...*Salina* is sunk, now?"

"No, no, what I meant was that *other* ship, the one Cap'n Parry cobbled from wrecks and some few sections of deck, sails, what-have you—a mast or two, even, seein' they have so many between 'em—and then budded off his and Cap'n Rusk's *first* ship, like a flower-cutting. Oh, 'twas a terrible difficult undertaking! Most 'specially so with those two hard at it all the time throughout, hammer and tongs, for I've never seen two such men for quarrels. Rather fight than talk, they would, though it's true enough how they do do a truly powerful sight of *that*, as well..."

"No surprise, there—ghost or no, a ship should have one captain only. 'Tis known."

"Aye, and there they'd agree wi' you, sir! Which is why they so long t'make two ships of their one, accordingly, and each sail far away, in opposite directions."

Humming to herself under her breath, Tante Ankolee let the two men before her talk, busying herself with a bit of 'broidery she'd tucked into a pocket of her skirt. And as stitch knit to stitch, needle dragonfly-flashing in the morning sun, she used the task's cover to reach out softly with her soul's fingers, rifling through that giddy skirl of worshipful fear-crazed memory and outright dream-lit invention Mipps currently termed a brain; there were all sorts of snatches of useful material here and there—albeit only half-glimpsed and barely registered, dimly, in the background of what Mipps considered far more interesting experiences—which she now commenced to pick through, sorting and cataloguing, sifting purest chaff from possibly fertile, only half-chaff grain.

At the top, she saw Parry stalk about restlessly, fair vibrant with impatience, as Rusk and his quartermaster went over the section of the ship's books regarding food-storage in finest, most niggling detail. New deprivations loomed, probably because their various crews had swelled so prodigiously over the past few weeks; Rusk counseled a push back into nearby shipping lanes, to gather supplies for those who needed them, even if he and Parry did not—take a fresh prize, the old pirate's answer to everything.

At the suggestion, Parry gave Rusk a look that might have been punctuated by spit, were he a different man. "This your fault, sir," he threw up at him, "somehow, and all of it."

"How, by the Devil's balls?" Rusk snarled back. "You be the wizard, here; ye know damned well I wot nothin' of magic savin' how to recognize the stink of it, when blown from your direction."

"Enough to curse me."

"Oh, aye? *All* men know as much, fool, just as all men would do the same, if only they knew ye as I do. Besides which—I *have* apologized, and that whole-heartedly, for any wrong I may have done you, back before ye saw fit to take my life in the most *unbefitting* manner possible...nay, do not dare t'lift your brow at me, sir! Ye saucy bloody knave!"

"Did I? No, please, do go on—I find myself interested where you mean to end, having already begun with a lie."

"Fish-wife! If ye did not so rail like a woman, ye might find yourself less oft treated like one."

"You do not impress me, sir, no matter how loud you rave. You never have."

"Oh, I do think I've managed, a time or two. Shall we test it?"

With this, Rusk took a step towards him—short by his reckoning, yet long enough by most others'—and Tante Ankolee saw Parry's fingers curl as though longing to warn him off, blue-green sparks striking from their nails. "You will stay in your place, by God," he ordered, "or—"

"Or *what?*" Rusk roared, not retreating. "Will ye kill me again? If only!"

"Would to God I could! Or *myself*, and be done with you, forever!"

Tante Ankolee felt her head nod, to hear it. Thinking: *But this will never happen. For punishments do not work that way...most 'specially them that seem, i' th' main, entirely self-inflicted.*

The two of them regarding each other now, panting slightly,

while the men around them kept strictly to their tasks, pretending total ignorance of what had just passed. For the overhearing of such arguments were obviously rule rather than exception, when working this particular voyage.

But: "As ye will, then," Rusk said, almost to himself. "Yet tell the truth for once, my Jerusha, and shame the bloody devil—in all these long years, who is't ye've thought on more oft than I?"

"None, admittedly. Given our circumstances, however, this is surely no great marvel."

"No mystery, either, seeing how ye yearn after me still, no matter your protests t'the contrary. Can ye deny it?"

"As Peter did Jesus."

"Ha! Well, we all know what happened t'him."

In Mipps's memories, Tante Ankolee saw Jerusalem Parry toss his head like a ruffled cat, hiss, and turn his back on Solomon Rusk, thus signaling that their argument was over, for the nonce. While Mipps himself bent even further to...whatever he might have been doing, something frankly unintelligible to her, save that it involved an adze. And now she was pulling herself back up into the here-and-now, where she found Captain Collyer asking, his patience audibly worn thin—

"But *how* did this new-made witch-ship of Parry's sink, yet again? And be *explicit*, this time; 'tis the king's business we're here on, man. England herself requires it."

Mipps touched his forelock, reverentially: "Oh, you can trust *me*, y'worship! Now, as to the sinkin'...'twas Cap'n Parry's project from the outset, albeit with my poor aid, and didn't Cap'n Rusk mock at him for it! Y'see, that ship of theirs *had* gone down once already, after Cap'n Parry was tricked into setting foot on a floating island; thought he'd beat his curse 'til the ship's magazine blew, with him too far away to stop it from slidin' t'pieces 'fore that shark-man he kept took a bite of him, big enough t'shoot cannon through—"

"Yet it sails still, this original ship, and multiplies."

"That's right! Cap'n Parry swore the place chafed on him, seein' he'd been trapped aboard almost ten whole tedious years, but Cap'n Rusk maintained he'd had the worse of it, bein' caught there just the same for at least as long, and ghostly all that while. An' though both of 'em thought Parry bein' dead too would finally loose their chains, by the time his bones'd hit sea-bottom *Bitch of Hell*'d already popped right straight back up t'surface an' started floatin' westward, with Rusk *and* Parry at her helm."

As Mipps told it, the *Bitch*—already well-used, as was Parry's habit-turned-hallmark while still alive, to being kept sea-ready with magically garnered donations from the same vessels he and his crew preyed upon—had immediately steered herself into the path of a hapless trader, which soon fell before Rusk and Parry's combined attack. No ship could long stand 'gainst a seasoned magician's assaults, while the sheer shock of being boarded by a one-eyed giant whose flesh blades passed straight through was enough to literally disarm the trader's occupants, 'specially once they realized his own blade seemed not even a fraction as insubstantial.

It was Mipps, who'd been part of that first group of "recruits," who suggested that Parry might be able to use much the same spells—helped along with some simple human carpentry, wherever arcane invention failed—to cobble a command of his own, thus finally separating his and Rusk's destinies forever. And they'd done fairly well in their attempt (the bulk of whose materials comprised all those missing ships whose absence Collyer had been first charged to investigate), by Mipps's professional estimation...right up until the moment they'd launched, only to find themselves becoming less stable the further they drifted from the *Bitch*'s side, as though every stitch of magic were melting away, leaving only an inadequate half-hull behind.

With all the seams sprung and bailing proven pointless, Parry'd turned to using sorcery for caulk, increasingly baffled by his own inability to keep this tub he and Mipps had sunk their labor into afloat. His last order was a brusque cry of *Abandon all hands!*, after which he'd been seen to *wink out*, immediately reappearing back by Rusk's side, only to find himself smirked at for his pains.

Obviously, such insult could not be borne—or so Mipps assumed, since the last sight he'd had of his former home involved Parry leaping at Rusk with teeth bared, a smoking blue-green blade starting to issue from one palm, followed by Rusk grabbing him under one arm and wrestling him up against the mast, pinning him there by his throat. They were still struggling when the last of Mipps's work gave way, prompting him to follow Parry's advice; by the time he resurfaced the *Bitch* itself was gone as well,

217

flickering away in much the same manner by which it had originally arrived.

"Snatched a cask as I went under," Mipps concluded, "and drifted, using it for ballast, 'til them as brang me here come by. Oh, I was main lucky, I can tell you—never did see any other o' the men I picked for Cap'n Parry's detail. But then, them waters is known for sharks."

"What sort of commander lets his crew flounder, and does nothing?" Collyer demanded, genuinely shocked. "Could he not see your distress? If his skills had returned, whyever would he not use them in your defense?"

"Busy!" Here Mipps gave a sobbing variety of laugh, odd enough to freeze most folks' blood. "Busy, aye, as they two always was—with each other. For I never did see two men fight so, alive *or* dead; Cap'n Parry'd rather stab Cap'n Rusk than talk to him, most-times, for all Rusk could pick him, throw him, and did. Yet 'tis easy enough t'see why for, when each fight always ends the same..."

Collyer paled. "Yes, yes," he put in, hastily; "so I have been informed. You may consider your tale told."

"Aye, I thank you for't, Cap'n. I'd cut these sights from my own head, if only I could."

Tante Ankolee shook her head, tongue clucking, and thought: *Ah, chah*—men. *Got no true stomach on some subject, all them brave talk regardless.*

Once Mipps had decamped back to his quarters, where rum enough had been promised him to provide a long, hopefully dreamless sleep, Collyer stood by the window a moment, wincing. Then said, at last, as to himself: "And these are the same shades we must convince to lay their mutual hatred down, at least long enough for them to go...elsewhere."

"Aye, sure. But did ya have aught else t'do?"

"Somewhat, yes—and you also, I suspect, for all you seem too polite to say so." Adding, as she grinned, and shrugged: "*Ghosts*, my good God. How I loathe all such spectral discomfitures...yet with no insult meant, madam, since I know they are part of your purview."

"None taken," Tante Ankolee replied, fluttering one dismissive hand. "Ghosts just people wit' no flesh, only dangerous as you let 'em think they can be—but neither of these no ordinary *men*, even when they still upright. So ta proceed wit' wariness an' caution a damn good thought, ta my mind."

"Thank you. Proceed where, however? This brother of yours, again begging your pardon, seems little amenable to reason, so logic dictates we apply to Captain Parry instead, to persuade them to cease their depredations. Yet my bo'sun tells me *he* once ran three witch-finders up his yard-arm and dangled them over a pod of true sharks, using them for bait while that creature of his watched, and giggled. If he's the one in the pair worth speaking to, therefore, we may already be at more of a disadvantage than I'd imagined."

"Ya miss the point. Why ask either, when 'tis the very ship herself won't let them leave?"

Here Collyer turned from his reverie, frowning. "What did you say?"

"The only possible answer. Ship bring 'em back up from below and herself along likewise, or so poor fuddled Mister Mipps say; ship keep me brother as captain even when Jerusalem Parry wear her colors, same as though she see no difference between 'em. So 'tis na she belong to either o' them, but t'other way 'round—they belong ta her, both, since she all unwillin' ta part wit' either of 'em, no matter how they tear at each other, not knowin' 'tis she keeps 'em bound."

"I fail to see how negotiation with a ghost-ship can be any more easy than attempting to enlist the help of those ghosts who sail her."

Tante Ankolee laughed. "Ah, but you forget: that ship a woman, fah all else, just like me, an' women everywhere know I do my best work for 'em, always. That how I make me livin', after all."

She had a plan already, of course. One of which, since Captain Collyer did not think to ask, she certainly did not think to tell.

When things fall foul of salt-water, common wisdom states, they are lost forever; down they go into the dark and wet, never to rise back up again. Yet the sea holds many mysteries. Indeed, with Her help—or hindrance—almost all things are possible.

Thus it came to Tante Ankolee how there were three things

she needed to make good the spell she contemplated: proof of the *Bitch*'s love for her two captains, first (poisonous-confining though it might be, as dictated the strangle-close twine and snap of whatever nameless tangle they still felt for each other), by which sympathetic parallel might be drawn 'tween them, Tante Ankolee and the good Captain Collyer, her unwilling partner in this venture—plus a token from either. Second, to raise two familiar spirits. Third, powers puissant enough they might summon the *Bitch* 'cross any expanse, however great, and wielding a love for Rusk and Parry which rivaled even the *Bitch*'s own.

In the morning, Collyer had promised they would cast off, back-tracing Mipps's report to the last place that vessel had made itself known. So Tante Ankolee began her work by taking the coral-set mirror off her consulting room's wall, its glass so rucked by the silver-mercury beneath that the images caught within looked almost water-logged, reeled up with hard-bought bait from strange fathoms, and cutting herself 'cross the palm with a knife made from drowned man's bone serrated like a stingray's spine, soft enough to bend, yet sharp enough to bring blood with a single touch.

The resultant mess she smeared over the mirror's wavy face to sketch sigils with, fluid as words in wet sand, falling straightaway into a scrying trance; she had only a moment to wait before the whole pale burgundy mess blinked open, showing the *Bitch*'s deck with its divided crew all uncomfortably a-doze, grumbling in their sleep—for they needed rest on occasion, being mere human men. And since neither of their captains shared that same hunger, they tended to retire during such periods; in tandem, as though to test each's ability to ignore the other while in close quarters.

Sinking through the cabin door like a mist, Tante Ankolee could see them both now, ghost-bodies fallen automatically into poses familiar from life: Parry propped up reading with his chair's back braced 'gainst the opposite wall, revisiting some book he must surely have perused 'til he could recite it by rote, while Rusk lay stretched on the bed in a sly parody of natural sleep, with both hands behind his head and his single eye closed. Yet even as she studied the scene, she noted how Rusk's lines began to soften, to blend with their surroundings, turn smoky and stretch longingly 'cross the distance between 'til at last he took shape behind and around the object of his affection simultaneously: a phantom pulse, cold flame-flickering, whose each caress stroked down through Parry's memory of skin to tease that of muscle, nerve, memory itself.

Rumbling, as he did: *Oh my Jerusha, constant treat and torment... so hard of heart, and else-wise. Yet diverting as these nightly conjugal fist-fights of ours have been, don't you tire of holding yourself always apart, as I do of laying siege to you? Why should we carry our quarrels ever-forward, even now, when we've already each managed to take such effective revenge on the other?*

To which Parry neither raised his head nor seemed inclined to shiver, even with the threat of those huge hands laid along either side of his jaw—though now she considered it, Tante Ankolee nevertheless thought she might have heard the barest suggestion of a crack in that cool voice of his, just poised on the verge of widening. Asking, in return—

What would you have me say? The great Captain Rusk, who apparently still cannot put himself out to remember my true name after almost a decade locked in mutual combat, let alone to use it?

And here she saw something never brought her way before, not before the man's death, or after: that not-so-little half-brother of hers look down as if genuinely abashed, bowing his black-maned lion's head in what seemed like regret, if never quite shame.

I do know it, and you, "Captain," he replied, quietly. *Better by far, I think, than you have ever known me...*

I have as much right to that title as any, sir! Perhaps more, given I held the position for twice the length of your own infelicitous tenure, at the very least—

Only because ye used guile and magic t'gain it!

And how were your colors rated to begin with, exactly? Through polite negotiation and diplomatic compromise? But here Rusk fell silent, leaving Parry to slump. *God, how you exhaust me!*

So I've seen, yes. Yet I might produce comparable effects in far pleasanter ways, if ye'd only see your way clear t'allowin' me.

I've no great doubt but that you think you could. A sigh. Shall I invite you to 'overbear' me awhile, then, given there's little else to divert us? Are you such a slave to your own parts you'd find that offer enticing, no matter how much contempt lurked behind it?

Did such things put me off, ours would be a very different story. But they have not, thus far.

221

Grip slipping down further, every finger shadow-nailed, brushing Parry's clothes aside like smoke to get at what lay underneath, in all its lifeless glory. *For only ghost can touch ghost*, Tante Ankolee's maman used to say, amongst so many other things. *That why them choose t' flock together, most-times, 'stead'a passing by t'the Nightlands or sailin' the Pearl-Bright Ocean, bound fah th'other side of All. 'Cause it mean more t' have just one person remember 'em the way they once was than any preacher's dream o' White Christ heaven, 'specially when them world grow so dark an' unfamiliar...an' that even if that other person an enemy, chuck, one 'em hate poison-bad when them both still upright. Fah death a terrible thing, you see, no matter when or how, whah or who—an' that no part of a lie.*

Parry caught his breath, or mimed catching it—he, who did not any longer need to breathe. Ordering: *You will take your hands from me, Solomon Rusk.*

Nay, Master Jerusalem. I think not.

The chair held them both now, re-sized to fit, stacked one upon the other; Rusk stroking down Parry's inseam with a rough palm, teasing in such a way as to make that stiff spine arch, rendering him blurred and boneless. 'Til at last he came settling into Rusk's over-full lap like a cat, wiggling shameless to find just the right angle, drawing a hiss echoed by Rusk as well—a shared spark hot enough to make them both flicker out, then reassemble on the bed, further entwined. They pressed their lips together, these two dead men, swallowing each other's snarls as Rusk pushed Parry back with a heave, a groan; Tante Ankolee saw Parry's eyes roll up, flush mounting, panting: *Oh, but I hate you still...*

I've come t'count on it, sweetheart. 'Twould disappoint me sore were you to change your mind now, after all this time and trouble. And here he nuzzled the twitching muscle 'neath the other man's ear, musing, with a lick: *Should've let ye sink with that bloody ship, I'd any sense at all, as many might tell ye. Yet common sense has never been my chiefest gift, neither then nor now—*

Damn you, sir, do me no favors! Just stop your tongue; to your task, and diligently!

Rusk guffawed, greatly tickled by such rank hypocrisy, 'specially when viewed at far less than an arm's length. *Be careful what ye wish for*, he warned him...

...then sunk down 'tween Parry's legs, applying himself so

heartily that at length that cold gentleman was forced to cover his eyes and cry out, hopeless—

Ah, aaah, Christ Jesus—Lord and God have mercy, who harrowed bloody Hell!

To which: *Amen,* Rusk agreed, grinning wide—and slid back up, rolling his much-beloved murderer's slack-gone fleshly illusion over, to take what was only his due. Presently, he barked his own climax and clutched him close, gently mouthing his nape while Parry sagged in his arms to bury his red face in the sheets, as though desperate to hide from the same Savior he'd only so recently conjured.

The mirror took it all, drinking deep, leaving nothing behind. And Tante Ankolee shook her head, amazed still by the sheer blunt *force* of it, after all that'd come and gone.

What need y'have of any Devil's playin'-ground, either of ya, she thought, *when this bed ya share already made so pitiful hard, this double-grave ya dug so deep?*

Almost as though he'd heard, Parry shifted, pulling himself free with a wince as Rusk entirely failed to flop one hand out fast enough to catch him; pride-goaded, he sat up, ordering himself briskly. Promising, as he did: *Yet this changes nothing—be assured, sir, I will find a way to sever from you, before the end. I will.*

I hope ye do, Rusk replied, muffled; for all his earlier gloating, Tante Ankolee almost thought he now seemed suddenly tired as Parry'd claimed to be, before their frolic ensued. A fact Parry appeared wholly unaware of, checking his re-tied hair, before continuing—

Aye, you may well mock, you object, now you've had your joy of me. But I might have done great things in this world, if not for our paths crossing.

Rusk sighed, heavily. *That ye might, I s'pose,* he agreed, without rancor. *Better than ye have done, any rate.*

(And I too, perhaps, all things being equal...once upon a time.)

Now you do jest, I think.

Ah, you would say that, ye false divine! But I had my better qualities, and much though I may relish th' mechanics of it, I've no great notion to spend my eternity playing out your very own personal ideal of self-punishment.

Parry raised a skeptical brow. *Since when?*

I will not be drawn. What you did was my due, and I accept it as such—have done, for years now. Yet for all that, I find...I cannot leave you.

With this, in one single snap both ghosts stood again full-dressed, each bent on staring the other down: Rusk with his looming height, Parry his imperturbable haughtiness, sharp as the sword he scorned to wear. Who huffed at his last statement, and replied, coldly—

You still could, I hazard, if you truly meant anything of what you've just said. If you tried, instead of talking.

Now it was Rusk's turn to snort. *How d'ye know I didn't 'try' every damn day of my time here already, and fail—how can ye, by Mary's bastard son? By your own admission, since ye could barely tell I was there 'less you drank yourself half-blind, ye'd never have known the difference.*

Which was true enough, they both knew, and Tante Ankolee as well. Yet as they all three also understood, Jerusalem Parry had never been a man who relished finding himself caught out.

I did take such things on faith, once, he allowed, at last, *just as those good church-mice who raised me preached—gave the benefit of doubt, even where least merited. But that was all quite a long time ago... and if you'll only trouble to recollect, sir, 'twas you yourself who finally taught me better.*

Then he was gone, unsurprisingly; away in a blue-green blink, leaving Rusk to stand there foolish with his mouth half-open, poised to toss the next retort straight back in Parry's absent face. Tante Ankolee watched him swallow it, instead, grimacing at the taste—sigh yet one more time, glance over at the very corner where her shade stood watching and cock an unruly brow, as if to say:

Ye see how 'tis between us yet, eh, cousin? Well, then: work whatever magic necessary t' come an' find us, and do what ye must to bring this long rout to its only proper end. For if I cannot help you, neither will I hinder...

A claim she much appreciated, empty as it might eventually turn out to be when push came to shove, like so many of her brother's promises. But now she had her first element, she wrung soul back inside shell with practiced ease and came to still hunched before the mirror like a savage before its god, all stiff and sore with her split palm throbbing—after which she rose up, wrapped the bloody glass in one of her maman's old scarves and stored it carefully away, saving it for later use.

One down, she thought, cracking her neck side to side.

Captain Collyer's ship was the *Malaga Victory*, a trim frigate with two masts and guns aplenty; he was unable to restrain himself from detailing its resources at Tante Ankolee a longish while before finally breaking off, seeing she did little but smile and nod in return. "Well," he concluded, at last, "I seem to've made a proper booby of myself and no mistake, since I doubt we will use our cannon for much more than ballast on this run. You are to be our primary source of ammunition, in such a fight."

And: "Perhaps," she allowed, twirling one stiff-locked plait 'round her finger, 'til the bells braided into it gave off just the very faintest of rings. "Or might be no fight at all, we only plan t'ings out accordingly. Yet I may need some small service, here an' there, in order t' guarantee me own particular store of powder ready fah action when at last we come to it..."

"Only ask, madam, and it shall be performed. 'Tis my charter in this affair to make certain you have all you need; use me as you will."

Once more, Tante Ankolee let her brow arch, smile deepening. "Be forewarned, then, Captain—for one way or t'other, I do aim ta hold ya to *that* promise."

Half-mad though his experiences might've left him, meanwhile, Mister Mipps proved a fairly good navigator; they made his last set of coordinates in good time, skirting one storm only to dive straight through another, with Tante Ankolee standing prow-set to switch its center-curl aside with a single fetish-clutching hand. Once there, however, they ran into doldrums that slowed them to a stop under a still and bloody sky. The crew murmured, blaming witchcraft, to which Collyer's gruff bo'sun merely snapped: "Is *all* weather to be judged unnatural, now, or only if inconvenient t'yer worships? Back to your work, ye dogs, and don't think t'bother th' captain or his guest wi' such foolishnesses!"

Yet in secret, he in fact did quiz Collyer as to whether or not the sailors might have a point, causing Collyer to later approach Tante Ankolee, in his turn. Night had fallen by then, exchanging shrunken sun for gibbous moon, and he found the decks deserted, crewmen choosing to brave below-decks' rank humidity rather than risk her overseeing their slumber, since she held much the same place as earlier. As though waiting on his presence, she turned at his approach to show herself wrapped to the tattooed collarbones in an ankle-length cloak of seemingly punishing weight, which—he only realized, upon drawing closer—soon proved to hide nothing beneath it but her own tea-colored nakedness.

"'Tis in good time you come, Cap'n," she told him. "Now, are y'ready ta make good on those vow ya made me, earlier?"

And: He did clear his throat a bit, poor man, ever-steady eyes gone a trifle uncertain under that bold gaze, in spite of 'emselves—yet for a moment, only, 'fore he squared his shoulders and came to attention, straight and tall as any good tin soldier: well-acquainted with the honor-standard his title required, him! On account of which, she all-of-a-sudden felt a stab of true affection, intermixed with just the slightest shred of pity.

For tonight, ya will see things an' do things ya never before thought on, she thought. *An' even if you prove more than match enough fah such trickery, as I do 'spect ya will, I still like ya far too much to lie that what's t'come will leave no mark behind.*

"If that is what's required, madam," he said, at last, "then... yes."

The cloak fell away then, unclasped in a trice, yet Tante Ankolee was somewhat impressed to see his gaze held steady; came sashaying towards him 'cross the deck, each part of her set all a-sway with much the same rhythm as the waves beneath, and stood there with her head tipped back, her own eyes full of mischief: so upright-stiff, still, this big, white man in his unseasonable clothes. Laid one teasing hand on his breeches' buttons, right under the triangle where one panel of his waistcoat met the other, and let her mouth curve even further, in open invitation.

"You nah a married man, Cap'n?" she asked.

"Me? Lord, no."

"But no innocent, either."

"Hardly."

"*Very* good."

So doff that coat o' yours, forthwith, an' let's us see whah may be seen.

Without his uniform to rein him in, the man seemed somehow

twice as large and yet more pale, freckled all over. To say it suited him ill would have been to tell lies, however, a habit which Tante Ankolee avoided indulging—less on principle than in the firm belief it was far easier to keep track of details omitted rather than outright inventions, under most circumstances.

"Y' should be flattered," she told him, gently. "It nah many men I'd take the bone out me lip fah, under any circumstance."

"And I do feel special knowing that, yes. But if 'twould better serve your purposes, madam...feel free to leave it in."

"Ah *ha*. You a man o' unknown depth, Cap'n Collyer."

"Call me Wilmot," he replied, his vowels tight—winded thin and dry, all on the instant—as he gathered her into his arms.

There was no great invention to what passed between them next, beneath the unwrapped scrying-mirror's watchful red-tinged silver eye—hung up beforehand on the prow's inner rim, just high enough so it would catch Tante Ankolee and Captain Collyer at their recreation, if angled where her cape's slack length had made a rude, hard bed. Yet both counted themselves well-satisfied by the time its predestined end approached, nevertheless...more so by far, at least, than those two ghost-gentlemen whose sad exploits it had last espied upon.

It was only then, meanwhile—at the veriest height of things, when she rolled atop and got herself re-seated, arching back 'til her hair's mass almost touched the deck—that she heard this brave young commander finally gasp out loud, his whole world literally turned upside-down. Shifting one of his big hands from hip to slippery fore-folds and guiding him where she needed his application most, prompting him to stir the pot first one way then t'other, fast and faster, 'til it came a-boil at last...

Beneath, as ever, the sea lapped on, so salt and deep and dark. And the will-working that same great power's adoptive daughter shed like shadow reached out accordingly in every direction at once, feeling through uncounted fathoms—abysses far beyond any human cartographer's scope to map—to stroke the various creatures whose service she required awake...

Then Captain Collyer gave out a whoop, to which Tante Ankolee added her own flourish, signifying that they were done. And they settled back together, laughing hoarse in their mutual glee, quite boneless-gone with pleasure.

"All magic works like ta like, as ya no doubt heard—from me myself, most recently," she began once they'd both regained their footing, along with as much clothing as either felt necessary for comfort (less in her case, naturally, though surprisingly not much more than that same pair of re-drawn-on breeches, in his). "So whah we done jus' now serve t'bind us closer yet to them we seek, by tyin' us neck-in-yoke wit' them own sharp-drivin' wants an' hungers—for loud as Cap'n Parry make protest, 'least wherever such-all like Mister Mipps can hear him, he an' me brother been twined fah too long an' fast in that net them weave together t' let go all of a sudden, let alone *never* comply when one of 'em most crave to take advantage of t'other."

Collyer sighed. "And you have *proof* of this troubling thesis, I suppose? ...Of course you do; nay, do not feel constrained to prove it me, I beg you. Very well, then—what next?"

She slipped a bag from her cape's pocket, brandishing it his way. "Next, we fill this back up wit' some few of the thing Cap'n Parry once keep in *him* hex-sack, just the way I taught him...one item in particular, knowledge o' which I have in from me brother's former bo'sun, Harry Vimes, in return fah a charm t' render him invisible in Parry's eyes once him finally flee while next let ashore fah provisionin'. You see, the tide have channels, like the land have lines—places o' power which them as find 'em can use to travel by devil-quick, there an' back in a day or less, no matter how far the distance. An' 'twas by one such channel Jerusalem Parry steer him new-won ship all the way back to Cornwall to retrieve somethin' he prize almost above all other things, on account of her it 'mind him of..."

"Some female? But I thought—"

"Shame on you, Wilmot-boy! Cap'n Parry handsome enough to turn most gals' heads, in him way—just like bold Solomon Rusk, as it happen, who never shied from pursuin' anything him take a fancy to, skirt-clad or no. But fah all ya might call th' one I have in mind Parry's first love, t' do so to him face would be...unwise."

Here Collyer's forehead creased but briefly, then smoothed again, almost as fast; he was a smart man, after all, as Tante Ankolee rejoiced to see thus re-proven. And—

"Ah," he said. "You mean his mother, I think. The hangéd witch."

She cut him a mocking half-curtsy, taking in herself as well, with much the same motion. Answering: "Who else?"

Sent that creature of his to glean it for 'im, he did, she recalled Vimes explaining, with a shudder. *Something hidden in the church they was to've gave him rule over, bricked up, in the wall. He wanted it bad, and 'twas us what paid for it...us after, and Cap'n Rusk before. Oh, if only I'd never told the cap'n what lay in that Navy-ship's cells, let alone sent him down t'see, with a bloody wink and nod!*

Ya knew whah him like best, I s'pose, she'd told him, shrugging, as the man just shook his grizzled head, eyes fair gone wet over her brother's awful fate. Thinking to herself: *And that was danger, always—a tussle's prospect, wi' hope of recompense near-equal t' the hazard's risk. Never happier than when him life hung i' th' balance, the great fool, be it wagerin' his own snapped neck on the fruit-tree's highest crop or takin' some French prize whose cargo seemed well-worth an eye's loss, so long as him still have one more t'spare...*

How she sorely did miss him, now and then, when she cared to let herself feel it. Like a stab under her breast, subtle yet sharp, up-angled towards the beating heart.

"All men do love their dams, 'tis true enough," Collyer agreed, eyes momentarily wistful, as though he might be thinking on his own. "Yet given these mysterious items must surely rest somewhere on the ocean floor, how do you propose to retrieve them?"

Tante Ankolee laughed. "With help from one who know such places intimately, 'course. And here him come now."

On much the same instant, something slammed 'gainst the ship's side from just underwater with a combination of wet thunk and unnatural rasp; a squeal of protest resulted, similarly liquid, and brim-full of hate. With almost comic speed, meanwhile, Collyer swerved to grab for his discarded sword-belt and drew, taking up a protective stance between it—whatever it might prove to be—and Tante Ankolee, who felt a genuine softening at the sight: *Brave man, this, along wi' all him other capacity. Brave, foolish young man.*

But: "Step back, lest you do yaself a mischief," she told him. "For in this matter, 'tis really I should be the one t' put meself 'twixt you an' harm's way, given the power this t'ing you an' I just call on wield, as well as the power give rise t' it."

"Madam, I've never run from danger in my life, no matter how unnatural. I do not propose to start now, even on your say-so."

"Then I counsel you hold fast, Wilmot-boy, no matter what-all come up from the Sea's own salty bosom—an' let me do the talkin' besides, fah Her sake, as well as yours."

Even as she spoke, within lamentably easy reaching distance, Collyer watched one webbed gray hand rise to grasp at the ship's railing, nailless pads digging deep, while—mere seconds later—another materialized to slap and strain likewise, beside it. With a groan of effort, something only roughly man-shaped hauled itself over the fragile wooden barrier to land, slippery yet four-square, on the folded-over "feet" of that haphazardly divided tail it called a pair of legs.

This, one might only assume, was a slightly more recent version of the creature Jerusalem Parry had once named Mister Dolomance—converted from shark to man, then back to shark, and insulted beyond measure to find itself once more caught midway through that first metamorphosis yet again. The shark-were turned its blunted parody of a face Tante Ankolee's way, hissing through a bared grill of teeth piled on teeth (two rows apiece, top and bottom), but found her unimpressed by the gesture, to say the least.

"Fah!" she spat, as though to cough up the very taste of this predator-fish's carrion breath. "Do nah dream ta 'proach me, ya shiftless duppy! Did you truly t'ink yaself forever freed from magic's reach, just 'cause ya kill him who laid the spell what make a plaything of ya? For 'tis nah so easy to 'scape its grasp, on land or sea...no matter how hot ya hate, or sharp ya bite."

Here the snarling hiss mounted to an angry teakettle shriek—yet though the mere sound of it sent Collyer a half-pace sidelong and his sword's blade an inch or so higher, Tante Ankolee held her ground.

"You keep that scaly carcass where I tell ya," she ordered. "Nah feelin' none too well, uh?" Continuing, as Mister Dolomance pressed both makeshift hands to where one might only assume his belly lurked, as though finally realizing where the pain that drove him was coming from: "Shouldn't've eat up that fetish o'mine, then, 'long of all the rest, when you trawled the muck fah the last of Cap'n Parry's corpse—for since 'twas I give him that to start wit', it will always come back t'me, if called. But as Parry could tell ya him own-self, 'tis most oft the very act o' seekin' on vengeance which drag ya furthest down, in return."

As Collyer stared, transfixed, Dolomance gave a last variety of begging grumble, to which Tante Ankolee responded by throwing him something he snapped out of the air, choking it down only to almost immediately hack it up once more, along with what looked for all the world like a lump of bloody ambergris. It fell to the deck before her feet and he shuddered, lurching unsteady, entire stumpy bottom-portion gone suddenly gluey-soft from crotch to where most bipeds' ankles usually lay, already beginning to knit itself back together, while those vestigial arms of his likewise shrank and flattened into flippers. As his ill-sealed gills popped open once more, Dolomance gasped and snuffled, barking a final plea his tormentor's way—only to hear her tell him, all unsympathetic:

"Be off wit' ya now; over the side 'fore ya drown on air, an' good riddance. Be grateful I consider ya debt paid, fah all the trouble you give me."

But for a creature so rapidly becoming devoid of anything like knees, the railing proved difficult to manage. Before he had quite formed the notion, Wilmot Collyer found himself lunging to assist, not even thinking to shield his palms from the shark-were's sandpaper hide. Grimacing as its thrashing drew blood, stripping him of several skin-layers in a trice, he heaved high and let what remained thump over the side, falling waveward with a mighty splash—then paused, exhausted and in pain, to drape himself over the wood for momentary respite, watching the same damned thing he'd maimed himself to aid's ungrateful top-fin streak back away into darkness.

From behind, Tante Ankolee's arms came softly 'round him, stroking sudden balm 'cross his abraded hands. "Fine hero indeed, y'are, me brave defender," she named him, "ta feel fah such a lost creature. So take this as payment, and give yaself but a moment, while I see what-all the sea brung us."

"Those...objects you were after, one hopes, given what effort you've gone to."

"Oh, aye. But one can always be wrong."

As it soon proved, however, her working had paid out exactly as planned: Tante Ankolee dipped the shark-ball into a shallow pan of brine, cracking it end-to-end and furling out a mess of muck she swished briskly, then separated—plucking forth first the promised fetish (dark wood and nail-studded with not one of its many rusty points still wet, as she kissed it and tucked it away), followed by two more treasures: an ivory eye set with skull and crossed bones in jet for her right hand, said trinket having once beamed forth from Captain Rusk's own skull, while her left was weighed down by a length of red hair braided nine times nine all wound about with chain-of-gold, like any holy relic.

"Good as new," she grinned, showing Collyer her haul, rightly proud of her own invention. "Just the keys we need fah raisin' spirits puissant enough t' lay our two bad gentlemen back down, right 'long wit' the ship who love 'em both best."

Collyer shook his head, discomfort so far ebbed he almost crossed his arms, before thinking better of what his own skin's salt might do to his lacerations. "If we can catch them, that is," he pointed out, wishing—as ever—to be practical.

"Oh, no great task there, I think. Seein' they on their way tah meet *us*, already."

Somewhere beyond compass's reckoning, meanwhile, Jerusalem Parry felt her magic prick at his without quite recognizing its source—cat-scratch rough, feverish, infectious—and lifted his bleak gaze to peer into the wind.

We are sought for, he told his co-captain, the which intelligence made Solomon Rusk's remaining eye flash with a nasty sort of joy. Suggesting, hand on sword-hilt—

Then let us seek them, *in return.*

A sniff. *My very thought, obviously. Make ready.*

I've never been not so, ye pinch-faced clerk.

The *Bitch* turned at their mutual pleasure, as always, bearing to breast this limbo they swam in's waves—made for where Parry pointed, towards that next most convenient point of opening, to breach the wall between worlds. And Rusk drew himself up full height, seeing two different skies and seas wrinkle like burning paper, one giving way to another.

All hands on deck! he roared to those below. *For though ye need not fight on either mine nor Cap'n Parry here's account if unwilling t'do so, be very sure, nonetheless—any traitors who look t'flee I'll kill meself, before they have a chance t' ruin our prize!*

At this, Parry raised a skeptic brow, perhaps about to comment.

But too late; their transit was made and done already, spitting them forth again into the waking world—

Predictably, it was Mister Mipps who first saw the phantom ship coming, and raised an alarum. Yet while Collyer and his bo'sun both turned to confirm this news, Tante Ankolee spared its arrival only a single glance; she was busy on the fore-deck, laying in the last few touches of her spell-trap, before she quite sprang it to.

The *Bitch Resurrecta* had both spread and sunk since Mipps last laid eyes on it, riding low in the water, just as its blue-green corona had spread, eddying aurora-style up and down each mast like St. Elmo's Fire. On its prow, an abominate multiplicity of figureheads formed one several-faced entity; above, Parry and Rusk stood glowering, and though her portholes were not turned the *Victory*'s way, the ring and clash of iron on iron nevertheless told a tale of cannon-loading that Collyer was loath to test.

"Gentlemen," he called, "I am Captain Wilmot Collyer, and I speak for His Majesty when I demand right of parley under promise of pardon for past bad acts, that we may discuss some peaceful resolution to your current prob...eh, difficulties."

"How do you expect to deliver on such an offer, sir?" Parry threw back, both palms flicking alight at one double finger-snap. "Being yourself palpably unmagical, and having not even a witch-finder aboard—but wait. Is that the fair Miss Rusk I see, lurking behind you?"

At this, Rusk perked up, more excited by such an idea than by the prospect of slaughter itself. While Tante Ankolee straightened, simultaneous, and corrected: "Nah fair nor miss, Jerusalem Parry, as ya well-enough know. Yet them did think ta bring me 'long nonetheless, by England-King's command, for that them know me far more acquainted wit' the two o' you an' your works than any other livin' thing...saving Mister Dolomance, that is, perhaps, whom I palaver wit' just last night gone."

"Oh? To what object?"

"Well," Collyer put in, far too pleased with his own wit, "there were one or two points of interest *brought up*, in the discussion..."

Rusk and Parry exchanged glances, equally unamused. "Be this man a full idiot, big sis, or only partway?" Rusk inquired of Tante Ankolee, who shrugged.

"No more nor less than any man o' him complexion, little half-me-blood. Yet in the matter of pure foolishness I reckon ya still ahead, if you was wonderin'."

A true barb: Parry muffled a species of smile while Rusk huffed, and Collyer crossed his arms. "Miss Rusk is our source for magical advisements, 'tis true enough," he confirmed, "leaving us not entirely unprepared to face whatever sort of attack you might care to levy, be it by arms alone or elsewise. Yet as I said, I come first and foremost bringing not a sword, but the ideal of peace. You have suffered much, I think—both of you—and the king would have that hurt balmed, as far as it may be..."

"Oh, aye," Rusk broke in, face split once more by his customary ferocious grin. "Very good of His Majesty, to think on Master Parry and me's comfort! The damage we've done to his shipping of late, though—that's got nothin' at all t'do with anything, I'm sure."

Collyer flushed. "It has...some bearing, yes. But if you would only—"

Now it was Parry's turn to intervene, head-shaking, an imperious gesture of dismissal splashing blue-green light like thrown water to mark a clear line between factions. "Enough. You have some hand to play, madam, I don't doubt—so do so, or prepare to be boarded. Neither Captain Rusk nor myself has any great pressing need the King of England can meet, nor any problem he can solve, considering how many different times and ways we've so ably proven unable to do so ourselves."

Tante Ankolee nodded. "True 'nough. Cap'n Collyer an' him charge aside, however, 'tis nah the wish of any earthly sovereign counts most, in this. Fah both of you been long self-deceived, in this matter; your quarrel wit' each other is secondary entire, whether birthed in lust, hate, or some sad mixture o' the two, t' the true, deep, an' terrible love a third creature still bear ya both. Thus 'tis to she we should address our arguments, wit' the help of yet two ladies more..."

And before any of the three men (let alone poor Mister Mipps, cowering in Captain Rusk's blind spot while simultaneously trying to make obeisance towards Captain Parry, though Tante Ankolee was fairly sure they neither were looking anywhere near him) could think to object, she had already turned the hex-bag she'd so long labored over inside-out, letting its contents fall free: the eye, the hair, both caught up on what appeared to be a boiling haze of mist, quick-ablaze as phosphor. As the others watched, she spun her hands like she was carding wool, separating one from the other—the eye floated right and up, folding itself inside a tight-wound ghost-peak that resolved, by slow degrees, into the image of a tall, grave woman boarded as severely in front as she was laced tight in back, her panniers broad and her gray-streaked hair combed high in the fashion of twenty years past. Rusk made a noise deep in his throat at the sight.

"Ma—m'lady mother," he almost mumbled, to himself.

To Tante Ankolee's left, meanwhile, the hair arranged itself to drape the small, sleek head of an only slightly see-through woman built like a bird, her fine bones due less to an aristocrat's elegance than simple lifelong privation, with a pair of red-fringed eyes that same fatal shade of silver as Captain Parry's own.

Morwennol, sea-sparrow, she had murmured when Tante Ankolee first conjured her, the night before, after Collyer was safely abed. *That was my true name. But most called me Arranz, for the color of my eyes.*

"Aye, and beautiful them eyes be too, madam. I have seen them before, in your son's face."

So he lives yet, my Jerusalem? Ah, but no—I see th'answer ye fear to give me. Do not keep silence, lady; we are never long for this world, those of my blood, no matter how we scheme otherwise.

"Well, sorry I am t' wake you from ya slumber. But I have certain business with that boy o' yours, an' him nah all too like t'listen to wit'out you stand beside me, when I tell it 'im."

I will do what I can, sister.

"Much thanks, then. As for yourself, Aphra-Maîtresse..."

I am glad to see you once more, Ankolee, but you know as well as any—I am no witch, never was. 'Tis not through me Solomon gained his power, much though I might've wished it, if only to deny him that burden.

"'Course not, Madame. Yet y'are the only one he'd ever stand still for, when he'd taken a mind t' nah be turned."

I...will do what I can, Ankolee. You have my word.

"An' you mine, that I will release ya both soon's I have what I need, to go whither ya will—accompanied, or un-."

In the here and now, Tante Ankolee waved these ghost-ladies on, ushering them to eddy towards their respective sons. With Rusk, his mother's disapproving stare caused him to bow that black lion's head, if only a little bit. But Captain Parry stood transfixed, fingers guttering dark, as his own dam's shade put up a ghostly hand to feeling soft along his fearsome clean-cut jawline, a stroke he palpably longed to fold into, like some great child. Crooning, as she did: *How tall you've grown, Jerusalem*, mabyn *mine. And how you do shine...*

Staring at her with a rigid face, instead, his pale eyes all further a-gleam, wet, and accusatory. Saying, to Tante Ankolee, over this phantom's shoulder—

"I had not expected such tricks from you, madam; that you should make sport of my weakness, even in your brother's defense... oh, it is vile, and crass. And disappointing, also."

"Little choice ya left me, fah how else might I gain your attention—who always know best, or so ya think—'cept to conjure the one creature you *will* listen to?"

Parry simply shook his head, apparently baffled to silence beneath that gentling touch. And Tante Ankolee took advantage of the opportunity, addressing him and Rusk both, while she yet could—

"Seein' such a great time elapsed already in ya confusion, me two fine fools, I come t' the point directly: Though both o' you long to see each other's back, it seem all things conspire t'keep ya bound together, doomed ta forever sail this ship ya both lay claim to. Yet in all ya wrestlin' 'tween yourselves, have ya never thought t' wonder *why?*"

"You sound as though you have an answer," Parry said.

"Aye, thus I believe. In alchemy, the qualities o' one substance may be rearrange ta create another—and just so, by a different process, two t'ings whah seem exact opposites may be shown t'have innate commonality by th' admixture o' a third t'ing, altogether." Here she caught sight of Collyer frankly goggling at her, and observed, acerbic: "Ah, put ya tongue back inside ya head! I learn me letters at the same knee as this great oaf, here—learn 'em better by far, too, truth be told. An' fah all me craft spring mostly from the natural world, a book *do* sometime pass m'way, if only now an' then."

Rusk nodded. "I'll not deny it. So...tell it through, big sis: What third thing *have* we forgot, in all our temper and muddle?"

"Why, whah indeed been the primest bone o' ya contention, savin' the obvious? This ship ya both lay claim to, 'long wit' the bond she help ya forge, since she love ya both so exceedin' well."

Parry glanced down, as though suddenly made aware of the very deck his boots seemed to rest on, whose swell-borne rise and fall was like some huge, submerged creature's breath. But: "No," he said, to himself. "It cannot be."

"Why, since *you* didn't grasp the trick of it first?" Rusk scoffed. "Nay, it does make a sort of sense. The *Bitch* watched me curse you, as you killed me..."

"...And while I cursed you, when I found myself so."

"Aye, and thus we made our troth together, I'll vow—for better your curse than any other's kiss, since 'twas more freely gave by far than anything else I've ever had of ye."

"*Good*, 'cousin' mine!" Tante Ankolee clapped her hands, admiringly, and added: "Let no one claim you incapable of learnin', 'specially when it's t' your own advantage. This, then, was the Salt Wedding ye fashioned together, wi' the *Bitch* herself as officiant... and 'tis *this* we must dissolve, wi' her own gracious help."

Chimed in Parry and Collyer both, almost as one: "And just how, exactly, d'you propose to—"

"Shush, nah, the pair o' you. Ladies, tell me—can she hear us, this great vessel? Will she be pled to outright, or do she require some further suppliance?"

"She hears you well, Ankolee," Mistress Rusk assured her. "Nor asks any price at all to treat with you, knowing you by sight as her sister, and her friend."

"Aye," Arranz Parry agreed, nodding her dim red head. "For this last passage has been a hard one, and she owns herself tired—as much so, almost, as these men she carries. She longs nothing more than to let herself go, resolve away, let all the varying parts of her return once more to the sea, from whence she helped my lad and Missus Rusk's boy pluck 'em."

"Hmm, I see. Yet why do she nah, then, if 'tis *her* dearest wish, as well as theirs?"

"Because she *must* have a captain to guide her, even on that last voyage, with nowhere to go but down. Even then."

The men all looked at each other. "Then I'll stay, and you go,"

Rusk announced, prompting a scornful snort from Parry, who replied—

"Yes, to be sure. For you must always have the last word, especially at my expense."

"Says the man who had the flesh scraped from my bones wi' bloody barnacles, for the grand sin of sticking my prick in his arse unsolicited!"

Parry went red, then white. "How dare you, sir!" he spat. "Insulting me with every word, every motion, these ten long years and more...and now, how *dare* you think to tweak at me yet further, by trying to put me in your debt once more—"

"Sweet Christ's own mercy! Then what else *do* ye want, in all this wide world, you contrary goddamned creature? We have both suffered enough to satisfy even your endless pride, yet if there can be freedom for only one of us so long's the *Bitch* needs her captain's chair filled, then 'tis my charge, just as she was my ship, long 'fore y'ever stepped foot onboard! Which is why I *will* make that sacrifice, and ye won't think t'stop me!"

"Will I not? *Watch* me."

Rusk shook his head, voice softening. "Oh, Jerusha—has this struggle for victory made ye so sore a loser, ye cannot even stand to win? For see, 'tis you mastered me, from the very outset—brought me down, took all I had and bound me to you forever more, no matter whether ye willed that last part, or no. Who else would I love, who never before cared for any but myself?"

"Your 'love' may kiss my hindparts, you pox-rid rogue!"

"My love *has*, and soundly, as I know ye well recall, ye sour-faced nun's fart."

Collyer threw Tante Ankolee a glance, putting in, weakly: "I believe we may be drifting somewhat off the subject, gentlemen..."

But to all concerned's startlement, 'twas Mistress Parry who raised her little palm instead, cupping her angry son's chin once more, as though to force his gaze back to hers. "Enough o' this," she ordered. "Jerusalem, decide: To go, or stay? Think on your troubles and trust this ship o' yours would not wish to keep ye, not if ye *truly* wish your freedom."

"When have I ever wished anything else? Oh, Mumma, I have tried so long with all my might to pry myself from this puzzle-trap without result, and God alone knows...I am so very weary."

Haughtiness doused and head drooping beneath this admission's weight, his silver eyes half-lidded—Rusk looked as though he longed to reach out a comforting hand, though a glance from his own mother sufficed to keep him still, as Arranz Parry nodded. "Yes, child, I know. But tell me this: Were you a terror to this world? Did you do wonders? Did you make the bastards pay, and suffer in the doin' so?"

"I...did, yes, to my best knowledge. Those who collared me learned their error, in the end, surely as this man did his. As those who swung you would have, had I only been able to dock on Cornish soil once more."

"Well, then—ye have more than done your duty, as our Master's old charge states. For sometimes, when it cannot be 'revenge yourselves or die,' it can be 'revenge yourself, and die.' There is no shame in it. And do not begrudge Cap'n Rusk the chance t' do but one good deed, in all his long, bad life; let go, let be. Rest, my dear one. Be free."

Parry just shook his head, helpless, stiff-froze still in his confusion's midst; Rusk crossed his arms and huffed, looking anywhere else, as Tante Ankolee threw up her hands and the *Bitch* itself gave out one great groan from stem to stern, similarly frustrated by her second captain-husband's stubbornness.

But: "Perhaps...there is another way," Collyer eventually began, tentative, feeling his way. "One in which neither of you must stay, and neither of you owe the other."

As though choreographed, Parry and Rusk turned on him both at once, fists clenched, primed to fight him, too. Cooler heads prevailed, however, along with their mothers' ghosts' restraining glares—and at length, under his cousin-sister's smiling eyes, it was Rusk himself (never known for reasonableness hitherto, though perhaps he'd been taking lessons) who replied:

"Tell on, sir."

That one time in Porte Macoute, Tante Ankolee—there, on the high seas, at the Pearl-Bright Ocean's very gate, where channel from one world ope into the next. Where the very Sea Herself let gape Her great mouth an' swallow down them lost, wanderin', contentious souls who finally find 'emselves willin' t' accept them own fate an' sink down forever, into sweet darkness. That one time, she.

Impossible ta tell if 'twas always her plan how Wilmot Collyer, so good an' true a man as ta feel sympathy fah monsters of all kind, should volunteer ta take him place at the Bitch of Hell's *prow an' let that same ship's other two captain go where they list. Though we all know 'twas she who stood beside him as a distraction while them two gentlemen made their final farewell, echoing it with kisses of her own, far sweeter an' less wounding...just as 'twas she who raise a wind ta blow them both home wit' the* Malaga Victory *followin' behind in their wake wit' the* Bitch's *old crew cram in an' doin' double-duty, once all four ghost had guttered away like snuffed candleflame. An' never was they heard from again, these hundred year an' more—neither in them part, all the islands from Port Royal to Tortuga-that-was an' all the many routes whah serve 'em, nor elsewhere.*

Indeed, once her fee been paid in full, 'tis impossible to deny how the favor Tante Ankolee done thah old, cold England-King last longer still than the empire he rule, in th'end. Fah which we o' her blood are grateful yet, seein' its collapse freed even those of us yet slave in them same days, an' take much merriment, ever after.

As fah the Bitch *an' her last commander, meanwhile...unlike Jerusalem Parry or Solomon Rusk, Cap'n Collyer was nah constrain t' spend out his life roamin' those warm salt waters, or doom t' prey on the same Navy he so-well serve fah prizes t' swell the* Bitch's *hold an' hull. Indeed, as they drew close to Porte Macoute's great dock, that same sad lady begun to sink outright, driftin' low an' lower 'til at last she come so waterline-close Collyer an' his witch-love have jus' time enough step onto one of the* Victory's *long-boats, 'fore splittin' apart altogether. An' 'tis said the varyin' wrecks thah make her up still lie there t'this day, wit' Rusk and Parry's hoard o' stolen gold an' jewels strewn out under sand an' stone fah any who care t' dive after 'em—always rememberin' how bad them waters are fah sharks, even so terrible near ta shore.*

Fah him part in the Bitch's *layin', Cap'n Collyer gain him a higher rank an' a better ship still, along wit' some land on Porte Macoute itself where him build a house large enough ta entertain guests in—one, at least, from time ta time. While nine month later, Tante Ankolee bring a son into this world ta carry on both her witch-blood an' the Rusk name—same as her slaver-father, aye, but same too as Alizoun Rusk, that gay, burnt girl who once danced on air an' laid waste to half o' Scotland, 'fore her own foolishness bring her down.*

That boy name Collyer Rusk, child, who live ta one hundred year exactly: me great-grandaddy, buried still out back o' our house on Porte Macoute. A witch's son like Jerusalem Parry, but born t'a sorceress-mother so puissant-powerful thah iron never wrap 'round him throat—not fah witch-finding, not fah slavery. Which is nah ta say him have no grief, in all him long, long life...but then, grief come at last t'everyone, cunning-folk or no. It cannot be avoided.

Yet we may still make merry, live on 'til we die, an' then die well. Thah, we may do.

An' nah, the story done—Tante Ankolee long dead as me great-grandaddy, an' meself grown old, likewise. Go make a tale o' ya own to tell, while ya still can.

Formerly a film critic, journalist, screenwriter and teacher, Gemma Files has been an award-winning horror author since 1999. She has published two collections of short work (*Kissing Carrion* and *The Worm in Every Heart*), two chap-books of speculative poetry, a Weird Western trilogy (the *Hexslinger* series—*A Book of Tongues*, *A Rope of Thorns* and *A Tree of Bones*), a story-cycle (*We Will All Go Down Together: Stories of the Five-Family Coven*) and a stand-alone novel (*Experimental Film*, which won the 2016 Shirley Jackson Award for Best Novel and the 2016 Sunburst award for Best Adult Novel). All her works are available through ChiZine Productions. Her novella, *Coffle*, was just published by Dim Shores, with art by Stephen Wilson. She has two upcoming story collections from Trepidatio Publishing (*Spectral Evidence* and *Drawn Up From Deep Places*), and one from Cemetery Dance.

CPSIA information can be obtained
at www.ICGtesting.com
Printed in the USA
LVHW020029131118
596825LV00007B/568/P